THE COLD LAST SWIM

GIBSON HOUSE PRESS
Flossmoor, Illinois
GibsonHousePress.com

ISBNs: 978-1-948721-10-3 (paper); 978-1-948721-11-0 (ebook)

LCCN: 2019951011

Cover and text design by Karen Sheets de Gracia.
Text is composed in the Whitman and American Typewriter typefaces.

Printed in the United States of America
24 23 22 21 20   1 2 3 4 5

⊚ This paper meets the requirements of ANSI/NISO Z39.48-1992 (Permanence of Paper)

The

COLD
LAST
SWIM

a novel

Junior Burke

GIBSON
HOUSE
PRESS

CHICAGO

for Bobbie Louise Hawkins

My friends are roaming or listening to La Bohème.

Precisely, the cold last swim . . .

   . . . the final glass of pleasure.

—Frank O'Hara, "Thinking of James Dean"

There is nothing much deader

than a dead motion picture actor.

—John Dos Passos, *Midcentury*

REEL
ONE

MARCH 1954–
SEPTEMBER 1955

ONE

Jimmy was looking out the porthole window, languidly playing his recorder, as the plane drifted down toward the hazy sprawl of Los Angeles. Nobody needed to tell Jimmy about LA. He'd lived there twice; the first time, when his old man moved the family west. But it didn't work out. Jimmy's beloved mother died and his prick father sent nine-year-old Jimmy back to Indiana on the same train carrying her coffin, to be farm-raised by Jimmy's aunt and uncle. Jimmy returned after high school, but that hadn't worked either.

Even though he told his New York theater friends he'd be back as soon as this picture was in the can, Jimmy knew it wouldn't go that way. Hollywood money was too easy, the people too pretty, the days too warm, the nights too soft. Having your image ladder-high in every movie house from Times Square to San Francisco; from Sheboygan to Tallahassee; the payoff was too sweet. Brando hadn't come back, had he? And Clift wasn't opening on the Great White Way, to emote to one house at a time, eight shows a week.

His eyes scanned the landscape below but he couldn't spot anything familiar. LA looked like a puzzle; most of the real estate disjointed and low to the ground. New York made more sense to him. Ninety-Sixth Street uptown; Fourth Street downtown; Eighth Avenue, west; Second Avenue, east. A cohesion to the chaos. But LA was a jumbled maze of small towns, each seemingly unaware of the ones right next to it.

Jimmy was most familiar with the west side; Santa Monica, where his old man lived, and Westwood, where he'd attended UCLA. He'd tried to fit in there, like he'd tried back in Indiana, he had even pledged Sigma Nu. There had always been a struggle inside him, between art or athletics. He'd played baseball, like any American kid, and basketball, being raised in Indiana. But art and theater were forever swirling, confusing him, conflicting his direction.

That last night in the frat house, Jimmy had abandoned his attempt at conformity. A smug upperclassman, Darrel Something, had ordered pledge Dean to take the wastebasket from the lounge and empty it in one of the outside trash cans. "Fuck you," Jimmy told him. "Empty it yourself."

"Wait a second, aren't you the one majoring in theater arts?"

"Minoring."

"I couldn't believe it when I heard it. We've never had a drama-fruit in the house."

Jimmy popped him, busting the guy's nose.

He'd rushed out and walked feverishly, all over Westwood. On Gayley Avenue, he came upon a gleaming Olds 88, unlocked, keys dangling from the ignition, too tempting to pass up. He drove for hours, east along Sunset, south on Vermont, all the way to Long Beach, making his way back on the freeway before abandoning the car at Pico and Westwood Boulevard, then walking back to the frat house in the gold-pink dawn to collect his few things.

At the door he encountered another pledge who told him, "I wouldn't come back if I was you. They've organized a lynch party."

Jimmy just smiled. He'd made up his mind. He hitched a ride west on Wilshire to his old man's house, relieved to find it empty. A little over three hundred dollars hidden in the dresser. Jimmy grabbed it. After an endless series of buses, he reached the train station.

Somewhere in New Mexico, he and a thirtyish nurse locked themselves in the bathroom where Jimmy had his first taste of reefer. East of Chicago, he shared a table in the dining car with a jittery young priest who wanted to hear Jimmy's confession. Jimmy begged off, not being Catholic, but ended up sharing the guy's sleeping berth all the way to Penn Station.

In New York, Jimmy did whatever he could to survive. He was on a mission. The theater was a bridge, the necessary means to earn respect as an actor. Had he remained in LA without the New York credits and training, he'd have been just another light-haired, lightweight pretty boy. But Jimmy wanted the kind of power that Brando wielded; the kind of power that made Hollywood knuckleheads—producers, columnists, starlets and leading men—eat out of his hand, and kiss his ass, and blow his joint, if that's what he felt like.

So he'd landed his contract with Warner Brothers and was slated to make three pictures. *Eden* was going to be all right because it had weight to it. To follow it, the studio was talking about putting him in *Rebel Without a Cause*, which had been kicking around for years. Warners was only doing it to cash in on the growing concern over juvenile delinquency. Jimmy was going to be cast as a mixed-up punk, which was the kind of image that would limit and restrict him. He had agreed in order to secure the contract, but he was already devising ways to duck *Rebel*. Jimmy wanted Shakespeare and Tennessee Williams and big-budget locations in Italy and France.

"We are preparing for our landing in Los Angeles," declared a female voice over the intercom. "Make sure your seat belt is fastened, and please extinguish all cigarettes."

It had been a long flight, nine hours, but Jimmy Dean didn't feel the least bit tired.

*

Ronald Reagan was sitting in his office at CBS Television, dressed breezily in an orange crewneck sweater with a powder blue dress shirt underneath. Behind him was an image from *Dark Victory*, where he stood alongside Bette Davis, evidence of what had been his once-substantial film career. Now he was on the downslope, relegated to Hollywood's red-headed step-child, the new and less-prestigious medium of television. On the *General Electric Theater*, a half-hour live showcase for melo-dramas, he served as both actor and host, bookending each presentation in his earnest, affable manner.

An open script was on the desk as he gazed into the imagi-nary camera. "What happens when an ordinary man, a decent man, is suddenly, inexplicably confronted with evil? Tonight's drama takes place in a quiet town on a quiet street on what, by all accounts should be—"

The phone chimed. Reagan seemed unfazed at the inter-ruption. "Ron Reagan speaking."

"Nancy wants you to pick up some Lea & Perrins on your way home. The grocer messed up the delivery." The voice, fil-tered and familiar, belonged to Guy Fletcher, Reagan's agent at MCA.

"That *can't* be why you're calling, Guy."

"I just came from breakfast with Charley Cannon. I'd like to suggest some terrific casting for that hepcat script you've got coming up."

"I believe it's cast already, but who do you have in mind?"

"This kid, Dean. Just finished a feature with Kazan. Charley's looking to keep him busy until the picture gets released."

"Can't say I've heard of him."

"Like Brando, but younger. From what Charley says, it'll be quite a stroke to get him."

A look of displeasure crossed Reagan's face. "Are we talking about one of those Actors Studio types, who mumbles and holds everything up? I made one picture with a primate, I'm not anxious to repeat it on television."

"The part is straight out of *The Wild One*, am I right? So you don't want to cast a choirboy."

"But I don't want to turn the show into a playground."

"C'mon, Ron. It could draw a whole new audience."

"I'll run it by our casting director." A moment, then: "Lea & Perrins? I thought we were having fish tonight."

TWO

Jimmy Dean, clip-on shades and motorcycle boots, walked late onto the set of the *General Electric Theater*. Cast and crew were there, as was Ronald Reagan, coproducer and actor-host. Jimmy was in character, although not precisely the one he'd signed on to play. He was deep into James Dean, New York stage actor, big screen Technicolor star, and not some black-and-white murmur from a television, from just another piece of living room furniture.

He'd already done plenty of live TV work back in New York, but considered it a trifle, a splash, not the sustained engagement of a Broadway run or a feature film. And while he had a sense of what this little melodrama was about, he hadn't actually bothered to read the script.

Nobody greeted Jimmy. In fact, they all glared at him.

"I think everyone here will tell you I'm a reasonable person," Reagan said. "Except when we're all kept waiting half the morning."

Jimmy lit a cigarette. "I'm here now, Pops."

"You just missed the first table reading. You'll rehearse today and you'll be here tomorrow at ten a.m. as scheduled or you're fired. Do we understand each other?"

After a moment, Ken, the hired-hand director, called out: "Places, everybody. Let's go to the moment when Sonny provokes Doctor Walker."

Reagan delivered the first line: "Sonny, I'm going to need you to tell me exactly what brought you here tonight."

Jimmy leaned in tight. He looked into Reagan's eyes. And he whispered: "You used to make *real* pictures, didn't you, Pops? What the hell happened?"

Reagan looked startled.

"And now you're hawking washing machines on the idiot box. You costarred with some of the big ones back when. Now, I'll bet Bette Davis wouldn't give you the time of day."

Ken and the crew couldn't make out the words, but they all sensed something happening as Jimmy drew even closer. "I only took this gig 'cause my agent wanted to give me something to do. But I've got a picture coming out. A big, fat one, that's gonna light up the world."

Reagan gaped, clearly not believing what he was hearing.

"That's the way it goes, Chief. Some cats are on the way up, while the has-beens, the once-upon-a-timers, they get left in the—"

Then Reagan lunged.

It took Ken and a couple of crew members to pry Reagan's hands from Jimmy's throat.

Reagan was crimson, apoplectic. "You'd better keep that creep away from me. I won't be responsible for what I might do to the little bastard!"

A glass of water was thrust toward him. Reagan's hand quivered as he raised it to his lips.

Ken looked over at Jimmy, who was smirking. The director had to keep from smirking himself. He'd never seen Ronald Reagan project that kind of raw emotion.

Jimmy nodded, then he strode off the set.

✦

That night, in his studio apartment, Jimmy sat on his bed and studied the script.

> DOCTOR WALKER
> I need to inform the police that you
> received treatment.

Sonny reacts like a cornered animal.

> SONNY
> That there's a very bad idea, Doc.

> DOCTOR WALKER
> (picking up the telephone)
> It must be a matter of record.

> SONNY
> It don't need to be a matter of nothin'!

Sonny desperately reaches into his jacket and pulls out a pistol.

Jimmy stared at the page, then crossed the room. *Sonny has to feel that this Doctor Walker is a threat to his very freedom. Needs to be ready to die before giving in to the Doctor Walkers of the world.*

He set the script atop the dresser, as though it was wired and ticking. In the top drawer, under frayed underwear and mismatching socks, was a .32 revolver. Jimmy weighed it in his hand, then placed it on the script in a kind of reverent offering.

Peeling off his clothes, he doused the light; stretched out atop the covers, asleep the instant he hit the pillow.

✱

Guest star dressing room. Jimmy, stretched on a cot, looking spent.

"That was an amazing run-through today," Christine, the costume designer, told him.

"You were amazing, all right," added the prop guy sitting next to her.

"Listen," Jimmy, coming to life, said to Christine. "I'm sure you've put a lot of thought into what you're having me wear, but it's just one outfit, right; no changes?"

"Uh-huh."

"I wanna take a look at what you've got in mind, then go through my closet and come up with something close. When I'm doing just a quick shot like this, I like to stay in character, wear the clothes twenty-four hours a day." A smile. "I'll probably even sleep in them."

Christine had never heard of such a thing. "Less work for me," she said, walking away.

Jimmy turned to the prop guy. "Allen?"

"Alvin."

"I'm lighting a few cigarettes, right—did you envision a lighter or a pack of matches?"

"Matches."

"What if I use my own Zippo?" Jimmy pulled the palm-sized, silver rectangle from his jeans, flipped the cap; fired it up. Flipped down the cap, shoved the lighter back into his pocket. "Now about the gun," he continued, "I'd like to use my own."

"Your own *gun*?"

"The script calls for me to pull it, not fire it. I've got a revolver I'm used to. Fits in my pocket." Out came the .32. "I'll feel a lot more motivated carrying my own heat. It won't be loaded. But when I point it at the doctor, it won't be a false moment, it'll be real." He placed his palm just above Alvin's knee. The guy didn't flinch. Jimmy smiled as they locked eyes. "It'll be our little secret."

✱

"Why aren't you asleep?" Nancy Reagan asked her husband in their dark bedroom in the Pacific Palisades.

"Mind if I turn on the light?"

Nancy didn't answer but after a moment, the lamp lit up on the bedside table and she saw her husband perched on the edge of the bed, gazing down, as though the floor was a pool he was working up the nerve to dive into.

"If you're headed to the bathroom," she said, "will you bring back a glass of water?"

He didn't reply but rose and crossed the room, stepped into the master bath, where another light came on. There were sounds and rustlings and then he was back with her water in a green plastic cup.

"It's Dean," Reagan said, sitting back down on the edge of the bed. "I hate to admit it, but he's getting to me."

"He's just another actor. And a punk on top of it."

"Over at Warners they're convinced he's going to be a major, major star. There's something about him that's . . ."

Nancy looked over at him. "This isn't like you, Ronnie.

You get mad at people," she continued. "Frustrated. But you never let them shake you up like this."

"When I was a kid, back in Illinois, we had tornadoes, you know, every spring and summer. The only time I ever saw one, I was coming from playing ball on a lot at the edge of town. We, the boys I was playing with and I, we looked out and saw this . . . force coming. It hadn't touched down, but was pulling things up from the ground, making them spin in every direction. We'd been hearing about tornadoes all our lives, but until that moment, we . . . myself anyway, never knew how destructive they were." He turned and looked at her. "That's what this Dean is like."

Nancy took a gulp, then set the cup on the night table. "He's a nobody, darling. And after tomorrow evening you won't have to give the little runt another thought."

*

The broadcast on live television.

Doctor's office. Jimmy, bleeding, while Doctor Reagan, bleary-eyed in a bathrobe, administered to him. "I have to tell the police about the gunshot wound."

"That's a very bad idea, Doc," Jimmy said.

Reagan picked up the phone. "It's a matter of record."

"It don't need to be a matter of nothin'."

Jimmy pulled out the gun.

"So that's the way it is," asked Reagan, "after I've sewn you up and saved your life?"

Dead air on live television. Reagan was supposed to put the phone down. Instead he started dialing.

Jimmy leveled the pistol at Reagan's chest. He pulled back the hammer . . .

*

Nancy Reagan was sitting in front of her television set, munching popcorn, eyes on the screen, watching her husband and Dean, who held a gun as Ronnie stood, telephone in hand. "Put that cap pistol away if you're not going to use it, Sonny." He reached out to grab Dean's wrist.

Dean's eyes flared. He thrust the barrel to Ronnie's chest as Ronnie pushed forward. The gun kicked. Ronnie's face contorted. He staggered, staring at Dean who had a deranged, mask-like look.

Nancy uttered, "That wasn't in the script." Popcorn and soft drink spilled to the floor.

She rushed into the kitchen with its sleek electric ranges, ovens and refrigerators, two of each, courtesy of General Electric. Her maid stood there. "Look after the twins," Nancy told her, "I need to go."

Nancy rushed outside, frantically climbed behind the wheel of her wood-paneled station wagon, jammed it in reverse, skidded down the driveway, and shoved it into drive.

*

St. Joseph's, Burbank. Police and hospital personnel, swarming the lobby.

Mayhem.

"I was told Mr. Reagan is here," Nancy said to the nurse at the reception desk.

"Mr. Reagan is with the doctors."

Nancy, moving.

"Where are you going? You're not allowed beyond—"

"Stuff it," snapped Nancy. She hauled through the doors,

in search of somebody in charge.

A doctor in his twenties; slight build, crew cut, was smoking in the hallway.

"I'm here about the Reagan . . . incident," said Nancy.

"He's being prepped—are you Mrs. Reagan?"

"Prepped for what—take me to him."

The doctor dropped his cigarette on the linoleum, stubbed it with a wing tip, then opened the door to a tiny, vacant room. Nancy stood her ground, glaring at him.

"You'll be more comfortable in here," the young man told her.

"I'll be more comfortable once I see my husband. What are you, an intern?"

He led her down the hall to a trauma room.

Nancy saw her man, tubes in his chest and arms, breathing with difficulty through an oxygen mask.

"Oh, Ronnie." She rushed to his side.

Hand quivering, he removed the mask. Lips dark, from spewing blood, he came out with the line he'd been saving. "Honey, I forgot to duck."

Nancy forced a smile. His hand felt cold, unfamiliar. "Be still, darling."

The physician in charge pulled Nancy aside.

"He's lost a lot of blood. When he came in, his systolic pressure was less than half what it should be. The bullet passed through his lower lung. It didn't pierce his heart, but it's lodged pretty close to it. There's no time to wait for consent forms. Will you grant permission for surgery?"

"You have my permission."

Nancy hurried alongside the gurney as her husband was rolled into the operating room, unconscious.

*

Jimmy was with Donald Lymon, his attorney. Besides a toilet, there was only a metal cot in the cell. Donald, a few years older than Jimmy. Tortoiseshell glasses, fresh razor scrape on his chin.

"I spoke to the cops. Some people are saying it was a real bullet and some say it was a blank. Which was it, Jimmy?"

Jimmy dragged on his cigarette. "Can you bring a carton in the morning? I've only got four left."

"Sure . . . Which was it?"

"It was real."

A parcel of air was drawn in, then released from Donald's upper body. "You'd better hope Reagan hangs on."

"Chesterfield or Pall Mall, either one."

Donald paced to the far wall in two-and-a-half steps.

"I don't want you spilling to anybody. Not any of your girlfriends. Not any of your . . . not any guys, either. Got it, Jimmy?"

"Yes, professor."

"You'll go before the judge in the morning. He'll either set bail or he won't. I wouldn't get my hopes up."

Donald buzzed for the guard.

Jimmy lit a fresh cigarette from the nub he was holding, then reclined on the metal cot, back against the wall.

He wasn't sure how the gun went off; the whole thing had a pulse of its own. *What the hell was I thinking?* He *hadn't* thought, that was the problem. In a world of shit now, no getting around it. All he could do was hang on for all he was worth. Jimmy took a deep drag. Exhaled.

THREE

Although it was half past three in the morning, light shone through the windows overlooking Grand Street on New York's Lower East Side. A young man, Garland Alpert, and the even younger woman, Oona Stickney, sat facing each other at the kitchen table. Rust-shaded hair and paler than Oona, Garland was wearing a gray sweatshirt, khaki pants and argyle socks; she wore a charcoal sweater over a plaid navy skirt and dark green leotard. Miles Davis's *Out of the Blue,* playing low on the hi-fi. A poster from Robert Rauschenberg's *Red Paintings,* tacked to the wall. Their faces, Garland's and Oona's, strained and tense. "I'd feel better," Garland was saying, "if you'd just be straight about it for once."

Oona's chin was resting on her right palm. She lowered her hand and placed it flat on the table, looking at it as though noticing something she hadn't known was there. She looked up. "See, Garland, when *you* do what you're accusing me of doing, you think that telling me turns it into a virtue." A high whistle rose from the kitchen. Oona stood. "The water's ready. You want some tea?"

"So you're finally admitting you balled him?"

"I can't deal with this right now. I've got a final tomorrow night."

"I should have known when you started having coffee with him."

Oona headed for the kitchen but stopped in the doorway. "Look, Gar, you're never gonna get past it, which is why I'm moving in with Sheila."

Garland's face, already strained, now registered shock.

"I'll clear out right before the holidays. Sheila's roommate is moving back to Buffalo."

"How am I supposed to swing the rent by myself?"

"I really like you, Garland. I even kind of love you. But it's going on a year and I can't see you letting go of this. So let's just be friends."

She ducked into the kitchen.

To the empty doorway, Garland said, "At least the sonofabitch is getting what's coming to him. I thought you were a sharper chick than that, Oona. How could you give it up to a creep like Dean?"

✽

Dear Mister Reagan,

You have always remained one of my favorite actors, always striking me as a good man, on the side of good. I cant believe what I saw on my TV. It was as though someone got mugged on our very block and the crime rate here is low. I hope your released before Xmas and that juvenile delinquent (Dean) gets whats coming to him. I further hope reading this has not made you too tired.

> Yours sincerely,
> Helen Marie Fawcett
> Manhattan, Kansas

p.s. I read somewhere that your friends with William Holden. I like him too but not as much.

Reagan looked up and saw Guy Fletcher, his agent from MCA, coming through the door. Another pair of suits were with him, as well as a photographer. Guy greeted him by saying: "How's the nation's most famous patient?" A hundred-watt smile. "I see, as always, you're in Nancy's capable hands." Reagan gave the card to Nancy who took it over to a stack of others on the corner table. "Ron and Nancy, this is Joe Ridley with BBD&O. He oversees all the advertising for GE. And this is Larry Beckman of Revue Productions."

"I've met Larry," said Reagan, sitting a little higher.

Ridley asked: "How are you feeling, Ron—are you eating, getting your strength back?"

"Liquids mostly, soup and the like." Slight laugh. "This morning, I had a craving for a ham sandwich. I took that as a good sign."

"We'll have a tray sent over," said Guy.

Beckman gestured toward the mound of sympathy cards. "Look at that. The network has a hundred times as many. Each one represents around ten thousand people who feel the same but haven't sent a note. Never seen anything like it."

"A heckuva way to gauge your popularity," said Reagan.

Ridley beamed: "We've got plans for you, Ron."

Reagan forced a smile, sending a glance to Nancy. "And what would those be?"

"We want you to go on tour—once you're back at full strength, of course. Get out and press the flesh of GE's plant workers all over the U.S. You'll be a real inspiration."

Reagan's smile tightened even more. "Am I being forced off the show?"

Laughter, all around.

Beckman picked up the ball. "You'll continue hosting

Sunday nights, but during the week you'll also be fronting in person for the sponsor. That's why we need you to regain every ounce of stamina."

Reagan, still thrown. "I don't like to travel. I hate flying on airplanes."

Ridley, undeterred. "One hundred thirty-six facilities in thirty-two states. A quarter million employees who consider you a national symbol."

Reagan laughed tightly. "I'm an entertainer. You make me sound like some politician."

"This thing that happened," said Beckman, "it's galvanized the public. They see you as representing the higher ideals of America, and Dean is the JD who's been slashing their tires and stealing their hubcaps and terrorizing their kids and God knows what else. It's turned into a morality play."

"People relate to you, Ron," said Guy. "They see you as one of them, yet above them somehow. Part friend and part hero. This has just shone a light on what was always there."

Reagan looked at Nancy who, ahead of her husband, sensed a seismic shift. "I don't know, gentlemen, I'll have to think about this . . . Nancy and I need to talk."

It scarcely passed his lips when Nancy spoke up. "He'll do it," she declared.

A flashbulb popped as everyone laughed.

FOUR

T he first shot Hiram Freeman ever took was of Mr. Simon's
unfinished Towers. That was his birth as a photographer
but, like all births, there was a conception.

Six months earlier at Snowden's Drugstore on 110th, three
blocks from his house, he was killing time, spending what little
change he had, when he reached for a magazine on the rack.
Life magazine. He'd seen it, of course. You couldn't miss its bold
cover with the loud red banner, always a big picture, always
white people, smiling or looking serious, the message being:
"This is what's happening in the world this week."

Fourteen and living in Watts, Hiram knew his world never
got reported in the *LA Times* or *Daily News* or *Herald Examiner*, much less a glossy national magazine. On this day, Mr.
Snowden was in one of his better moods and not inclined to
shoo him or any other kids out of the store right away.

Hiram opened the sprawling, important-looking copy of
Life. The usual. Cigarette ads with couples—white couples—
glamorous and oblivious. Articles about Washington politics
and New York plays. About to put it back, he turned a page
and something jumped out and grabbed him.

A picture of a woman in a rocking chair—a black
woman—ancient, regal, in elegant profile as she clutched a
cane in her right hand. Looked like any number of women
Hiram would see in Watts on a daily basis.

And, my God, there was another picture. A group of black men and boys—five of them—hanging in a doorway—hats cocked, hands pocketed, shoulders slouched, but more out of impudence than resignation. One held a dog on a leash in the foreground. Hell, these were his people, the ones he sometimes waved to but usually avoided because they could be friendly or not, mess with you or not, depending on what they were feeling at any moment.

Excited, Hiram's eyes moved to the name on the lower right below the photograph. *Gordon Parks*. Checked the other photo and it was the same: *Gordon Parks*. Certainly sounded like a white name; he'd never met anybody named Gordon. But no, hell it couldn't be—no white man could see like that. That's what his uncle once said about white people. "They look at you but they don't ever see." Well, this man saw, all right.

In the weeks that followed, Hiram spent every day after school and all day Saturday collecting pop bottles all over Watts, turning them in for the refund. Even tried one Sunday afternoon, but his mother drew the line—the Lord's Day after all.

He came home from Gilmore's Pawn Shop one Friday, dizzy and practically out of breath. He'd bought himself a Voigtländer Brilliant, although it looked like any old camera to his mother, for fourteen dollars and fifty cents. A lotta pop bottles, as it turned out.

Hour after hour, Hiram just looked at his camera, touched it, carried it around the house like a new pet he was getting to trust him. Then Sunday, after church, well into the afternoon because the choir had gone especially long that day, he walked to the Towers as he'd done countless times.

Like most every resident of Watts, Hiram loved the structures being constructed by Mr. Simon. Didn't know if it was his last name or first. The man built his edifice each day after work and on the weekends, laying in seashells and glass, ceramic chips, bottle caps and pottery shards, fashioning a set of steel towers covered with mortar—winding, rising, twisting, bending—whose design one simply had to gaze at in awe.

Mr. Simon was quiet and not all that friendly as he worked, using his tile setter's tools, strapped to his creation with a window washer's belt and buckle. Although Mr. Simon was Italian, Hiram heard that he preached fire and brimstone at a Mexican tent revival. The man's artistic statement was proud, colorful, outlandish; and it was taking shape in a neighborhood the soapy denizens of Beverly Hills and Pasadena would be reluctant to venture into even on the sunniest of days.

After snapping the Towers, Hiram began a study of the neighborhood. He'd been born there seven years before the war when it was more racially and ethnically mixed. Three years after the war, Watts was mostly black. But it was nothing like Harlem, or ghettos he'd heard about in Chicago or Philly or Detroit. Watts was still kind of an easy, sleepy enclave with cozy bungalows and quiet streets and tidy yards. It felt more like a small town than part of a huge sprawling city whose tentacles reached through valleys and over mountains, clear to the ocean. There were gangs, and men out of work, and women (Hiram's widowed mother, for instance) raising children by themselves. But if you didn't want real trouble in Watts at that time, it could be avoided. He hadn't had a fight since second grade when Clarence Randall jumped him on the way home to continue a dispute started during recess.

The Voigtländer felt powerful in his hands. He'd get intoxicated conceiving a shot, then peer through the lens like a hunter taking aim at his prey. He'd wait, wait, wait, wait, before clicking the shutter; what had been in his line of fire would be captured forever. Quiet and dreamy for fourteen years, Hiram found his purpose and was all aflame.

But eventually he grew tired of combing the streets and alleys of Watts in search of unique images. Also, it was getting expensive, for although he owned the camera, it needed to be fed—with film and materials to develop it.

So Hiram made a sign, which his mother allowed to hang from the porch: *Freeman Art and Photography*. He spread the word—at school, knocking on doors—that he was available at very reasonable prices for any event worth commemorating: weddings, birthdays, graduations, family or personal portraits. It was slow the first few months, but soon he was not only paying for materials, he was putting money away for when he'd be done with school and ready to open his own studio.

Hiram didn't even consider college. They didn't teach photography anywhere he knew about, and by the time he graduated (class of '51), he figured that, like his brother, he'd have to go in the army; just hadn't figured it would be so soon. Two months after graduation, the notice came.

Even though he was sent to Korea, even though there was a real war going on there, in many ways, it was the best thing that could have happened to him. He got on the staff of *Stars and Stripes* and spent the war shooting not a rifle but a camera. Saw plenty of action, enough to prove that even in freezing temperatures, with mortar shells bursting and rifle rounds whistling, his aim stayed steady.

Hiram wasn't like so many of the men he'd served with who had to decide what to do in the civilian world. He was going to make his living as a photographer, but not the safe course of posed portraits and staged events. He would be an artist whose purpose was nothing less than chronicling the time he was living in, no different than da Vinci or Rembrandt or any of the masters. Only he wouldn't be doing so with oil and canvas, but on photographic paper in living black and white.

Within a week of his discharge, seated at his mother's desk, Hiram set about writing the letter he had, in effect, been composing for years. He'd send it care of the address that appeared every week in every issue that hit every newsstand in the country.

Dear Gordon Parks, I am a young photographer from the Watts section of Los Angeles who is relocating to New York.

Hiram stared at the word after he had written it. *Relocating.* Where the hell had it come from?

Although clear at the other end of the country, New York was the fulcrum of America. That's where all the news was beamed from, all the fashion, all the art and commerce. Hell, if he was serious, he needed to get there for someone like Gordon Parks to take him seriously.

So even though Hiram knew nothing at all about what New York was really like, he tucked the letter in a suitcase, along with everything else that had become essential to him, and, twenty-one years old, camera in hand, dream stitched into his heart, he boarded the hound for its lumbering dash across the country.

*

Asleep when the bus reached Manhattan's Port Authority Terminal that December morning, Hiram stumbled out stiff, hungry, sleepy-eyed . . . but all discomfort was instantly wiped away as he stepped onto the streets of New York. *Man, what a circus!* He felt like whipping his camera out right there.

In Times Square, as the crowds were swelling just before lunch, a bearded, toothless guy—white, not that old either—was hoofing up a hurricane while his brown-skinned, derby-hatted buddy strummed a ukulele and sang "The Darktown Strutters' Ball."

A group swept by who looked like fashion models—six, seven of them—cheeks rouged, lips smeared red, flowing coats, dresses and heels, all around six feet tall; Hiram was pretty sure they were men.

A tug on his arm and a black man, eyes glazed, face sweaty, uttered: "I won't kid you, brother. It's chilly out here, but I'm burnin' up with fever and I sure could use a fix." Hiram fished out all the change in his pocket.

Hours passed that seemed like minutes and, sunlight fading and shadows falling, Hiram found himself downtown on Third Avenue. Figured he would run into a YMCA sooner or later but so far, he'd either not hit one or had been so caught up he'd failed to see it. He'd look in the phone book. But he hadn't eaten since the night before, and his stomach was giving him a talking to.

＊

In the harsh glow of the Parthenon Diner, Hiram was at a table by himself when Oona Stickney, first name tagged on her waitress uniform, came over.

"What'll it be?"

Hiram glanced at the menu. "Is it too late to get eggs?"

"It's never too late to get eggs."

"Over easy then. Rye toast and whatever kind of potatoes

you have."

"Congratulations. You just ordered the breakfast special. Coffee?"

Hiram laughed. "This *is* breakfast for me. But orange juice, instead of coffee."

"Just get to town?"

Taken aback, Hiram said, "How did you know?"

She shot a glance to the floor where he'd placed his suitcase and camera bag. "Back in a sec."

Oona walked to the kitchen to put the order in. She emerged almost immediately, then went to a corner booth where Garland Alpert was sitting. The sharp light rendered his pale skin even paler, bringing out traces of what had been adolescent acne. A bouquet of red roses lay across the table like it had been slain.

From across the room, Hiram had the sense that the two of them were, for some reason, talking about him. In a few minutes, the cook rang the bell and Oona brought the eggs to Hiram's table. "Somebody would like to join you for a moment. That okay with you?"

Hiram shrugged. Oona sent a look to Garland.

Hiram sized him up as he approached. Five-eight or nine, he bounced in a way that seemed like an effort to make himself taller. Faded jeans, a pair of once-white Jack Purcells. Nothing sinister; his expression loose as his clothing. He pulled back the chair opposite Hiram. "My name's Garland."

Hiram had a piece of egg poised on a fork. "First or last?"

A smile. "Garland Alpert."

"Hiram Freeman."

"What kind of artist are you, man?"

"Who says I'm an artist?"

"I do. I'm an artist. I can pin another one a block away."

"What kind of artist are *you*?"

"Writer . . . Journalist, to make a living." He nodded toward Oona who was hauling a stack of plates toward the kitchen. "So is Oona, although at the moment, she's otherwise occupied." Another pause. "So what kind of artist?"

"Photographer."

"Sounds cool. Tough to get established here, though. Any contacts?"

"Not a one."

Garland reached for Hiram's half-consumed glass of water and pulled it to his lips. This startled Hiram, who recalled a moment during basic training when an Irish kid from Wooster, Mass., reeling from heat exhaustion, had refused a drink from Hiram's canteen.

After taking a sip, Garland said, "Oona used to be my chick."

"Why are you telling me this?" asked Hiram.

Garland chuckled. "I need a roommate and you need a pad. Your own room, of course. Share the bath and kitchen. Wanna take a peek?"

Thoughts crowded Hiram's brain. He glanced at Oona, who was smoking as she sent a smile.

Garland leaned forward. "Nights like this, when the owner's at his other joint in Jersey, Oona will let us eat here for free."

"Sounding better all the time," said Hiram.

FIVE

O ut of earshot of guards and prisoners, Jimmy and Stan, a young Warners exec, walked the yard.

"Jimmy, Jimmy—how the hell did we get here?"

"The goddamn gun went off."

"What were you doing on the set with a loaded pistol?"

Jimmy pulled hard on his cigarette.

"It took you long enough, man. Is the studio behind me or not?"

"We're with you a thousand percent."

"How do I know that?"

"Let's talk, one guy to another. The studio's got millions riding on you. One picture in the can; two on the boards. They're arranging bail as we speak."

Jimmy said nothing.

"We're about to orchestrate a little pretrial campaign. You're gonna go home for a while."

"To New York?"

Stan laughed. "That's the last place you wanna be, man. No, home is Indiana."

"I can't face those people. They all think I'm crazy."

"That's what we want everybody to think. You've always been too weird for them anyway—sodbusters, right?"

"Don't look down on them, man, there's some good people there."

"You get what I mean. The studio's gonna arrange for somebody from *Life* to come out and spend some time with you."

"*Life* magazine—in Fairmount?"

"It's gold for the opening of *Eden*. All indications are they're gonna put you on the cover."

Jimmy smiled, suddenly the hayseed. "You mean it?" His expression clouded. "I gotta see what my lawyer says."

"Donald's already on board. Nuts about the idea, excuse the reference."

"But I'm not crazy."

"We need you to *seem* crazy. When you get off, it'll be rest and relaxation and a round-the-clock headshrinker. That gang picture we're developing for you will go through the roof."

"You sure about this? It sounds phony."

"We wouldn't take this route if we weren't sure. Just brace yourself for *Life* mag to tell the world what a nutcase you are."

"You're the expert. Hell, man, people think I'm crazy already."

The bell clanged. Stan shook Jimmy's hand. "You'll be out before you know it. You're a genius actor. Get ready to go back home and act loony for when the people from *Life* show up."

*

Hiram was working at a framing shop in Chelsea. One gray afternoon, Bianco, who owned the place and worked up front, stepped into the framing room.

"Phone call for you, Hiram."

Surprised, Hiram picked up the receiver. "Hello?"

"It's your lucky day, Freeman." Garland's voice.

"How's that?"

"Cameron Duff, up at *Life*. I've been bugging him for months. The poky bastard finally came through."

"You got a story? That's great, Gar."

"We, baby. *We* got a story."

Hiram was speechless. Then: "How'd you manage that?"

"I know him. He got loaded one night at a party and I put him in a cab uptown. He digs my stuff . . . And I told him Gordon Parks is crazy about your work."

"What?"

"Don't sweat it. Gordon's on assignment out of the country. Listen, you need to score some gone-time to be on location."

"Where?"

"Illinois. Indiana—one of those *I* states out in the sticks."

Hiram glanced at Bianco who was eyeing him, all but tipping forward.

"I'm in. What's the subject?"

"James Dean, that punk actor who shot Ronald Reagan on television. They want a show-and-tell on how crazy he is. Apparently, nobody wants the gig, but I figure we'll have some kicks."

✶

Wearing glasses, a black beret, leather gloves, and a brown leather flight jacket, Jimmy was at the wheel of his uncle's pickup, open fields on either side. It was just before dark, the light sharp. Garland and Hiram shared the front seat with him, each wrapped up against the February cold. Jimmy dug the photographer well enough but the writer was a drag, not half as hip as he was struggling to pull off.

"My aunt's cooking us some supper," mumbled Jimmy, cigarette between his lips. The truck swung onto a mud-covered road that led to a classic white farmhouse. "Before we go in," said Jimmy, "I need to soothe the cows."

He pulled over, went to the back of the truck. Picked up a large canvas bag; peeled off the canvas. Inside was his conga drum, brown and white fur covering the sides.

Garland and Hiram climbed out of the truck.

"Looks like a cow, don't it?" Jimmy grinned. "I used to pound on milk pails but this here drum will be a lot more soothing."

He rushed to the fence, drum cradled. Garland and Hiram followed. Jimmy entered the pen, chose a spot and sat. Drum across his lap, he soloed.

Garland appeared agitated as Hiram clicked away.

*

In Hiram's motel room, Milton Berle was getting big laughs, wearing a dress on television. "This whole scene is a real shuck," Garland said, rolling a joint.

"How you mean?" asked Hiram.

"Dean acts out of his nut and we're supposed to play along with it. Goddamn insulting."

"Gonna cash the check, aren't you, man?"

"If I wanted to write ad copy, I'd be at J. Walter Thompson."

"But you agreed to do the story the way they want it."

"I just said that to get the gig."

"You're sounding funny, Gar."

"It's some kind of bullshit trade-off so Warner Brothers can protect their investment." He struck a match. "You won't even try a hit?"

"I'd rather you do that in your own room."

"I can't believe you've never gotten high."

"I like to have a few things to look forward to."

Garland waved out the flame. "You ought to loosen up, Freeman."

"I don't know about you, but this assignment felt like a break."

Uncle Miltie's sponsor, Texaco, was running a commercial.

Garland stood. "There's more to life than *Life*," he said, as he opened the door and headed for his room.

✴

In bed, Hiram tried to shut down but his mind wouldn't let him. The only places in America he'd spent any time were Los Angeles, New York, and Camp Cooke, where he'd scarcely left the base. Rural Indiana was quite a new experience. The people of Fairmount were polite but distant, regarding him and Garland as the outsiders from Bigger-Than-Life Magazine. Plus, Hiram had never been more aware of his skin color, even in Korea. The Fairmount locals stared at him, as though they'd never seen a black person before and never wanted to see one again.

Hiram could tell that Jimmy himself was an outsider, which was surely why he got out of Fairmount at the first opportunity. Plus, there was the cloud of his having shot Ronald Reagan on national television, which didn't exactly qualify him as a local hero.

So, wherever they went there was a kind of simmering suspicion. It didn't help that the story's premise was the unhinged artist who had committed a national outrage. Bizarre images were being provided: Jimmy standing like a sentinel beside a massive hog, or posing as a corpse at the local funeral parlor. When Hiram took that shot, it unnerved him somehow. The guy had death all around him, you could feel it.

After supper that evening, they'd gone with Jimmy to a Valentine's dance at the high school. One of his former teachers, perhaps the only non–family member in Fairmount who still held some fondness for Jimmy, had invited him. Jimmy kept off to the side as he must have done as a schoolboy. The kids, caught up in living their lives, carried on as though he didn't exist. Jimmy struck Hiram as a ghost revisiting a scene he had never really been part of.

Hiram came fully awake, having heard something; footsteps, voices. He got up and opened the door.

Standing across the parking lot, like some hideous statue, was a figure decked out in Ku Klux Klan robes and hood. Hiram grabbed his camera to be certain he wasn't seeing things.

He didn't know what he or they—he assumed the fool wasn't alone—intended to do; burn a cross in the parking lot or scrawl some scurrilous message on the door. As soon as he clicked, the figure drifted into a wooded area to the left.

*

Cameron Duff   February 25, 1955
Features Editor
Life Magazine
Rockefeller Center
New York, 36, New York

Dear Cameron:

Like you, I was distressed by our telephone conversation.
Yes, you hired me to do a story. That story had a premise
you wanted me to reinforce, and my account regarding Dean
clearly differs from what you want me to portray. If I don't
report what I see, then journalism loses in the face of public
relations.

The powers-that-be at Warner Brothers set this up to be
presented with a certain slant. The fact that I haven't delivered that might indeed put them (and Life) in what you characterize as "an awkward position." You decry that there's too
much anticipation to kill the story and it's too late to hold it
back.

Think of what's at risk here. While you're pleasing these
Hollywood types, you risk losing the esteem of every writer
in New York, where the written word matters. "How the hell
would I lose that?" you might ask.

Kill my story, and I'm prepared to go to every major news
source and say how you sold some powder puff version of
reality that belongs in Photoplay rather than the respected
and esteemed Life magazine. I'm not kidding, Cameron. I'll
buttonhole every journalist and editor from Bleecker to the
Hundreds. I'm aware that I will never get another assignment
from your publication, but I can only do what I know is right.

Journalistically yours,
Garland Alpert

SIX

C rouched in a toilet stall, Specs Pelham was shaking like a table lamp during a five-point quake. He had rushed into this perverse sanctuary after the Shifters ran him out of the lunchroom.

Most kids in his high school had thought the name was because of the horn-rimmed glasses or wraparound shades he invariably sported. But he hadn't worn glasses until seventh grade. He'd gotten the tag when he was around eight, hanging out with older guys on his block. Started out as Speck but mutated into Specs. He looked at his watch, the Hamilton worn by his father. He'd been in there less than two minutes and it seemed like forever. Specs felt like crying, then checked himself. He hadn't cried when his father died and he wouldn't cry now.

The Shifters, golden-haired, rippling-necked cretins, were after him because of what Specs said about one of their member's new car. Used car actually, that his thick-walleted daddy bought for him. It was an MG, a green one, to match the money, not to mention the envy that flooded through Specs upon seeing it in the parking lot the day before. The Shifters were ogling it like it was some luscious, gigantic centerfold as Specs slunk by. Not one of them had so much as glanced at him, and Specs could have left it alone but no, he had to sound off like he always did. Smart-mouth, wiseacre; the story of his life. This time he could have let them relish their ludicrous moment, gazing at the newest and flashiest addition to their car club. But That Thing came over him. That Thing he'd grappled with for as long as he could remember, since kindergarten and before.

"Where'd you get the Tinkertoy?"

They were too stunned to respond, too dim to have done anything right then. But Specs knew there would be a delayed counterstrike. He fretted about it all night, carried a cold, close dread all morning. They waited until lunch, as he was coming out of the line, balancing his tray of mock pizza pie and cream-of-asparagus casserole. One grabbed his arm and steered him to a corner where the others were waiting—all five of the Shifters.

"Outside, Pelham," ordered Winthrop, their leader. "You're gonna kiss the tires and gas cap of the MG. Then you're gonna tell us how cherry it is."

Specs summoned strength from somewhere and flung his tray upwards. He bolted before any of them could react, darting from the lunchroom like he'd been shot out of a cannon.

He slid on the linoleum of the hallway, then dashed around the corner. His goal was to keep pumping until he reached his house, only a block away, where he could shut the door behind him, safe in his bedroom for a while at least. Instead, he impulsively turned into the boys' bathroom and headed for one of the stalls.

He immediately knew it was foolish, a horrible mistake. If they came in and found him, he'd be trapped, away from faculty intervention; they could whale away at him until his face was shattered. "Just don't break my hands," he feverishly rehearsed, knowing he needed them to play his instrument. Who was he kidding, he didn't want *anything* hurt.

Footsteps on the cement floor. Doors pushed open. Getting closer. Checking the stall next to where Specs was crouched. His chest felt like some hand was gripping him from within. He had to struggle to keep from coughing to relieve the tension. The dull metal door, his only shield, swung toward him. The Shifters were standing there, mouths drawn into tight, evil mockery. Hands and bodies forced him against the wall. Specs clamped his eyes shut. This was going to hurt.

But they didn't beat him.

They each took their turn, laughing maliciously, treating him as though he were nothing more than the toilet bowl in that dank, hideous stall.

Specs did not know how long he lay there; it must have been over an hour before he stumbled home. The house was empty. His mother wouldn't return from work for another five hours. He peeled his clothes off, stepped into the shower and steamed and scrubbed until it felt like his skin again. He gathered his tainted clothing—shoes, socks, underwear, T-shirt, the whole soaking mess—and dropped them in a grocery bag. Specs got a shovel from the garage, dug a hole in the yard and buried the bag about four feet down.

His mother came home and fixed dinner, but when she slipped in to tell him it was ready, he groaned that his stomach was upset.

Later that night, Specs told her something terrible had happened and he would not be going to school in the morning. She didn't say anything, just sat stunned. In his final senior semester, he wasn't planning on college, had gone to court reporter school in preparation for when he got out. Fastest in his class; fastest ever in the program. He'd been promised a job at the Van Nuys courthouse starting in June, but he would go there tomorrow, start right away. He refused to talk about what had happened—not now and probably never—but the only reason he would ever go back to that school would be to bomb it or burn it down.

✱

In a small conference room, Donald Lymon stood with Stan from Warners, a copy of *Life* open in front of them. Jimmy was on the glossy page, beret tilted, cigarette dangling, standing in mud and cow dung, eyes closed in apparent ecstasy, palms flailing a conga drum. Caption: *Crazy Like a Fox: A Young Star Faces the Music* by Garland Alpert.

"So what's wrong with it?" asked Jimmy, glancing at the two men.

"Everything," groaned Donald.

"Read it," said Stan.

Jimmy picked up the magazine, pulled out his glasses. The right earpiece was missing; the lenses settled at a precarious angle. "Pictures look cool," Jimmy said to nobody. "The one of me in the casket was my idea." He skimmed.

James Dean, twenty-three . . . must somehow convince a jury . . . no responsibility for his actions . . . Will defense attorneys establish . . . not responsible for very nearly taking another man's life . . . merely hiding behind a premeditated pose meant to be taken as insanity?

Jimmy knows what he's doing all the time, declared Edgar Brawley, proprietor of Smiley's, an Upper West Side watering hole that Dean frequented as a struggling New York actor. *I've never seen anybody more in command of himself.*

"You've never even talked to me, you old lush," Jimmy screeched at the magazine.

"Watching Jimmy perform," said Broadway director Mark Grogan, *"is like watching a highly skilled tightrope artist . . . every second . . . he might fall, but . . . he's far too accomplished to allow himself to slip."*

So what was in Dean's mind that December night when he brandished a loaded pistol and . . . (continued, next page)

Donald took the magazine.

The enormity of what he was facing came freshly down on Jimmy like a freakish downpour. "So what does this mean for me?"

"The jury's not sequestered, I argued very effectively against it," said Donald. "You know they're gonna see it."

"*Life* magazine," Stan said, "everybody sees it."

Jimmy looked ready to bust through the wall. "I thought you had this clown under your thumb."

"We thought so too," said Stan, misery in his voice.

Donald paced. "Everything hangs on an insanity plea. We can't reverse now, there's no time."

Jimmy's face was flushed and contorted. "If the jury thinks I did it on purpose, I could go away for twenty years."

Donald turned to his client. "That's right, you could."

Jimmy yanked off the lopsided glasses and locked eyes with his attorney.

"So you're just gonna go on as planned, except that your plan has already backfired."

SEVEN

A BC, CBS news cameras in the courtroom. A ten-man, two-woman jury, Judge Sterling Billingham presiding. Live on radio. One hundred sixty seats, one hundred twenty filled with press. Jimmy in a blue suit; Donald Lymon in gray flannel, heavy for springtime California.

Jentzen, head prosecutor, addressed the court. "Witnesses will testify that the defendant was antagonistic toward Ronald Reagan from the first day they met. 'Why?' you ask. Because James Dean despises authority. Humiliated and antagonistic toward Mr. Reagan, he chose to lash out in the most sensational way possible—on national television. Again, why? Because he's pampered and egocentric, and used to getting what he wants. We will prove that James Dean willfully and knowingly brought a loaded gun onto the set that night to fulfill his demented plan of mortally wounding Ronald Reagan, the man who had called him out for his infantile and loutish behavior."

Striding confidently in front of the jury box, the prosecutor offered a tight smile. "When a firearm is used in the commission of attempted second-degree murder, the charge automatically becomes a first-degree felony, punishable by a maximum of thirty years in a California state penitentiary. That comes with a twenty-year mandatory sentence if, as it is with this case, the gun is discharged. The state does not have to prove that the defendant had the intent to cause death.

"Under California law, we also have something called implied malice. This is when no considerable provocation occurs, or when the circumstances attending the attempted killing show evidence of what California penal law refers to as an abandoned and malignant heart. Now, what is that, you might ask. It's an odd phrase and an old one, but it speaks to an act with a high probability that it will result in death, and is performed with an antisocial motive that has a wanton disregard for human life. Looking at the defendant, showing that he committed an act that resulted in the near-lethal wounding of Ronald Wilson Reagan, we intend to prove beyond a reasonable doubt that James Dean does indeed have an abandoned and malignant heart."

✦

Christine Lademus, costumer, was on the stand. Donald, cross-examining: "So you had no idea that the gun the defendant was using was real."

"No, I did not."

"Had you known, would you have intervened?"

"How do you mean?"

"Would you have, for instance, told the director, or told the producers?"

"Yes, I especially would have wanted Mr. Reagan to know."

"Because there was the possibility of it going off?"

"Well, you saw what happened."

"No further questions," snapped Donald.

*

Alvin Noyce, prop manager, looked discomfited as he offered testimony: "You have to understand that stars have a lot of power during a production."

Jentzen, pacing: "So when Mr. Dean requested that his use of a real gun would be 'our little secret,' you decided to keep that confidence."

Alvin turned to the bench. "Am I going to get into trouble?"

Judge Billingham: "Just answer the question."

Alvin seemed not to know what to do with his hands, folding them in his lap before drawing a deep breath. "He told me it wouldn't be loaded. I trusted him."

Jentzen took a moment. "Mr. Noyce, would you characterize Mr. Dean as a person who is capable of manipulating people?"

Donald was up: "Objection, Your Honor."

*

"The state calls Doctor Delbert Mongeon."

A fresh alarm went off in Jimmy as Mongeon took the stand. Thick, salt-and-pepper hair. Bushy eyebrows, Jimmy remembered him all too well.

Jentzen approached. "Doctor Mongeon, you interviewed James Dean approximately eleven months ago, is that correct?"

"Yes."

"What were the circumstances of that interview?"

"I was hired by Warner Brothers to determine whether

or not they should insure him before principal photography began on their motion picture."

"And that picture was *East of Eden*, which the defendant did, in fact, complete?"

"Correct."

"What was Mr. Dean's demeanor during the time you spent with him?"

"He appeared aloof. He kept igniting scraps of paper with his cigarette lighter."

"Was he, in your opinion as a professional, distracted?"

"No, I felt he was doing it in an attempt to intimidate."

"Objection," said Donald.

"Overruled," droned the judge. "The doctor was observing the defendant in a professional capacity and therefore can render an opinion."

Jentzen smiled. "Doctor Mongeon, didn't you advise the studio not to insure Mr. Dean?"

"I certainly did."

"Because you felt he was unstable?"

"Because I felt he was loathsome, reckless, and untrustworthy."

"Objection."

"Sustained. As stated, it's too subjective."

"Did you have the impression that Warner Brothers would have preferred you to endorse him?"

"Yes, but I told them to find another doctor if it was just a formality."

"You felt that employing Mr. Dean was against their best interests?"

"So much so, that I've never been called again by that studio to make an assessment."

"But you held firm."

"My professional credibility was at issue." Mongeon glared at Jimmy. "I have never met such an odious, self-absorbed and potentially dangerous young man."

"The behavior that has been attributed to the defendant," said Jentzen, "would you characterize it as normal, doctor?"

"I would characterize it as antisocial."

"Have you, in your clinical experience, ever encountered people who could not control their actions?"

"Yes, but usually such individuals are marginalized to the point that they can't function in society."

Jentzen paused, facing the jury, then flung the next question. "Having already interviewed the defendant, and having administered a set of diagnostic tests, would you say that such a condition applies to Mr. Dean?"

"Object, Your Honor," piped Donald.

"Overruled. Professional assessment."

Mongeon took his time. His big moment. "James Dean is someone who exhibits chronic antisocial behavior, but who can be composed, calculated, even charming, when it suits his purposes."

"So you would say he tends not to be out of control?"

Mongeon turned fully toward the jury. "On the contrary. I would say that Dean is in control at all times. What he has developed is a sense of privilege regarding his willful and ultimately destructive behavior. He chooses to be the way he is."

"No further questions."

✦

Restaurant, downtown LA, a block from the courthouse. Jimmy, with Donald and Barbara; mid-thirties, unconventionally attractive, serving as assistant counsel. Jimmy, looking both agitated and despondent, was saying: "That head-shrinker destroyed us. The jury ate it up like they were paying good money for it."

"Now we get our turn," said Donald.

Jimmy: "This trial scene, it's a lot like my line of work."

Donald: "How do you mean?"

"You go up there and say your lines and the audience, the jury, either buys it or not. It's a performance, that's all."

Donald, alarm bells. "What's your point, Jimmy?"

"I want to go on the stand."

Donald, to Barbara. "What did I tell you?" Back at Jimmy. "What if the jury—even one of them—doesn't like the way you're dressed, or that your hands fidget, or your eyes shift, or that you remind them of somebody who used to taunt them back in school. Sorry, Jimmy. We can't risk it."

Jimmy, about to leap across the table. "Look, man, you may have been to Harvard, but I know a helluva lot more about getting in front of people and drawing them in."

Donald turned to the other lawyer. "Do you have an opinion on this?"

Barbara dabbed her mouth with her cloth napkin. "We're getting clobbered in there. We damn well better come back with something as strong as what they've already heard."

EIGHT

"State your name please."

"James Byron Dean."

"Do you swear to tell the truth, the whole truth and nothing but the truth, so help you God?"

"I do swear."

Donald, dressed in a tan suit, pale blue shirt, dark blue and yellow striped necktie. Jimmy had on his blue suit, white shirt with black tie, black belt and shoes. Blond hair tousled, he resembled a boy summoned to the principal's office after a schoolyard scuffle.

Donald: "What do you do for a living, Jimmy?"

"An actor," Jimmy mumbled.

"A little louder," ordered Billingham, "so that the court reporter can hear you."

Jimmy glanced at the kid taking testimony. Fingers on the keys, he was peering at Jimmy through horn-rimmed glasses.

"An actor," Jimmy repeated. "I'm an actor."

"Do you think you're a good actor?"

"Objection, Your Honor!" boomed Jentzen.

"Overruled. Let him offer an assessment of his talents."

Jimmy smiled. "I think I'm the best actor in the world. Best my age, anyhow."

"Have other people supported this claim?"

"Objection. Subjective and irrelevant."

"Overruled. Answer the question."

"I've got some reviews that said as much. *New York Times.* Gadge Kazan thinks I'm good."

"And who is Gadge Kazan?"

"My director in *Eden.*"

"Let us remind the court," said Donald, "that Eden is *East of Eden*, the motion picture James Dean completed for Warner Brothers."

"Right," said Jimmy.

"And you're scheduled to do two more for them?"

"I sure hope so."

Some laughed, including members of the jury. The judge didn't like Jimmy's response. "If you find these proceedings lighthearted and amusing, Mr. Dean, I assure you the court doesn't."

"Sorry, sir. Your Honor."

Donald turned to his client. "When you were performing on the *General Electric Theater*, on the night of December twelfth of last year, did you know what was going to happen?"

Jimmy squirmed in his seat. "Well, I thought I did. Guess it turned out a little different."

"Did you prepare for the part?"

"See, acting doesn't just take place onstage. For instance, Ronald Reagan wasn't Ronald Reagan to me. He was Doctor Walker, that part he was playing. I was Sonny, the part I was playing. But I was playing it all week, not just for the half hour in front of the camera."

"The script called for you to pull a gun and point it at your costar, Mr. Reagan, isn't that right?"

"Yes."

"Are guns unusual items to be seen on a set or a sound-stage?"

"No, they're around all the time. Especially in Westerns."

Another titter from the audience, which Billingham let pass.

"But those are what are called prop guns, are they not?"

"That's right."

"The gun you pointed at Mr. Reagan, the one that discharged and wounded him, that was a real gun, wasn't it?"

"Unfortunately, yes."

Donald asked, "Why did you use a real gun instead of a prop?"

"To be a great actor, you've got to not only convince the audience you're somebody else, you've got to *become* somebody else. I hadn't planned on loading it, but I'm sorry to say I did. See, when there's a threat of violence in what is supposed to be a true-to-life drama, the threat has to be real. In a supposedly realistic scene, like the one Mr. Reagan and I were performing, I needed to feel that the emotions I was carrying inside me, and the gun I had in my pocket, were real, that there was the possibility somebody could get hurt or even killed."

"No further questions."

Billingham called a recess. As Jimmy walked back to the defense table, he took a longer look at the court reporter, at Specs Pelham, although he didn't know his name. Clark Kent glasses, dark brown hair brushed forward, pale white skin, an undertaker's suit. Jimmy knew another freak when he saw one. There was something imperceptible from the kid; not a nod, exactly, but some kind of tacit approval. *Whew*, thought Jimmy, *maybe I've got a friend here after all.*

*

Back in session. "Mr. Dean," Jentzen droned, "you didn't like Ronald Reagan the first day you met him, did you?"

"I didn't dislike him."

"You called him Pops that first day of rehearsal, did you not?"

"I may have. Sounds like me." This time, nobody chuckled.

"You have a disdain for anyone in authority, don't you, Mr. Dean?"

"Objection, Your Honor."

"Sustained. Please limit the scope of the questions to the parties involved."

Jentzen came at him a different way. "You didn't like Mr. Reagan from the first time you laid eyes on him. From that moment, you decided to bring a loaded firearm onto the set and began working up the—what shall I call it, certainly not courage—the *nerve* to pull the trigger and make your ultimate statement to America. Isn't that how it went, Mr. Dean?"

"No, sir. I was just an actor caught up in the realest performance I could do."

"Just an actor?" The prosecutor sent a smirk toward the jury.

"People act all the time, every day of their lives, I just take it farther," said Jimmy. "The folks on the jury there. Say, the boss comes in with some big idea. They know it's foolish, but they might say, 'Boss, you're a genius.' Or a husband gets served a dish his wife has cooked for the first time. She's made a mess of it, they both know it, but he might say, 'Honey, this is delicious.'"

"Your Honor," Jentzen sighed. "Can we get him to stay focused?"

"Just an actor," Jimmy added, "just like you."

"Oh, I'm an actor now?" mocked Jentzen.

"A great actor."

"What makes you say that, Mr. Dean?"

"Because you know it was an accident, I wasn't trying to hurt anybody. Just because I take my work seriously, you're trying to put me away for it."

Jentzen glared at Jimmy. "No further questions, Your Honor."

*

Conference room in the courthouse. Jimmy, at a table with Donald and Barbara, was smoking, jumpy. Donald: "Why don't you go home and get some rest, Jimmy? We'll call when we get the word."

Jimmy: "I'd rather wait it out."

Barbara stood. "I'm going for coffee. Want me to bring back anything?"

"It's getting pretty late, and who knows what's open," said Donald. "You should take somebody with you."

Jimmy stubbed out his cigarette. "Why are they taking so long—is that a good sign or a bad one?"

Donald, distressed, fussed with his tie. "I won't bullshit you, Jimmy. This one could go either way."

*

Editorial, *Los Angeles Herald Examiner*, March 30, 1955

. . . In the wake of James Dean's hung jury, we need to seriously examine our judicial system. Have we turned into a society where one man can shoot another in front of all of us with what appeared to be nothing less than cool, murderous intent, and we are somehow not able to reach a conclusion? The district attorney has no recourse but to try Dean a second time. While it will again incur a great expense to the taxpayers, the cost of allowing a homicidal act to go unpunished is a much greater expense to the people of this city and indeed, the nation at large . . .

✦

Meeting with Joe Ridley at his and Nancy's house, Ronald Reagan was furious.

"How can there be any doubt but that Dean was guilty? It was on TV, for God's sake, millions of people saw it."

"Too bad they couldn't play it for the jury."

"You mean it's too bad some idiot at CBS misplaced the kinescope. I'd love to find out who was responsible for that." Reagan shook his head. "I should have let them hear my side directly from me."

"Dean's not getting away with it. I got that straight from the DA."

"Well, if and when there's a retrial, I'm going to make sure I testify. I can sway a jury as well as that little worm." Reagan's voice took on fresh emotion. "Clear-thinking people need to start making and enforcing the laws. James Dean and his ilk should be locked up where they belong, away from decent and law-abiding citizens." A fresh look came over Reagan's face. "How about if I include that in this first set of speeches?"

Ridley, bent over his legal pad. "Include what?"

"My perspective on the non-outcome of the trial. Yet another example of government using the public trust and still not functioning effectively."

Ridley shook his head. "The company just wants us to support the line of products, Ron. Save that kind of thing for offstage."

NINE

In the screening room of his house in Beverly Hills, Glenn Parnell, feature film producer, stood before thirty or so guests, mostly fellow members of the Hollywood community, working on his third gin and tonic. "Tonight you'll be seeing something I'm told is very special. Our friends over at Warners were good enough to slip me a copy. While we in the industry usually have the privilege of viewing films before they come out, this is one whose release status is uncertain because its star received a lot of bad publicity. But all that aside, I understand it's a wonderful picture and it's a tragedy that the young man in question made the unfortunate choice of shooting himself in the foot—not to mention Ron Reagan's torso. And now, let's all enjoy *East of Eden.*"

The lights were dimmed; the film began. Jill Parnell, Glenn's lovely, fawn-haired, sixteen-year-old daughter, first saw James Dean with her eyes, but felt him in her hips, pelvis; the base of her spine.

Jimmy in the role of Cal; beige sweater pulled over a white shirt with a drooping collar. Wrinkled khakis. Blonde hair uncombed, but even that struck her as perfection. Eyes, pale one instant, dark the next, a stray cat backed into a corner, hungry and wary, but longing to be soothed by a touch.

Scene after scene, shot after shot, he communicated as much by gesture and glance as by the lines he spoke. Jill felt a stab of jealousy when Cal sat beside his brother's fiancée, played by Julie Harris; close, legs touching, locked inside a Ferris wheel. During their lingering, onscreen kiss, Jill nearly evaporated.

Although he couldn't see her, she could drink in every luscious part of him on the screen. He was deep and sensitive and vulnerable and caring; a luminous soul that shone like no other.

The lights came on and Jill sat blinking amidst murmurs: "Dean, James Dean, Jimmy Dean . . . Monster, crazy, menace . . . nearly killed Ron Reagan . . ."

*

Jill had never been in love but she'd had one sexual experience. Up in Big Bear, the previous August; the last night of camp. One of the counselors, Leland Marsh, a twenty-year-old Stanford guy, had been the star of the summer. Jill decided on him the final Saturday of the final weekend when he was swimming between the rafts. He looked like he could swim for hours if he had to. Anybody who could swim that long and that smoothly and forcefully, you'd think he'd have known what to do.

Jill invited him to meet her by the picnic tables that night. They talked for a long time and Jill thought maybe he wasn't picking up her signals. Just before dawn, they stretched out on the grass and . . . what? What *was* it? It didn't exactly hurt but it didn't feel that good either, not like her friend Kim told her it would. But tonight changed everything.

She would love James Dean forever.

*

Stan sat in his office at Warners, looking out at the mountains. Telephone in hand, his manner neutral, distant, like he was reading a prepared statement. "I wanted you to hear it from me, Jimmy. The DA's office just informed the studio that they're going to try you again for shooting Reagan. With the public response to the hung jury, there's not a lot of love out there. The studio is exercising the clause that renders you uninsurable. *Eden's* been shelved. *Rebel's* green light just turned red. The part in *Giant* is going to Paul Newman. The only good thing, they're paying you forty-five grand to cut you loose."

*

Jimmy, in his apartment, on his back, mic in hand, talking into his new tape recorder. "At a stoplight today, this car pulls up beside me. A couple and a kid, no more than six or seven, who's standing on the back seat. Has on a cowboy outfit, pulls a gun from his holster. Points this long barrel at me and pulls the trigger. 'Put that thing away,' the father tells him. Mother looks at me, says to her husband, 'The boy's only doing what he saw *that one* do on television.'" Jimmy raised up on one elbow, stared at the pair of whirling, caramel-shaded cylinders. "That's the jury, right there. The state's not gonna blow it next time. I'm pretty damn sure Donald won't even plead my case again, he's so convinced it's a loser. So, till judgment day, they've got their little maze set up for me. No more films anymore; that's gone. Nowhere to go, but gotta keep moving as fast as I can. Get all the kicks I can. Once those bastards are done, they might as well put me away for life, because this one, the one I've known up till now, is gonna be over."

*

Competition Motors, Hollywood. Jimmy paid cash for a white Porsche 356 Speedster, 1500 c.c.

He first got the speed bug back in high school when he owned a Triumph bike and felt all that surge and power between his legs. The feeling was better than sex and almost as good as being up in front of an audience.

He always knew he could drive, but now he'd prove it. Driving required focus and commitment, but different than what he brought to acting.

One wrong turn could get you killed.

*

Pacific Palisades, Jimmy's first race. Bent forward over the wheel, he couldn't help grinning as he flashed over the finish line, well ahead of the field.

At Pomona, Jimmy let out a whoop as he sailed past the checkered flag, winning by three car lengths.

As he'd planned it, each race was ever more challenging. Faster track, better drivers. He entered as Byron James, using his middle name and flipping his first to deflect his infamy, although some of the drivers and mechanics recognized him and the word soon got out.

Jimmy expected them to be skeptical, even dismissive or hostile. But once he was on the track, he earned their respect. That's how it was in a world where, unlike acting, you either crossed the line first or you didn't. There was no faking it, and everyone there knew it.

At Palm Springs, he was seething as he steered into the pit, his mechanic telling him: "Nice race, Jimmy."

Jimmy lunged out of his car, ripped off his helmet, flinging it toward the infield. "Don't tell me that when I came in
second. I wanna win, man, that's the whole lousy point!"

*

Jimmy, in his new digs; a one-room cabin in Sherman Oaks.
Bullfight posters on every wall, Wagner booming as Jimmy,
stretched out on his bed, droned into his tape recorder's
microphone: "Bakersfield. I had the pole position, shoulda
won hands down. Came in . . . third. Is it me—is it my car?
Doubt will kill you, man. Doubt will fucking kill you."

*

Labor Day weekend, Santa Barbara.
Jimmy stood in awe as a black Porsche Spyder 550, sleek
aluminum body, rounded a turn in the qualifying lap, smooth
as a panther.
By lap sixty-two of sixty-seven, it was a three-way between
Jimmy, a Ferrari, and the black Spyder. Jimmy was lapping a
yellow and black Lotus MK9. "C'mon, sucker, get out of the
way."
The Lotus drifted toward the bales of hay that lined the
infield. Jimmy gunned it even harder. The Lotus kept drifting left. As Jimmy came up behind, it veered into his path.
"Goddamn idiot!"
His left front bumper brushed the first set of bales. Straw
flew as Jimmy thudded against them, swerving onto the
infield, struggling to keep the Speedster from flipping.
He glanced ahead and saw the Spyder and Ferrari sailing
on without him. Jimmy accelerated, guiding his car back onto
the track, the rest of the field surging from behind.

Eyes on the Spyder, Jimmy leaned forward, gripping the wheel. He streaked past the halfway pole, was into the back-stretch when his car jerked, the engine knocking like a hammer had been flung into it.

The speedometer receding, Jimmy groaned. Blown piston, done for the day.

The Spyder, a football field ahead, pulled away even further. Jimmy's Speedster limped into the pit. He ripped off his gloves, hurled them to the dirt. Looked over at Rudi, the Spyder's mechanic. *What's the fool grinning at?* Was he making fun of him? Jimmy stalked over. "What the hell is with you?"

"You made miscalculation," Rudi said, in a German accent.

"And what was that?"

"You felt that the Lotus would see you and make way. A driver should never rely on such. You can control your car, but you cannot control what other is going to do."

Jimmy had thought as much himself once he'd collided with the bales of hay. "Yeah, well I don't need a lesson right now." Headed back toward his car.

"You are the most natural driver here, my friend," Rudi called out. "If you had Spyder, there would be no one who could beat you."

Jimmy froze, turned slowly, deciding he liked the guy.

"You're absolutely right, Rudi. I'd give my left nut to have a car like that."

"You may not need to go to such extreme. One has been ordered. I work for Competition Motors. I could suggest you as buyer. We could trade for your Speedster."

Jimmy's system, up several watts. "When is it getting here?"

"Before end of the month. Shall I inform sales department that you wish to be first to see it?"

"Yeah, Rudi, by all means, I'm your man."

The mechanic laughed. "I knew, of all people, you would be most excited."

"What color is it?"

"What color?"

"So I can picture it in my mind."

"Do not worry about color, Jimmy. Think about the engine."

"You're right, baby. I'll just think about the engine."

Jimmy was grinning as he strode back toward the pit.

TEN

August 25, 1955

Dear Jimmy,

I hope this finds its way to you, that your family in Fairmount
will forward it. I've thought of you many times since I saw
you last. I felt put down and pissed off that I didn't mean as
much to you as I might have hoped.

You getting arrested was a real bring-down, but know
in my heart that it had to have been an accident. Bad news,
since your career was starting to move. What I want to tell
you is: that article in Life that made it sound like you did it on
purpose was written by my former boyfriend, Garland Alpert.
Because of me, he was out to get you and really tried to fix
you with that article. I was going to tell you at the time (of
the trial) but didn't know how to reach you.

If I was ever really mad at you, I'm not anymore. I hope
you don't end up having to go to the joint. I'm not a lawyer,
but maybe you could state in your retrial that somebody, for
personal reasons, tried to sway public opinion and keep you
from being acquitted. The last thing you need is some jealous
fool poisoning the well for you the next time. Underneath it
all, you're a good enough cat.

Don't take any,
Oona

＊

Jimmy strolled into Googie's on Sunset, took a table, shared a pleasant exchange with Gilda, the waitress, leaned back and lit a cigarette.

Specs Pelham sat alone in a corner booth, with a BLT and triple-chocolate malt.

Jimmy kept thinking *where do I know him from; the racetrack, the beach? No, no* . . . and then he remembered. He crossed the room, slid into the opposite seat. "You were the only soul in that courtroom who seemed to think I wasn't guilty."

Gilda bustled out with Jimmy's order—burger, fries, cola. He motioned from his new location. "Musical chairs tonight," she muttered.

Jimmy took a quick sip, said to Specs: "This Pepsi here—I did a commercial for them once. After everything that's happened, they'd never let me do another spot for them in a hundred trillion years." Took a fry from his plate. "What do you do, man?"

"You know what I do."

"I know what you do for a living. What do you do to express yourself?"

"I write songs," said Specs, like he didn't quite believe it himself.

"How many you written?"

"I dunno. Twenty maybe."

Jimmy drew hard on his cigarette. "They aren't any good yet, are they?"

"I haven't really played them for anybody."

"They aren't any good yet, I can tell."

Jimmy pulled out Oona's letter, rumpled from repeated readings.

"The clown who penned that *Life* article really tried to screw me. That's how I ended up on the stand."

"Well, they didn't convict you."

Jimmy smiled faintly. "I got this from a chick I used to run around with in New York. Told me the writer, Alpert is his name, was jealous 'cause I'd been with her." Spit a tobacco fleck from his lower lip. "So he tried to put the screws in."

Specs took a sip of malt from the bottom of the glass. Slurping sound. Set it on the table. "He wanted you put away just for that?"

Jimmy looked around for an ashtray, dropped the cig butt on the floor, pressed down with his shoe. "See that chick over there?"

Specs's eyes went to a pretty girl with long brown hair reading a newspaper, pulled up to a table in her wheelchair.

"One night she tells me how lonely she is; how if she could be walking around like other people, she'd be fighting guys off with a stick. But no guy's ever touched her because she'd had polio. Anyway, we went back to her place on Laurel, and I gave her seven hours of the best stuff I've got and now she won't even look at me."

Specs stared at her. She was reading the paper like there was nothing else in the room.

Jimmy drained his Pepsi. "Give a little square to somebody and they want the whole damn puzzle. People can't accept that nothing lasts forever. They hold on to shit till dooms-day. That lousy magazine writer did it and that girl's doing it. It's poisonous." Fired up a fresh cigarette. "Hey, why don't we blow this place." Already on his feet, food all but untouched on the mint-shaded, Formica table, Jimmy dropped some dollars beside his plate. "That ought to cover us. Let's get out of here."

✱

Santa Monica Pier, Jimmy stood with Specs beside the carousel.

"When I first came to town," said Jimmy, "I felt these horses were the only friends I had. Each one is solid wood. Hand-carved in Germany."

Out of nowhere, a slight, baby-faced guy appeared at Jimmy's elbow. "Reliving old times?" he said.

Jimmy, startled but cool. "Oh, hi there."

"Congratulations on still being out in the world."

Jimmy lit a cigarette and said nothing.

The guy glanced at Specs. Then, to Jimmy: "Got a new buddy, I see."

Jimmy glared. "Something I can help you with?"

The guy stepped back like he'd been shoved. Over his shoulder, walking away, he said to Specs, "Watch yourself, kiddo. Jimmy leaves skid marks when he stops for you, then leaves 'em again when he goes."

Jimmy sent his glowing cigarette into the air. "Let's split, man. It gets kind of rank down here."

✱

PCH, driving north. Ocean on the left; mountains, right. Specs, like he was looking to duck under the dash, as Jimmy pushed a hundred, a hundred ten. They flashed by a sign and Specs said, "We're going to Santa Barbara?"

Jimmy, eyes on the road. "Just south of there. Somebody I gotta see."

Twenty minutes later, Jimmy swung into a parking lot that served a one-story building with a broadcast tower adjacent. Shut off his engine. "Come meet somebody."

Front door, unlocked. They passed through an open reception area, then down a tight hallway. Left, behind a pane of glass, a woman around thirty with striking red hair sat behind a control board. Bebop, emanating. The woman smiled, motioned for them to come in. They entered, Jimmy and Specs, and she threw her arms around Jimmy. "You made it, baby,"

He grinned. "How could I turn down a return engagement? Patsy, this here is Specs Pelham. The man is destined to be a great songwriter."

"We could use more of those."

Specs nodded. "Pleased to meet you."

"You boys want some lush?"

"Naw," said Jimmy, "I'm just here for the Q and A."

"What about your sidekick, has he got eyes to watch?"

"He's just gonna tune in," Jimmy said, "along with the rest of your audience."

"Cool," said Patsy. "I've pulled some sides."

Jimmy led Specs out the way they came in. Crossing the parking lot, Jimmy said, "Just sit in the car and dig the show. Patsy's got great taste."

"How long you gonna be in there?"

Jimmy ignored him, switched the key, igniting the radio without turning over the engine. Tuned the dial until a piano progression overtook the static. "See what I mean? Monk. I'll be back in an hour or so."

Specs, left sitting there, bop piano filling the small speaker.

*

Zooming south, two hours later.

"C'mon, Jimmy, what'd you do in there, smoke reefer or something?"

"Naw, Patsy's a juicehead. Gin and Orange Crush is her thing."

"Why'd you leave me hanging outside?"

"It's like this. She booked me as a guest after I shot *Eden*. Afterward, she announces a music marathon and cues up a couple of LP sides to play straight through. She has a little pad she sets up in the corner; foam rubber mat, silk sheets, scarves over the lamps, the whole bit. While the music is spinning and her audience is digging the uninterrupted presentation, Patsy is balling the subject of her interview."

"So while I was listening . . ."

"You got it, baby. It's how Patsy gets off, and man, does she."

"So this is with lots of guys?"

"Chicks sometimes. There's a chick singer from San Francisco who Patsy got so into, her listeners were treated to half an hour of dead air." Jimmy downshifted, the glow of Los Angeles in front of them. "Man, I'm thirsty. What say we go for a drink?"

*

Jimmy pulled over on Sunset, east, practically to Chinatown. He parked and locked the Porsche. A bar, with some kind of Polynesian motif: *Little Sam's* in purple neon.

Specs followed him in. Hand-in-front-of-your-face dark. Lime green lights around the bar, figures on stools and at tables. Jukebox droning: *You give your hand to me, and then you say hello.* "What you want to drink?" asked Jimmy.

"Beer, I guess."

Jimmy, to the bartender, "Two bottles of Falstaff."

Specs looked around. Couldn't make out much of anything. A pair of figures dancing close, a few feet away. Both pretty tall. *A couple of guys?*

Jimmy tapped Specs, handed him his beer. "Let's go down to The Smoking Room."

Specs followed.

Downstairs, dark, but not black, like above. Amber light, shadowy. Jimmy led them to a small table. Around twenty others in the room; all appeared to be men. Specs, a little rattled, took out a cigarette. "Don't do that, baby," ordered Jimmy.

Specs peered across the table. "I thought this was The Smoking Room." He indicated a guy at an adjacent table. "Look, *he's* smoking."

Jimmy took a swig from the bottle. "That isn't the point."

Specs, thrown, as Jimmy continued: "Down here is where you declare what you're into. If you like to pitch, you pull out a cigarette and leave it unlit till somebody offers to fire it up. Lighting it sends the message that you're more into catching. Looking for a driver, if you get what I mean."

Specs, perplexed.

Jimmy nodded toward a door bordered with out-of-season Christmas lights. "Then the two of them go in there and play however they want to play. Or, you can watch from the gallery. Some nights get pretty crazy. There's one guy likes to have butts stubbed out on his body. The Human Ashtray, they call him." Grinning as he took out a cigarette. "You want a light, or you wanna light this one for me?"

Specs shoved his cigarette back into its pack. "Let's get out of here."

Jimmy took another gulp. Pushed back from the table.

They didn't say anything to each other on the way out.

Outside, Jimmy chuckled. "Man, you're really wound tight. I started going in there to observe people, you know. Great research when you're preparing a role."

"I'm not an actor, Jimmy."

"But you're an artist, right?"

"That just isn't my scene."

Jimmy laughed. "Something tells me you have yet to exhaust all of the possibilities." Climbed into the Speedster. "You're not tired, I hope. There's another spot I want to show you."

✦

And then they were in Little Tokyo, inside the Seven Steps, more teahouse than restaurant, at a table with Miko, the proprietor. She was wearing a kind of sheer wrap, jade in color, coral necklace, and several rings. Hair was up; around forty, but looked ten years younger. Smiling at Jimmy. "You not acting anymore—they make you finish with that?"

"I only act as much as everybody else does," said Jimmy. "No, it's speed now. Racing. That's the thing."

Miko smiled. "Speed is good. Fast is good. They still try to put you in jail?"

The only patrons, a pair of middle-aged couples, were drifting toward the door. Ignoring her question, Jimmy asked: "Do you have any of the house brew?"

"On low flame in back." To Specs, smiling: "He told you of house brew?"

Specs shook his head.

Miko playfully slapped Jimmy's hand. "Jimmy, man. You should tell him before making such suggestion."

"What is it exactly?" asked Specs.

Jimmy: "A Far Eastern delicacy."

Miko rose. "I will prepare." Holding up her index finger. "One. One serving is all." Headed toward the back.

Jimmy took a drag on his cigarette as he looked at Specs. "Don't worry, it's just tea."

＊

Later. How much later, Specs didn't know. His gaze was fixed on the unframed landscape on the wall. Night scene, the facade of some lantern-lit, Japanese temple. Jimmy and Miko were talking, laughing; distant voices from some other shore. Specs sipped the green liquid. It was steaming, but had cooled. No taste, no odor, but it coated the throat and was soothing. His neck and chest felt warm. Limbs light, not easy to control. Wanted to get up from the table. Needed to summon his will. Wood surface, smooth. Lute plucking from an overheard speaker. Up now, moving. Going where? Had in mind the restroom but was floating toward the front door. Jimmy and Miko, still talking, laughing, but growing even dimmer. His mind seemed to blink.

He was outside, on the sidewalk in front of the Seven Steps. No traffic. Specs melted against the wall, the bricks probing the fabric of his jacket. Tilting, tipping, aboard some hopeless wooden boat. His whole frame—arms, legs, everything—spilled onto the pavement.

*

Specs, washed up on shore, salt in his mouth and nostrils. His hand brushed the sand; smooth, but now there was a pebble, or perhaps some kind of tiny, fallen berry from some swaying, tropical tree. He held it between his thumb and two fingers. Felt it growing subtly, in response. A sound, a low purr. He opened one eye, then the other.

Miko, eyes closed, luxuriating in some world of her own. Miko, naked. No top sheet or blanket. Specs released her nipple, pulling his hand back as though it had been singed. He was naked himself and how did he, how did *they*, get that way?

Beyond her, Jimmy, also naked. Blond hair on his chest and belly, a mound of beige around his crotch. Erection pointed toward the skylight like a mushroom sprouting from a long, thick stem.

Specs rolled from the bed. Clothes on the floor, he flung them on as though the room was ablaze.

Jimmy stirred. "Hey, man. What's shakin'?"

Specs, dressed in a flash, was staring down at Miko and Jimmy. "What was that stuff?" he demanded.

Jimmy, sitting on the edge of the bed. "Nothing, nothing. Lay back down."

"What *was* it?"

"Nada, man. Some of Miko's nectar, that's all. You seemed to really dig it."

"What was in it, Jimmy?"

"The Ivory soap of beverages. Ninety-nine and forty-four one hundredths percent pure. What's with the third degree?"

"How did we all end up like this?"

"We went to sleep, that's all. Good, clean fun."

Miko, awake and smiling. Jimmy gazed at her fondly. "Sweetie, would you please make us some regular, old, time-honored tea?"

Specs, at the door. "Just get me out of here."

＊

In Jimmy's Porsche, gliding west on Sunset. Gray, mid-morning.

Specs, to Jimmy: "Hang a left. The DeSoto there, on the right."

"Look, man," Jimmy said, pulling up beside it. "I don't know what you're bugged about. But you know what I'm up against. I can't waste any time."

Specs opened the door.

Jimmy: "You wanna be friends or not?"

Specs turned back, looked at him. "Yeah, I wanna be friends."

"Okay. I'll see you 'round Googie's."

"How about I call you sometime?"

Jimmy smiled. "Sure. Go ahead."

"What's your number?"

Smile faded. "Nobody has my number, baby."

Jimmy pulled the door closed. Peeled away.

＊

That evening, Rudi called.

"I have been trying to reach you all day. Spyder is here, immaculate and waiting."

First thing Jimmy said: "What color is it?"

ELEVEN

Jimmy stepped outside. Lighting a cigarette, he blew out smoke, watched it drift. Glorious morning, a Friday, last day of September; glowing sun, vivid colors.

He was slated to race that weekend, yet Jimmy had this shadow with him. Spinning around a dirt track at deathly speeds, was he hoping he'd crack up and end it, beat the bastards at their own game?

Needing to shake this, Jimmy gazed at his new car. What a beauty. Dusk gray. Racing number *130* in black, on the rear.

He drove down Ventura Boulevard to Laurel Canyon. Turned right. Glided by Gloria Swanson's old mansion. At Sunset, Laurel Canyon became Crescent Heights. Took that down to Melrose, swung over to Fairfax to the open-air farmer's market.

When Rudi arrived, Jimmy was at a small table in a flimsy wooden folding chair. Jimmy ordered three eggs, ham, whole wheat toast with grape jam on the side, home fries, black coffee, and orange juice. Rudi, just cantaloupe.

Jimmy smoked as he ate. The two didn't talk much.

*

Up Grapevine Pass north of LA, onto Route 99 near Bakersfield. Spyder, performing beautifully. Jimmy, pushing it, preparing for the track. His eyes went to the rearview mirror as a state patrol car eased out from behind a thicket. No siren, but a twirling red light. "I'm only ten miles over. I oughta outrun the sonofabitch."

Rudi shook his head. "He would radio forward."

Jimmy had a tight look as he steered the Spyder to the side of highway

The cop strode to Jimmy's window. "Where you headed?"

"Salinas," Jimmy replied. "There's a race up there on Sunday."

"Seems like there's a race here today. Eleven miles above the limit."

Jimmy laughed. "I was crawling, officer. There were people passing me, little old ladies, school buses full of children, all of them going eighty, eighty-five. You're just busting me 'cause my car looks different."

Cop pulled out his book.

Jimmy leaned toward him. "C'mon, don't write me up. I'm doin' everything I can to stay clear of trouble."

The fool didn't recognize him.

"Admit it. You just wanted a better look-see at this little beaut. No top, no bumpers—never seen one like this, have you?"

The cop handed Jimmy the ticket. "Don't make any plans for October seventeenth. See you at the Lamont courthouse."

"Thanks," Jimmy grumbled. "For nothing."

✱

They stopped at a town, nothing more than a traffic light, general store and gas pump.

In the store, they ordered at the counter, beside a tight serving area. Rudi got a cheeseburger, fries, and iced tea with lemon; Jimmy, a glass of milk. Then Jimmy stepped over to the modest produce section, bought a bag of apples. At their table, he rubbed one on his white T-shirt.

"This is what I used to eat in high school before a basketball game. Ever been to the Midwest, Rudi?"

The mechanic shook his head. "My father brought us straight to California—Santa Monica, where he knew some people."

"The basketball games out there—the tournaments—whew! Intense as anything on the track. People would trip each other, spit at each other, gouge each other's eyes; then afterward there'd be a big punch-up in the parking lot before the visiting team got on the bus. Everybody jumps in—kids, parents—including mothers." Jimmy bit the apple, chased it with a gulp of milk. "I felt like belting that cop back there. I'll bet he believes this is a free country."

"Well, Jimmy, there *are* speed limits. That is why for one such as yourself, track is best way to burn aggression."

A boy of about ten, T-shirt and bristly flattop, appeared at the table. "Is that your car out there, mister—the silver one?"

"Yep," Jimmy replied.

"Can I take a picture of it?"

Jimmy glared. "You've got a camera there around your neck. It's got film in it, right? Go take the shot." Bit into the apple. "And listen, kid. When you ask for something simple as that, the answer is usually no. When you just go ahead, the answer is always yes."

As the boy retreated, Rudi took a long sip of iced tea. "That seemed unnecessary to me, Jimmy."

"I did him a favor. Maybe next time he'll grab what he wants and not be so hung up about it."

Rudi pushed back from the table. "It is getting near dusk. I want as little night driving as possible."

"You're the boss, boss," said Jimmy.

Strode out to the Spyder.

＊

Afternoon light, waning. Gliding west on 466, into the setting sun. Two lanes, bordered by telephone poles and fence posts, they were snaking through San Luis Obispo County.

Jimmy pounded the Spyder—a hundred, a hundred ten. "We will get there," Rudi told him. Slowing to ninety, then eighty, Jimmy held it at seventy-five.

No matter how he tried, Jimmy just couldn't clear his head today. He had a whole career—fame, money, sex—and he ruined it. He'd turned into a pariah, and now he's streaking up to nowheresville to spin around a track with a bunch of nobodies.

As though reading his thoughts, Rudi turned from the passenger seat. "I received a letter from my uncle, my father's brother, who is at Porsche factory in Stuttgart. He has offered me a management position. I am considering accepting."

Jimmy didn't respond, stared ahead.

"If you are found innocent, and are made free, perhaps you could come to Porsche. They are always seeking skillful test drivers. I could likely arrange it."

Jimmy let out a breath. "Rudi, you know as well as I do, this is as free as I'm gonna be for a long, long time."

The sun was nearly gone but they were still pushing into it, swiftly approaching where 466 met 41, two roads forming a Y. Rudi saw the car even before Jimmy, a massive black-and-white Ford sedan, swinging across their lane.

"What the hell is that guy doing?" Jimmy said, urgency in his voice.

The Ford slowed its turn, blocking them.

"React, Jimmy. React!"

Jimmy gunned it, spun the wheel and swerved. The Spyder, all but sideways, missed the Ford by a breath. Tires shrieked as Jimmy righted his course, sliding back into the northbound lane. Rudi turned to Jimmy, a grin of relief across his face.

Eyes on the road, Jimmy pulled a cigarette from its pack. *Whew, that could have been it.* He fired up his Zippo. The wind whipping fiercely, Jimmy kept the flame from being extinguished.

REEL TWO

OCTOBER 1955—
JULY 1957

TWELVE

Jimmy didn't race that Sunday in Salinas. During Saturday's qualification, he spun out on the first turn and, though he managed to avoid the wall, the Spyder made two and a half twirls, coming to a stop facing the opposite direction. He didn't immediately right himself to make up for the time he'd burned. Instead, Jimmy sat frozen for an agonizing ten seconds before spinning the wheel and turning in a tepid, uncertain circuit of the track.

He and Rudi decided not to stay and watch the race, leaving at dawn on Sunday, the mechanic at the wheel.

Although Rudi assumed his protégé was humiliated at not making the field, Jimmy was consumed, not with the botched turn, but with the close call on the way up, when that huge ugly Ford had crept like a turtle into their lane. He was convinced the guy had not seen the silver, low-to-the-ground Spyder in the gray-shadowed dusk and, had Jimmy not responded with pure instinct, he and Rudi would have bought it. Jimmy freshly realized that not only did he not want to die, he wanted to live, and not just for these months before the state of California locked him up for nearly as long as he'd already been in existence.

*

At Googie's, Jimmy and Specs sharing a booth. Jimmy: "So when am I gonna hear these songs of yours?"

Specs, after a sip of malt. "I don't know, man. I write something, then I can't play it the way I hear it."

"You're not good enough on guitar?"

"Guitar's fine. It's just that I hear records in my head. Arrangements, effects, the whole gumball. It's not possible to reproduce what I'm hearing with just one instrument." Specs leaned forward. "Like, when I buy a record, I always buy two copies. I've got a pair of turntables in my bedroom, rigged to run simultaneously. Actually, one's a hair behind the other. So it's two records spinning at once and you get all that depth. I want my music to sound like the bottom of the ocean. Not just hear it, but feel it, you know?"

Jimmy stood. "Come on, we're splitting."

"I still got all this malt left. For where?"

*

Specs hit the final chord with a flourish. Seated on his bed, he looked at Jimmy, who sat on the floor, back pressed against the bedroom wall. Jimmy shook his head. "Sorry, man, that doesn't make it either."

Specs—deflated, frustrated, pissed. "That's it then. Those tunes are the best I've got."

"Don't be a baby. Play another one."

"You're not into this kind of music, Jimmy. You only dig jazz and classical. This just isn't your kind of thing."

Specs, off the bed, set his guitar into its open case.

The door opened and Specs's mother stood there in her bathrobe. Hair uncombed, eyes haunted. "I heard voices," she declared.

"Hi, Mom. This here is Jimmy. He's my friend."

"Hello, Mrs. Pelham," Jimmy offered.

"What time is it, Stephen?"

"It's late, Mom. After two."

"I shouldn't be up," she said. Floated away.

Jimmy, to Specs, "I gotta go myself."

"Wait, I'm not tired."

Jimmy smiled. "I'm not either. Gotta split."

✦

Jimmy was at Googie's. Going on nine in the morning, his last stop after being out all night. Gilda called out from the counter, "Phone call for you."

Jimmy took a gulp of coffee. Rose, crossed the room.

Gilda, handing him the receiver: "Gonna start charging for office space."

"Hello?"

"It's Specs."

"Sure, baby. What's up?"

"My mom died."

Jimmy didn't seem to react.

"She was cooking breakfast. Cooking for me, and she just . . . Her heart, I guess. I didn't see it, I was upstairs. An ambulance came and they took her away. I don't know what to do. I'm all by myself here."

"Sit tight, baby. I'm on my way."

✦

Living room. Specs, pacing.

Jimmy, sitting on the floor, back against the wall. "You need to get a grip, man. This kind of thing can level a guy. You need to decide."

Specs looked at him. "Decide what?"

"Whether you're an artist or not, that's the only thing that's gonna save you."

"Jimmy, my mom just died."

Jimmy, on his feet, grabbed Specs by the arm, pulled him toward the stairs. "C'mon."

"What's going on?"

Jimmy tugged Specs upstairs to his bedroom. "Pick up your guitar."

His Gibson L-5 that his mother had bought him at an estate sale, on its stand in the corner. Deep brown finish swirling into sunburst, beautifully carved f-holes. Specs stepped over and lifted it. Sat on the bed, cradled the guitar across his body.

"C'mon, man, play something."

Specs strummed a C chord, a languid tempo.

"Now sing the first thing that comes into your head."

Specs stared at him, tears in his eyes.

"Sing, baby, or I'm splitting."

Specs, lips quivering.

> *Because I knew you,*
> *My life will never be the same.*
> *Because I knew you,*
> *I'll never feel this way again.*

"Beautiful. You got me. Keep going."

> *Because I knew you,*
> *My heart will never be at rest.*

"Beautiful."

Because I knew you,
Now I've . . . known . . . the very best.

Fingers formed B flat, then A minor, and suddenly he was at the bridge; singing, crying as he sang, from some place deeper than he'd ever gone.

And though I can't see you now,
And though I couldn't be how
You wanted me to be,
The story we share
Is written somewhere
In eternity.

Bang! G augmented, then back to C for the final verse.

Because I knew you,
I know you really can't be gone.
Because I knew you,
Somehow you'll help me carry on.
And every day, that's just the way it's gonna stay,
Because I knew you.

"Amazing. Now don't let go. Keep playing so you won't forget. Print it, baby, own it."

"Shouldn't I write it down?"

"It's already written. Just keep playing it."

Specs rolled into it again and there was the song, pure and perfect as when it first revealed itself. The window was open and a gust breathed into the room, causing the curtains to part.

"Feel that, baby? I'll bet she's right here with us."

Specs, laughing and crying. "You think so?"

Jimmy, laughing too. "Why not, man? You just made something immortal."

THIRTEEN

Six hours she'd been at it and Jill couldn't get Jimmy's face right. She nailed Reagan, that was easy, but Jimmy's expression was multidimensional—angry, confused, determined. One minute she'd feel she'd captured it and then it would transform into something deeper and more confounding. She was working with oil on canvas, a *Time* magazine photograph from the *General Electric Theater* thumbtacked onto an easel. She felt ready to quit but knew if she walked away now, she'd never be able to capture it again. Then, shit, the door creaked open.

Jill turned and her father was standing there, martini in hand. What time was it anyway; she'd been out here since morning. She wondered if he was loaded. Glenn always downed the first one fast and the second came quickly on its heels. Had to be on his second or third.

"Since when," he said, "has the cabana turned into an art studio?"

Jill set her brush on the rag-strewn, wooden table.

"Nobody used it all summer."

"That's not the point. If anybody wanted to use it, it's a mess."

"Just let me finish this piece."

She figured her father would leave after that, for their conversations were invariably brief and seemed to be getting briefer. But he sat down on a wooden bench that protruded from the wall. "I'm guessing you didn't make it to school today."

Jill looked at him and shrugged.

Glenn gazed down at his drink as though searching for something floating on the surface. "So when they call, what excuse do you want me to use this time? A cold, a fever; another ailing grandmother?"

"Dad, I really need to finish this."

Glenn rose. "What have you got there; let me take a look."

Jill stood in front of the canvas.

"It's not ready for anyone to see."

"C'mon, let your old man take a peek."

He all but butted her out of the way as he took in the image. "What the hell is this?"

Again, Jill shrugged.

Glenn's face was reddening. "You think that was funny, Ron Reagan getting shot like that?"

"No."

"Then why are you making a goddamn cartoon out of it?"

"It's . . . I just thought this was a compelling image."

"Well, I can't imagine who you'd show it to. Strikes me as pretty sick." He headed toward the door, then stopped and turned. "What I came to tell you . . . Brad Remington is casting kids for an episode of his new detective series. He called the office to see if you might be interested."

"Definitely not."

Glenn's face, already pouting, fell even further. "You have to start thinking of something to do with yourself, Jill. You're screwing up school, and if that's the kind of thing you're painting . . ."

"Brad Remington? Isn't he the one who was here for that start-of-the-season party you threw?"

Glenn's expression brightened. "He challenged you to a game of Scrabble and you spent two hours in the den with him."

"Uh huh. And when I was done beating him, he asked if I'd ever played poker. When I said I had, he asked if I'd ever played *strip* poker, and might I be interested in coming by his office and playing some time. So no, Dad. Appearing on that jerk's idiotic TV show is the last thing I'd want to do."

✸

Cantor's on Fairfax. Jimmy and Specs, in a booth. "White Christmas" droned in the background. Jimmy, grinning. "Don't you dig that Irving Berlin laid that one on the world? Jewish guy pens the biggest Christmas tune. Sweet revenge." Sipped his coffee, continuing. "You oughta try your hand at one, baby. Every year, you'd rake in royalties from all corners."

Specs, grim. "Who knows whether I'll ever write anything else. 'Because I Knew You' might have been a fluke."

"Fluke or not, it's a classic. Now we just need to prove it."

"And we do that, how?"

"Get it down on tape with real musicians."

Specs took a sip of chocolate egg cream. "Sounds expensive."

"I got a buddy named Mart Lidman whose old man has some recording gear in their garage. Cat wants to be a sound engineer. Old man's a musician, a drummer. I know him too."

"You're not talking about *Shel Lidman*, are you?"

"Why is that so surprising?"

Specs leaned back as though on a train picking up speed.

"That cat's on half the jazz I own—Chet Baker, Art Pepper, Julie London. Played with Bird when he came out here; the coolest touch on the Coast."

"I'm going back to Indiana for the holidays. It looks like that retrial is gonna start next fall. This is the last Christmas I'll be able to spend at home for a long time. Will likely stay past New Year's, do some work around the farm." Sipped his coffee, then smiled. "This is my Christmas present to you, baby. Next week, you're gonna get that tune of yours recorded."

*

Pasadena. Residential block with plenty of trees and on-street parking. Specs eased his pink and black DeSoto beside the curb. Chilly outside, early evening. Out of the car now, nerves jangling as he lugged his guitar case from the back seat.

As Specs trudged up the driveway, he reached into his corduroy jacket, pulled his shades out, slipped them on. He opened the door on the side of the garage. Stepped inside to a dark, tiny room with a recording console and a couple of chairs. A pale guy about his age was in one of them. To Specs: "I'm Mart Lidman. C'mon, everybody's ready to hit."

Everybody?

Mart sprang out of his chair and opened the door to a larger room, separated from the control room by an expansive pane of glass. "Specs Pelham, this is my dad, Shel."

"Pleased to meet you," offered Specs.

"Jimmy's not coming?" said Shel Lidman from behind the kit.

Specs took in the rest of the room. A massive black guy was thumping a single bass string, tuning to a younger, scrawny white cat, hunched over an upright piano.

"That's Doug Bledsoe," said Mart, "and that's Horace Raymond on bass."

Specs nodded, his mind whirling. *Butter Raymond.* Specs felt like bolting.

"We wanna get a little jammin' in after we lay down the tune, so let's get to it," said Shel. He turned to Specs. "Can we see the chart?"

Specs tried not to gulp. "Chart?"

Shel's eyes darted to the others. "This is a recording date, right? An original tune, right? We don't wanna end up writing it for you."

"Okay," said Specs. "But it'll take a while."

Shel got up from his stool behind the drum kit. "Just sit here and play it and Doug will call out the changes for us to scribble down ourselves."

Two minutes in and Specs has to perform, all eyes and ears trained on him. He set his guitar case on the floor. It suddenly looked enormous. He unfastened the steel latches and pulled out his L-5, polished to a glistening sheen.

"Nice box," said Butter Raymond. "Looks like the axe Barney Kessel's got."

"Hope he can play like Barney," said Bledsoe, with a grin.

Specs sat on a stool, balancing the guitar on his knees. E minor, his favorite chord to tune to. As he tuned the B string: *Just pretend they're not here.*

Strumming C, descending to A minor, to F, resolving to G, which he augmented, before going back home to C.

Did they really expect him to sing?

Eyes on him, waiting, all right.

Because I knew you, my life will never be the same.
Because I knew you, I know I'll never love again.

Bledsoe called out the changes to Butter and Shel.

Specs, into the second verse, braced himself for the bridge, a vocal stretch—sometimes his voice held, sometimes it cracked.

And though I can't see you now,
And though I can't be how you wanted me to be,
The story we share
Is written somewhere
In eternity.

Home free, into the final verse, Shel's voice cut through.

"A repeat of what went down before, right? We'll improvise a tag. Okay, Marty, set some levels and let's cut this bambino." To the musicians: "It's 'fish gotta swim, birds gotta fly' all over again. Let's run it down and see if we can find some spots that won't be so predictable." To Specs: "We gotta lose the guitar, kid. Your time is too shaky."

The band slipped on headphones. Specs did too, once he'd awkwardly set his L-5 on the floor.

Shel put his sticks aside, picked up a pair of brushes. Counted the tune down. Specs, a mannequin at the mic, started to sing.

"Wait a sec." Mart's voice, coming through the phones. "This isn't working."

Mart left the board and bustled in. "I've got the instruments on one track and Specs's voice on the other and everything's bleeding into his mic. I'll never get a clean vocal mix."

"What do you suggest, Marty?" Shel asked. "We don't have an isolation booth."

Mart yanked the cord to Specs's phones. "Follow me."

Specs did. Mart set up a vocal mic in the control room. Shel counted it down once again.

Still wearing shades, Specs closed his eyes as he sang. By the second verse, the piano player was dropping ninths and sixths and diminished chords throughout the progression. When they got to the end, Shel said: "How did that feel to everybody?"

"Very cool," said Butter Raymond.

"Solid," said Bledsoe.

"Okay, Marty," ordered Shel. "Let's take it this time."

He counted it down once more and they floated into the tune.

Specs gritted his teeth as the embellishments continued. *Distracting, unnecessary, wrong—taking away from the words.*

"Beautiful, Horace," said Shel. "Impeccable as always." He turned to the control booth. "Did you get it, son?"

"Got it, Pops."

Shel: "You can dub him a copy later." To the other musicians: "All right, let's take five then start shedding for the gig this weekend."

Face burning, brain flashing red, Specs left the control room, shoved his guitar into its case, started for the door. Shel looked at him. "Hey, kid."

Specs turned.

"Aren't you forgetting something?"

"What's that?"

"How about a thank you?"

From behind his shades, Specs almost caved in, almost said it. But some current ran through him. "For what?"

Shel smiled. Was this little shit putting him on? "For having the hottest players in LA lay down your song."

"You didn't play my song. You played your instruments."

Shel smiled tightly. "What the hell are you getting at?"

Specs turned for the door.

"Hold on a second."

Specs stopped, turned back.

"Jimmy told Marty you really had it together. Well, come on, you've got all the answers. Why don't you show us how you want your little tune to sound?"

Everybody was looking at Specs. He sucked in some breath, set down his guitar case, unfastened its latches for the second time that evening. Turned to Mart. "Reset the mic for the guitar. I won't sing, let's just lay the track."

Shel sat back down behind his kit; picked up his brushes.

"I'll count it down this time," said Specs. To Shel Lidman: "Forget the brushes. Play with sticks and lay behind the beat. Feel what Butter is doing." To Bledsoe: "I want you to mirror what I'm playing on guitar. Straight chords, so when you hit the augmented it won't be just another flashy color. Okay, from the top—one, two, three, four."

The band played, deliberate but effective, water into a cup. At the end, Shel: "Well, that was what I'd call basic."

Mart, from the control room: "Wanna come in and listen to that?"

"Not yet," said Specs. "Play it back in here through the speakers and hit 'record' again." To the musicians: "Butter, play exactly what you played before, right on top of it." To Shel: "Lay out except for a simple roll followed by a cymbal crash at the end of each verse. When we get to the bridge, tap out eighth notes on the hi-hat."

Shel grinned tightly. "Whatever you say, Mozart."

Specs, to Bledsoe: "Major chords only, in at verse two. Just lay on the sustain pedal so it washes over everything." Turned to the booth. "Mart, during playback, record all this with whatever echo chamber you have, left wide open."

"Specs, this is a two-track machine. You're not leaving yourself any room to sing."

"Don't worry about that," Specs told him. "Just get it on tape."

FOURTEEN

S pecs and Mart in the control room, a few days later. As
Mart was patching into the board, he said: "That was a
pretty rough session, Specs. My dad's got a gig up north at the
hungry i. I waited till the coast was clear to bring you back in
here."

"Your father's the greatest drummer in jazz, Mart. But
when it comes to a hit record, he doesn't know his ass from
his eyeball."

Mart looked at him, unsure of how to take it. "What about
you, Specs? We've got two tracks filled up with no room left to
sing. The song has lyrics, as I recall."

"Any way you can get hold of another two-track?"

"There's the old one in the closet."

"Cool. Let's patch the machines together."

"Two machines?"

"We'll sync them up—"

"Specs, I'm not sure I—"

"—then we'll have four tracks, won't we?"

Mart dug out some cords and linked the new machine
to the older one. Hadn't listened to what they'd recorded but
when the playback kicked in, he was astounded. The basic
track was solid but the overdubbing, instruments augmenting
parts that had been laid down, provided a wash of sound. You

couldn't hear the surge of the music, as much as you could feel it. The track pulled you out of your chair, demanding that you come closer. The echo Specs insisted on caused everything to glisten; doubled instruments creating a pulse that throbbed like a living organism.

"Okay," Specs ordered, "set up a vocal mic and I'll lay down a lead, then harmonize with myself."

Specs stepped out into the studio and slipped on headphones. Sang it through once and they listened back. Specs turned to Mart. "The sound isn't sheer enough."

"Sheer?"

"It has to be like somebody's talking to you through a screen door on a summer night. Afraid to come outside until . . . they feel ready to face the world." A moment. "Gotta be something that could suggest that picture." Then: "Could you get a pair of your mother's nylons?"

"What for?"

"Just get them, okay?"

Mart went into the house, then came back with two beige stockings.

"Perfect," chuckled Specs. He dangled them over one arm, went back into the studio. Slipped them over the mike, then sang: *Because I knew you, my life will never be the same.*

When he laid on the harmony, a third above the melody, the vocal was all the more compelling. Specs's voice sounded like . . . well, somebody talking to you through a screen door on a summer night.

"Amazing," said Mart, listening to the playback for the seventh time. "It's like something that's always been there."

"Inevitable," uttered Specs.

"Excuse me?"

"Art has to be inevitable."

Mart nodded, lost in the track. "You should take this to Moss Levan."

"Who's that?"

"Has a pop label. Had a bunch of hits."

"You've got his number?"

"Sure. When you call, make sure you tell him it came from me. He's my uncle."

"Your father's brother?"

"Yeah. They haven't spoken in years."

✴

Hermosa Records, a division of Moss Levan Enterprises. Hollywood Boulevard, right off Vine, in the shadow of the Capitol Records building. Tenth floor. No receptionist or secretary. Stark and tight, a pair of gold records on the wall. The man himself had no hair to speak of, broad shouldered and big-chested, hands that a couple of cantaloupes would just about fill. Flowered shirt, open at the throat; blinding white slacks and matching shoes.

"Marty said you should call—how is the little guy? Haven't seen him since I bumped into him and his mom at the Brown Derby, which, by the way, serves as my real office."

"He's good—a great engineer."

A cloud crossed Moss's face. "So long as it's not a musician, especially a goddamn drummer." He settled his massive frame behind his messy desk. "What have you got?"

Specs handed over the tape. "An original song."

"A demo."

"It's ready for the radio."

"We'll see about that. Who's the artist?"

"I am."

Moss smiled. "So the Renaissance isn't dead." He stood, threaded the tape, hit play. The caramel-shaded circle hissed as it spun. The track unfolded. Good speakers, fidelity superb. Specs closed his eyes behind his shades. When he opened them, he expected to behold Moss breaking out champagne or lunging for his checkbook. But the man was just sitting there.

"Not terrible, not terrible," offered Moss.

"Not *terrible?*"

"I like how you phrased it—'Because I knew you.' It suggests fucking without *saying* fucking. Very clever, man." Moss pulled himself up from his chair, then hit rewind. "You're not an artist—you know that, don't you?"

Specs gulped. "I . . . don't know what you mean."

"You're a writer, that's your talent. Who produced this?"

"What do you mean, produced?"

"Who directed the session, told the musicians what to play, got the sound onto tape?"

"That was me."

"Okay then, you might also be a producer. But you're not an artist."

Specs's head was swimming. "I don't agree, sir."

"Don't take my word for it. Run over to Capitol or Liberty or RCA, see if they sign you up. You're dorky and weird and your voice sounds like a terminal head cold. Kid, you're not Sinatra. Doesn't mean you don't have talent. Gotta go with your strong points. In fact, I'm willing to publish the song for you."

"You mean sheet music—who buys that?"

Moss chuckled. "Publish it as in secure the copyright with the Library of Congress. See it gets in the right hands and is recorded by an artist who's gonna sell some records. Make sure all the performances get logged through BMI and the royalties get collected and accounted for." He chuckled again. "Publish it."

"And what do I get?"

"Your fair share of whatever revenues I collect. Meanwhile you won't be bogged down with paperwork—and believe me, there's mounds of it. This takes off, you need to come up with a follow-up smash. A cliché, but true—you're only as good as your last one."

"You really don't think I can sing it?"

"Look, kid, at those two gold records up on the wall. I've actually got ten times more, but I don't like to be too opulent when the pain-in-ass IRS comes sniffing around. You gotta trust somebody to get your music out of the drawer. Yours truly can see it gets done."

"So it's a hit?"

Moss Levan shook his massive head. "It ain't nothing yet, just a fucking sound on a tape. A hit is something you hear on the radio enough times it's permanently etched into your brain, along with nursery rhymes and dog food commercials and dirty limericks." Moss smiled. "But yes, I can make your song a hit. By the way, how'd you get that vocal effect?"

FIFTEEN

B lack-and-white postcard. Tony Bettenhausen, qualifying for the '55 Indianapolis 500. Scrawled on the back: *Got your letter. Great that Mart's uncle signed up your song. Hope he knows what he's got there. Heavenly home cooking here, but farm work is hard. Soon, Jimmy*

*

Specs was driving his DeSoto. Alone, three a.m. At Vermont and Franklin, lightning struck. No intro from the DJ. Specs, absolutely nailed when the opening lines kicked in:

> *Because I knew you, my life won't ever be the same.*
> *Because I knew you, I know I'll never love again.*

Girl vocalist, a couple of other girls in the background. The phrasing and atmosphere mirrored his demo perfectly. Pride, bewilderment. During the fade, the DJ: "That's new from the Dreamsickles—think I'll slide that one into rotation." Then a commercial for Safeway.

At dawn, Specs went to a coffee shop on Melrose and called his coworker Bev, one of those people who couldn't say no to anything, and persuaded her to cover for him at the courthouse. He tried to eat but couldn't. Read the *Times*, scarcely took in a word. Minutes crawled. At ten a.m. he drove to Hit Man Harvey's; was at the curb when Harvey turned up. The man—bald, shirtsleeves rolled, smoking—looked startled. "Specs, my first victim of the day. What you doing out so early?"

"Do you have a new record?" Gulp. "By the Dreamsickles?"

"Came in Monday."

"How many you got?"

Harvey opened, went directly to the bins. "A half dozen."

"I'll take three."

Harvey walked to the register. "You must really dig this tune, Specs."

"I wrote it." The words held some kind of echo that rolled back to him.

"You're kidding." Looked at the label, handed all three records to Specs. "You *co*-wrote it, I see."

Specs grabbed them. Stared at the one on top. *Because I Knew You—Hermosa Records. One minute, fifty-seven seconds. Published by Lemonaid Music, BMI, written by Levan/Vinetta/ Pelham.*

Specs's hands trembled.

"Your name," said Harvey. "Last, but there it is."

"Why is Levan's name on it—and who is this Vinetta?—I wrote the song myself."

Harvey laughed. "Moss Levan puts his name on everything. Vinetta is probably one of the thugs he's in bed with. Pretty fast company, Specs. That'll be two forty-four."

❋

Specs steamed until noon, parked in a lot on Hollywood Boulevard, stormed into the Brown Derby. Had never been there, although he'd seen it mentioned in the *Times* and the *Examiner*. One of the spots the stars went. The place was dark. Specs told the maître d': "I'm here to see Moss Levan." Was led to a table at the far end of the restaurant.

Levan, having lunch with a pair of guys as beefy as he was. Moss squinted at Specs's slight figure as his jaws worked a chunk of rib eye. Something resembling a smile swept his broad face.

"My young prodigy—how goes it?"

"I saw a copy of my song," hissed Specs.

Moss's mouth churned. "Record's a turntable hit already. Jocks can't get enough of it."

"What's your name doing on the label?"

Moss glanced at the pair sharing his table. "My name appears on all my product, kid. Last time I checked, I owned the company." Set his fork aside, dabbed his thin lips with his napkin. "Meet a couple nice guys for a change—this here is Sergio Baldoni; across is his younger but even bigger brother, Dominic. Got a company called Streamline Distributors, responsible for getting your record into the stores."

Specs, to Moss, "Who is Vinetta, and how did his name get on my song?"

"Let's continue on some other occasion."

"Who *is* he?"

"If you gotta know," Moss said, as though addressing someone who has a concussion, "Skip Vinetta is the most powerful promo man in Chicago. It's two hours later in the Midwest. Unlike these gentlemen and myself, he's undoubtedly *had* his lunch and is buttonholing every jock and program director in a seven-state radius to make sure your song becomes a regional breakout." The fork, back in his hand. "Now let us finish."

"You're a thief, Levan—you'll be hearing from my lawyer."

Moss replied, his jaws still working the food. "Don't make me laugh, punk—this steak's too good to choke on."

Sergio, gazing at Specs, sizing him up. "You want us to remove this gnat, Mossy?"

Moss: "He was just leaving." Ice and steel. "Ain't that right, Mr. Pelham?"

Specs spun away, turned back: "A thief, Levan!"

The restaurant babble halted as Specs steamed back the way he came in. Moss, to his companions: "Artists will drive you as crazy as they are."

"Undoubtedly," Dominic said. Back to business.

*

Hermosa Records publishing contract
Page 16, clause 24

. . . In the event that the Label, through its best efforts, causes the Composition to enter the Top Forty sales charts as calculated by Billboard, Cashbox or Disc World within one hundred eighty (180) days of release, Label shall exercise the right of first refusal regarding the exclusive services of the Writer for a term of seven (7) years from the rightful and lawful signed and dated execution of this agreement. This includes, not only the aforementioned Composition, but all facets of music creation, performance and production with which the Writer might engage, currently in practice or through mediums yet to be devised. This shall apply in the aforementioned Territory (The Universe). If, at the end of any seven (7) successive year term, the Writer does not, with at least thirty (30) days' notice, inform the Label by certified or registered mail of any intention to terminate this agreement, it shall be renewed automatically for another seven (7) year term under all conditions and clauses contained herein. . . .

✳

"You can't sue my uncle," Mart Lidman said, not for the first time that afternoon. He and Specs were in Griffith Park, scooping frosty malts beside the merry-go-round.

"It's a free country," Specs droned. "I can sue whoever I want."

"What about that contract you signed?"

"Toilet paper. Nobody cosigned, and I'm still a minor."

"Let's walk," Mart said, grimly.

He led Specs to a path that wound into the hills. A warm afternoon. Mart had on a T-shirt and khakis; Specs, a long-sleeve black turtleneck. Cotton, but hardly the thing to wear that day.

"I've hired Donald Lymon as my attorney," said Specs, then spun into embellishment: "He kept Jimmy Dean out of prison. Watching him in court is like watching Sugar Ray in the ring. He'll take your uncle apart."

"Shouldn't do it, Specs."

"I don't wanna make your family look bad, Mart. But the guy's a crook."

"I told my dad you were suing Moss—he was gonna hear it anyway. He told me a story he's kept inside for a long time. For your protection, I need to tell it to you."

"My *protection?*"

"My uncle used to own a club down in Hermosa, the Blue Point, it was called. When Dad got his first trio together, they played there, Wednesday through Sunday, twelve sets altogether. End of the week, Moss told Pop how great it was, too bad there wasn't a dime to pay him."

"That's outrageous."

"Dad's trio was scheduled there the following month. They canceled, of course. The other guys in the band put the word out that Moss had stiffed them and a few other acts canceled. The club had to close. Moss held Dad responsible, felt he should have kept a lid on it." Mart drew a breath. "My uncle had a couple of goons drag him under the Santa Monica pier. Broke both wrists. Dad had to learn to use the sticks all over again."

Specs halted. "Why didn't you tell me this beforehand?"

"The story Dad put out was he'd tried skydiving and his chute opened late." Mart walked away in the direction they'd come. Over his shoulder: "I put you next to my uncle, Specs, but if you get yourself hurt, you did it on your own."

✳

Top of Mulholland. Narrow, steep, and snaky. The glow of Los Angeles from the basin below. Jimmy at the wheel of the Spyder; Specs, shotgun.

"I can't believe I split town and you let things get so far out of hand," said Jimmy. "You need to decide what you're gonna do."

Specs said nothing, seemingly talked out.

"An artist has a responsibility to his work. And somebody just stepped in and stole yours. If you were married and somebody stole your wife, would you let them get away with it?"

Specs, sulking. "I'm not married," he said.

Jimmy veered to the right, stopping perilously short of plunging the Spyder over a ravine.

"What's going on?" asked Specs.

Jimmy, out of the car, rushed over and yanked open the passenger door. "Get behind the wheel," he ordered. "You're driving."

Specs got out. "C'mon, Jimmy. I haven't driven a stick since driver's ed."

"Long as you can steer and work the clutch, this baby does it all for you. Climb back in there."

Specs, immobile. "Where are we going?"

"That's not the point. The point is you not turning into mush. So put your mitts on that wheel and your foot on the gas. I want you to hit eighty by the time we reach the bottom."

Getting in. "This is crazy, Jimmy."

"I'm trusting you. If you cave, I'm going down with you. You don't want that on your conscience, do you, man?"

Specs, behind the wheel, pressed the clutch. Put the Spyder in first.

"C'mon," said Jimmy. "Time's ticking."

The car bucked once and they started downward. Specs took the first turn tentatively. Jimmy: "C'mon, baby, push it— No balls, no blue chips." Hitting fifty, swinging into a curve. "Don't let up. I'm with you, man. I know I'm with a winner." A straight stretch, sloping down. A hill pressing from the left; a steep ravine to the right. "Pour it on, man. Nobody can park you and take away the keys—you're an artist—they can't stuff you in a box." *Sixty.* A set of headlights swung around an upcoming bend. The Spyder whooshed by at *sixty-five, seventy.* Speedometer rising. "A big curve coming up, leads right to the bottom . . . Don't let it stop you, baby—just become part of it."

The Porsche sailed around at *eighty.* As the road straightened, Specs took his foot off the gas, coasting to the bottom where there was the red glow of a stop sign. They bucked to a halt at the intersection.

"You did it, man—made it like a pro. How do you feel?"

Specs, laughing. "I feel good, Jimmy."

"Why, man—*why* do you feel good?"

"Because I can't be stopped—nobody can park me or tow me away."

"Because?"

"I'm a goddamn artist!"

Specs was grinning as Jimmy got out and stepped over to a set of bushes along the road. "I've gotta piss, baby," he said. "Never been so scared in my life."

*

Disc World: **Hot Cakes Column; March 29, 1956**

"Because I Knew You," Top Five, on its way to a million units, has been the subject of a legal tussle between label and writer. Specs Pelham, a former court reporter who claims to have inked the tune solo, further claims that Hermosa Records owner Moss Levan listed himself and associate Salvatore Vinetta as cowriters without his knowledge or permission. Levan, who has been the defendant in scores of similar lawsuits, was ordered by the civil court to prove his and his associate's authorship under threat of perjury.

Levan told this column: "If the guy thinks one measly song is so important, let him get every last dime coming to him. I know there's more where that came from, but I'm not so sure he does."

SIXTEEN

In a life filled with surprises, the last thing Jimmy ever dreamed would happen was taking shape.

He was being offered another film.

And not just any film: *Rebel Without a Cause*, the one he'd had on the boards with Warner Brothers.

He felt ambivalent about the material. Brando had once screen-tested for it, but then Warners considered him too mature; another way of saying too old for the part. At twenty-five, Jimmy felt too old for it himself. Had he still had a career, he would have seen it as he always had, a trap, a way to keep casting him as the troubled, mixed-up, screwed-up youth. He'd have woken up one day and the best parts would be handed to actors who hadn't taken the bait when they were starting out.

Yet the thought that he'd get another one hundred twenty minutes of his image burned into celluloid seemed like a big Fuck You to the bastards who were rubbing their hands in anticipation of locking him away. So he'd already signed on in his head, but wasn't about to turn that card over.

He pulled up to the Chateau Marmont. The valet saw the Spyder, then approached wide-eyed and wary. "Just tell me where to park it," uttered Jimmy. The guy pointed, and Jimmy glided around to the lot. He pocketed his keys, strolled to the lobby.

The desk clerk. "May we assist you, sir?"

"I'm here to see Mr. Ray."

"We have a Nicholas Ray."

"That'll work."

Desk clerk handed him a map, circled one of the units. "Mr. Ray would be here."

Jimmy went out the way he came. Marvelous day in LA, early April. Jimmy, at the cabana door. Partially open. Pushed with his palm and stepped inside.

Living room, kitchen, stairs. Ray was lounging on the sofa, close-cropped silver hair, white deck pants, bare feet, like he was docked at Huntington Harbor. Rose to shake Jimmy's hand.

"Jimmy—may I call you Jimmy? So pleased you came. A drink?"

"I'm okay." He plopped onto a massive, cushioned chair.

Ray floated back to the sofa. "I saw you in *Eden*. They should never have shelved it. Like I said on the phone, I've purchased the rights to *Rebel*. An actor of your caliber, I'm sure you're up for making another film."

Jimmy, poker-faced.

Ray grabbed a folder off the coffee table and thrust it at him. "No script yet, just a synopsis. The studio took to calling it a gang picture. There's a gang, but it's really one kid—one guy. His parents don't dig him. The other kids don't dig him either. A total loner, like you."

"I know a ton of people."

Ray, on a roll. "Those chickenshits at Warners were never going to make it, but they gouged me anyway. I know time's an issue, so I'll have principal photography completed by the end of the summer."

Jimmy put his hand forward like he was sticking it into a cage and something might bite it. Ray gave him the folder. Jimmy thumbed through the thin document, knowing that without glasses, he couldn't decipher the words anyway. "I'm gonna need to see a script before I commit."

Ray seemed to brighten. "I've got two writers working independently. I'll take the strongest elements from each. But I have an approach in mind that should really get your juices churning."

Jimmy handed back the folder, looked down at the rug.

"On top of each scripted scene we'll include an improvisation. You know, jazz. I'll surround you with a cast I can get to really blow."

Jimmy, on his feet. Turned toward the door, which he didn't close behind him. "I gotta be someplace."

Ray shadowed him. "Regardless of what happens with your situation, Jimmy, this will be a film for all time; for the world to see what an incredible artist you are. I'll take good care of you, baby."

Some current passed between them, then Jimmy was out the door, into the air.

✦

The Hollywood Recorder, **May 7, 1956**

Dean Inked for Ray Pic

Troubled actor James Dean has agreed to star in director Nicholas Ray's new gang picture, "Rebel Without a Cause." The script will be adapted from the nonfiction book by Robert M. Linder, a prison psychologist and purported specialist in juvenile delinquency.

Ray intends to shoot on location in Los Angeles this summer. While some roles have been tapped, including child star Natalie Wood, a number of gang members will be cast from open auditions involving unknown high school students. Ray will also serve as producer, committed to significant funding for the project.

Protecting that considerable investment, one of Dean's contractual stipulations states that he will refrain from participating in any automobile races during principal photography. Competitive racing is largely how Dean has been occupying himself since being released from his Warners contract in the wake of the sensational shooting of Ronald Reagan, which resulted in a mistrial, as well as a national outcry. Some industry insiders contend that Ray's inking of the controversial Dean, who will be retried for attempted murder starting on November 5, will backfire, citing that the actor's currency with the general public has been irreparably tarnished.

"I wanted the best young talent available for the lead in 'Rebel'," contends Ray. "And Jimmy Dean is definitely it."

Will Ray's gamble pay off? The jury is out.

*

Dinner at the Parnell house, quiet and strained. Jill's kid brother, Perry, sullen as ever. Jill's father, Glenn, truculent as usual. Stephanie, Glenn's wife, seven years Jill's senior. Beef stroganoff, being served by Irma.

Glenn, talking: "It can't all be miserable, son. They must be teaching you something."

Perry slumped even deeper into his chair. "You'd sure as hell think so."

Glenn: "There's always military school. More vegetables, Irma, if you don't mind."

Jill drew a breath. Now or never.

"I saw something interesting in the *Recorder* today."

Her father, surprised. "Since when do you read the *Recorder*?"

"I don't—I just . . . spotted something."

Glenn and Stephanie, listening.

"They're making a movie called *Rebel Without a Cause*."

Glenn pressed his fork into a piece of broccoli. "Nick Ray put up the better part of the funding. Sold his house to do it, I heard. Moved into a hotel or some damn thing."

"Sold his house?" chimed Stephanie. "He believes in it that much?"

"I think Nick's gone loony," Glenn said. "Ever since his son ran off with Gloria, he's been off-kilter."

"Who's Gloria?" asked Perry.

"Nick's wife. Ex-wife now."

"Just forget it," said Jill.

"Forget what?" said her father.

"No, Jillsy," said Stephanie. "What about the article caught your attention?"

Jill took a moment. "May I have some more water, Irma?" She fortified herself with a sip. "It's a story about young people."

"Nick has signed Jimmy Dean for the lead," said Glenn. "Who the hell would pay money to see that little shit?"

"Can I be excused?" asked Perry, pushing back from the table.

"We'll talk later," his father told him.

Stephanie looked at her husband. "I thought you liked Dean in that picture we screened."

"He's talented, just . . . demented. Besides being a criminal, he's . . ." Glenn made a gesture that caused his wrist to droop.

Stephanie turned back. "So what about it, Jillsy?"

Jill, thrown off. "What?"

"What was interesting—you haven't told us."

It came tumbling out. "It said they're having tryouts. I thought I might show up."

"Audition?" said her father.

Jill nodded.

"Glenn Parnell's kid doesn't audition—"

"But I thought it sounded—"

"—I'll call Nick myself. Better yet, I'll have Bogie call him.

"Why Bogie?" asked Stephanie.

"He made that picture with Nick. The one where the screenwriter gets accused of murder."

SEVENTEEN

On location at the Griffith Observatory, the LA basin sprawled below; cast, crew—including Jill Parnell—not to mention Nick Ray himself, were waiting on the star.

Jimmy sat in his trailer, absently blowing his recorder, the script open beside him. In the initial drafts, his character had no name. Ray thought that was more universal, more relatable to kids. But Jimmy said he wouldn't play some nameless symbol and insisted on Jim Stark, the last name an anagram for *Trask*, the last name of the character he played in *Eden*. He improvised a snaky line of notes, set down the recorder, and looked at the script.

> JIM
> (indicating Buzz as he opens the trunk)
> You watch too many lousy movies.

> BUZZ
> Oh, he's deep, this guy. Real abstract.

> JIM
> Yeah, and I'm a handsome devil.

He opens the trunk and pulls out a jack.

JIM

(continued, as he turns to Judy)
You always in the peanut gallery?

Judy glances at him, unsure how to respond.

ON BUZZ, who senses something between Jim and Judy.

BUZZ

Whaddya say we play the blade game—you got
a blade don't you, amigo?

JIM

That's none of your business.

BUZZ

Oh, but I think it is.

Buzz pulls a knife out of his jacket. With the CLICK
of the exposed blade, you can almost feel the gang of
teenagers draw a collective breath.

BUZZ

(continued)
Either pull one or we'll give you one.
But you're not getting out of this, amigo.

JIM

I don't want trouble.

BUZZ

(taunting, drawing closer)
Oh, I'll bet you don't.

CRUNCH

(from behind Jim)

Maybe we got us a chickie, Buzz.

MOOSE

Yeah, maybe he's a chickie.

Jim whirls on them.

JIM

Are you talking about me?

BUZZ

Sure we are.

JIM

You shouldn't call me that!

BUZZ

(flicking the blade toward Jim)

Then prove it.

Jim reaches into his back pocket and pulls out his knife. He and Buzz face each other, the gang tightening around them.

BUZZ

(continued)

No sticking, just flicking. Comprende, amigo?

Jimmy closed the script, then strode out into the daylight.

They were strewn about the small parking lot adjacent to the observatory. All eyes on Jimmy, as he approached. Supporting player Sal Mineo fell in behind. As Ray shouted instructions to the DP, Jimmy seemed in his own universe.

The camera, from Natalie Wood's point of view. She's Buzz's girl, but has eyes for Jim, and is perched on the hood of Jim's '49 Merc, whose right front tire has been flattened by Buzz's blade.

Ray had already shot the scripted version; this improvised take was to see if he could capture anything more immediate and exciting. Jimmy felt he'd nailed the scene already, so he offered nothing in terms of dialogue, simply went about opening the trunk, yanking out the jack, shooting hostile looks to Buzz and Judy and the gang.

With Jimmy not riffing, the young actors were thrown off, unable to come up with anything on their own. The scene resembled a silent film; Jimmy brandishing the jack, then finally some mumbled taunting, until the knives came out.

Jimmy just wanted to get this over with. He lunged and Harley Dale, playing Buzz, parried with a move that caught Jimmy just below the ear, the gash immediately streaming. Jimmy's hand went to the wound. Seeing blood, he yelled, "Cut, goddammit!"

Harley, to Jimmy: "What'd you stop for, man? That scene was cooking."

Jimmy called out: "Where's the prop guy?"

A distressed looking fellow stepped forward.

Jimmy sprang like he was about to slug him. "You were supposed to dull the blades, you moron. I'm all sliced up here."

Harley grinned as he looked around at the cast and crew. "Dull the blades? Where's the realism in that?"

The first-aid man appeared and looked at Jimmy's wound.

Jimmy glared at his director. "You'd better get control of this set, Ray, or I'm not doing another scene with these idiots."

Ray said, "Let's break for lunch. We'll pick up at two o'clock."

As Jimmy headed back to his trailer, he held a gauze pad to his wounded neck. Harley said, loud enough for Jimmy to hear: "What a bringdown. I thought the cat was for real."

✱

As part of the "gang," all Jill had done was stand around in stupid saddle shoes and goofy poodle skirts and ridiculous bobby socks. Her one big line got jumped by that twerp Nick Adams. No contact whatsoever with Jimmy. Since that day at the observatory when that idiot Harley Dale (a friend of her brother's—big surprise) slashed him with a real blade, Jimmy would hide in his trailer, come out to do his bit, then disappear again in a puff of smoke. This whole thing had been a drag, a disaster.

And speaking of drags, the production was dragging out, dragging on; might spill over to shooting on weekends, even after school started. Jill was thinking of quitting. Why couldn't she be like Natalie Wood, who clearly felt movies were what mattered and put Life Itself a distant second? Word was, Nat was even sleeping with Director Nick, their fearless leader, who was what, thirty years older than her? If Jill didn't snag Jimmy's attention by the time they were ready to wrap this turkey, the whole thing had been for zilch.

✦

Cast and crew, assembled on the soundstage. Nick Ray, addressing everyone.

"Chickie run is the climax of the film. The ultimate challenge to Jim Stark's manhood. A rite of passage. We got this from Freddy, our gang consultant during preproduction." Ray appeared excited. "Two guys get behind the wheels of stolen cars and drive toward a cliff that drops off into the ocean. Each kid has to roll out of the speeding car before it plunges over the side. It's an action scene, but we'll be shooting on a soundstage, as well as on a ranch near Chatsworth. When the two cars swan dive into the ocean, we'll have ramps on location north of Zuma Beach and use stunt doubles, having already covered the actors. Any questions?"

"Just one," said Jimmy.

All eyes on him.

"Forget stunt doubles. Why don't you shoot the final take above the ocean as me and Harley actually drive? Really roll out onto the ground. Chickie run for real."

Ray shook his head. "Too dangerous, Jimmy."

"Me and Harley are the ones risking our necks. Realism. Whaddya say, Harl?"

Harley gulped. "I'm game."

Jimmy turned to Ray. "Then it's set?"

"We'll see what we get from the soundstage and the ranch. We may not need it, Jimmy."

"I need it," Jimmy told him, ice in his voice.

"Let's talk about it later."

But everyone, Ray included, knew it was going to happen.

EIGHTEEN

S pecs, in his bedroom, wearing his bathrobe, guitar cradled
across his lap as he strummed and sang:

> *When my friends want to know*
> *What I see in you,*

Phone rang.

> *All I ever tell them*
> *Is diddy diddy doo.*

Another ring.

Specs stopped, looked at the phone. Rested his guitar on
the messy bed. Picked up the receiver mid-ring. "Hello."

"Well, I've finally reached the Phantom." Jimmy's voice.
"I've been calling all week. You shacked up with somebody?"

Specs, excited. "Jimmy, I'm having a real breakthrough."

"Tell me."

"Songs, man. They just keep coming like a . . . waterfall.
Every one of them's a hit. They're like records already."

"Sounds good, baby."

"Every time I finish one, a fresh one comes right up
behind it."

"I hear you, baby. You've caught a wave and you wanna keep riding it."

"Feels like a whole career worth of tunes. Like, fifteen in five days. I've been ordering food in 'cause I don't wanna break the spell. I thought I was done but it feels like there's a few more hanging around."

"It's the muse, baby. You gotta be showered and shaved when she comes a-knockin'."

"When She Comes A-Knockin'—great title."

"You're on fire, Specs."

"When this is over, I'll need to borrow your tape recorder."

＊

Jimmy and Nick Ray in El Mocombo, talking above the music. "Listen, Jimmy. This thing you're looking to do is really reckless."

"Don't worry about me, man, I'll be fine."

"I'm not worried about you. You're a pro. It's that fool Harley I'm concerned about."

Jimmy leaned forward. "I want people to see this movie, Nick; otherwise, what's the point? This kind of scene, speeding off toward the ocean with us really driving, that'll get people talking. Harley and I will roll out of our cars and become buddies, just like in the script."

"What about the agreement?"

"What agreement?"

"That you wouldn't be involved in any competitions involving automobiles during production."

"Wait—whoa. This isn't professional. It's just kicks."

"Kicks could get a boy killed. Harley's only eighteen."

Jimmy grinned. "Let me tell you somethin', daddy. This

here's a matter of honor. Just set your camera down on that beach, and when you see those two junk heaps fly over the cliff, Harley and I will be rolling in the dirt, laughing our asses off. But young Harley will have learned a valuable lesson."

Ray glared at his star. "And what would that be?"

"Nobody messes with me, man."

*

Jimmy's pad. Specs was patching cords from Jimmy's tape machine into the hi-fi speakers. "As you're listening," said Specs, "you've gotta hear beyond just the voice and guitar. So read the notes I made. Got all the arrangements worked out. The instrumentation. Doubling, tripling. What should have echo and what should be dry. Like I said, I don't just write songs, I write records."

Jimmy peered down at the marble notebook. "So this producer thing is a lot like directing a film. You've got a script but you gotta get it off the page. Paint a picture, but with sound."

Specs took a tape out of its box, threaded it onto Jimmy's machine. "Twenty-one songs, all of them hits. Half of them smashes. It took me three full days to record them all."

Jimmy: "When your 'Because I Knew You' royalties come in, you oughta buy the Speedster. The guy who bought her from me is selling it. She's sitting there on the lot at Competition, just waiting for you. Every time you fire up the engine, you'll be telling the world to kiss your ass. You'd like that, wouldn't you, man?"

Specs chuckled. "Yeah, that car would be nice." As he hit play: "I'm gonna leave this here so you can really listen. Tell me whether I'm crazy or a genius."

Jimmy smiled. "You can be both, you know."

✻

Gorgeous LA morning. Specs, in bathrobe and sneakers, walking down his driveway, approaching the mailbox. As he opened it and pulled out a handful of mail, a guy emerged from a car parked across the residential street. Around thirty. Scrawny—no, wiry. "Hey, I guess you're a pretty popular fella."

Specs stood, squinting, wearing neither glasses nor shades. "Do I know you?"

"I'm nobody. You're somebody though, that's for sure."

Specs, not liking the feel of this, started back toward the house.

"There's a big fat royalty check in that stack there."

Specs turned. "How would you know that?"

"I'm from Western Union. Here to give you a message."

Specs waited.

"Somebody else considers a lot of that to be their money. You cash that check, you'll be in for a big sack of hurt."

The guy was grinning. Specs had to say something. "Are you threatening me?"

The guy started walking toward his car, some kind of Ford. "We know you got talent, Pelham. Let's just hope you got the smarts to go with it."

Behind the wheel now, he started the engine, then glided away. Specs watched him go, eyes fixed on the license plate. Duct tape over the numbers.

Specs hurried back inside.

✻

"You've got to," Jimmy's voice on the telephone. "If you don't cash that check, I will."

Specs, on his end. "I don't wanna get my arms broken like Shel Lidman."

"That's your bread, you earned it. Plus, you've really hit pay dirt with those new songs, man. The melodies are catchy. The words are dumb but real. Dumb, but sincere. Just like your audience. You're gonna be bigger in the music biz than Moss Levan and company ever dreamed of. So you're gonna cash it, right?"

*

Googie's. Jimmy by himself in a corner booth, a finished plate in front of him.

He hated to admit it, but he was having serious second thoughts about the chickie run. Why the hell had he pushed it? He knew damn well why. Working with Jimmy was the closest Harley and that bunch of amateurs were ever going to get to real art, real truth. He couldn't let a smug little punk like Harley get away with questioning his authenticity. Despite his misgivings about the material, Jimmy was turning in a magnificent performance. Fully in his power, every line and gesture, ringing true.

Jimmy knew he'd stay behind the wheel right until the very edge, while Harley would bail out with plenty of safe ground between himself and the unforgiving cliff, likely pissing his jeans in the process. It would almost be worth plunging over the edge just to humiliate him.

Specs entered and offered a cool wave—right hand, palm flat, smooth as taffy, left to right—then slid in across. "I've made a decision, Jimmy. I'm gonna take the new tunes to New York, let the Greek hear them."

Jimmy pulled on his cigarette, stubbed it into the ashtray.

"So come by this weekend and pick up your tape. Who the hell's the Greek?"

"Alex Kampeteris. Gulf Port Records. He's got talent and taste. About the only suit in the business you can say that about."

Jimmy's eyes were fixed on some point through the window on Sunset. "Parked out front there . . . that what I think it is?"

*

They stood outside at the curb, beside the white and gleaming Speedster.

Jimmy beamed. "That you scored this car is poetic."

"Not only that, I've got a date this weekend. Things are really cooking."

"Take me for a spin and I'll give you a few pointers."

"About the car?"

"Yeah, and about this date. Like, where are you taking her for dinner?"

"I haven't thought about it."

Jimmy smiled. "See what I mean?" He pulled out a Chesterfield, lit it with his Zippo. A moment. "I need you to make me a promise." Jimmy pulled hard on his cigarette. "I told you about this scene I'm gonna do. Just promise that if anything should happen, like if this chickie run thing goes bad for me tomorrow, you'll follow through with your music. Do whatever it takes."

Specs shook his head. "Nothing's gonna happen to you, Jimmy, you're the greatest driver in the world."

He put his hand firmly on his younger friend's shoulder. "Promise me."

Specs shrugged, trying to lighten the moment. "Okay, Jimmy, I promise."

Jimmy laughed harshly, no joy in it at all. "Or if I get locked away, I want to know that you're out there, really living."

But secretly, Jimmy had no intention of going back to court. Soon as this final scene was shot, he was gone. Where? He hadn't decided, but it would be someplace that even if the fools came after him, they wouldn't be able to haul him back.

NINETEEN

Friday evening, the Villa Capri. Specs sat across from petite and pretty Deborah Margolin, dark hair to her shoulders. Specs ordered veal; Deborah, lasagna. First date chatter. Deborah: "I'm going to be a psychologist. It's a growing field, especially here in California. My dad says he'll pay my tuition at USC, but I'll have to cover room and board. That's why I'm working at his store, saving up for next year."

"I don't believe it."

"What?"

Gazing out the front window, Specs uttered: "Somebody's stealing my car."

The Porsche was rolling onto Sunset. A dark-haired guy behind the wheel had the top down. Must have lifted the keys from the valet. Specs rushed out into the sizzling twilight. "Hey, asshole, come back here!"

He sprinted into the street. The light at the intersection was red. The Porsche eased up to it, then stopped.

Blood pumping, Specs was twenty yards from the light when a car glided by in the Porsche's lane, then swung abruptly left, stopping directly beside it. It was long, dark and gleaming, black or deep blue; a Lincoln, maybe a Chrysler. Two guys inside. Specs, hell-bent on his white Porsche and the greasy, dark-haired thief at the wheel, was mad enough to tear the bastard apart. An arm extended out the passenger window of the dark car. BLAM, BLAM, BLAM, BLAM, BLAM!!!!! The dark-haired guy slumped against the driver's side of the Porsche. He convulsed, then went still. The dark car lurched into the intersection, swung right, around the corner, tires squealing, smoke hanging in the air.

Specs couldn't stop running, was too wound up. He stopped when he reached the Porsche. The leather interior, splashed with blood. The thief's mouth was twisted, eyes fixed, his motionless body grotesque behind the wheel. A horn blared. Another. Somebody shouting. All around, traffic was stopping on Sunset.

*

Jimmy in the Spyder, driving Topanga Canyon's darkness. Winding curves that dropped off into nothing.

At Pacific Coast Highway, he turned north. Not a lot of traffic. Hillside right; ocean left. Jimmy pushed—ninety, ninety-five. The Spyder purred.

He slowed somewhere in Malibu Canyon. Valets with flashlights. Jimmy parked on the road. He took a deep breath; wasn't even sure what he was doing here, except he had time to kill.

*

Tad Harbor, the night's host, was back by the pool, talking to a blond-haired young man, cocktail in one hand, the other resting on the young man's shoulder; their eyes locked. Another blond guy—they were everywhere, Tad himself blond—caught the host's attention. "Hey, Tad," he said, with a bitchy lilt. "Look what the wind blew."

Tad did a double take. "Jimmy, long time, no see."

"Tad," Jimmy countered, with a calculated nod.

Sipping his cocktail, Tad said, "You've made it tough for us, sweetie."

Jimmy: "How's that?"

"The studios are starting to impose the morals clause. Got a call from my agent suggesting I find some nice girl and settle down. All because of that big bang you made. Warners paid you off to get you outside the system."

"What's your point?" Jimmy replied.

"Outside is outside," said the bitchy friend. "You're not welcome here."

"Wasn't talking to you, Goldilocks."

"Not welcome, get it?" Grabbed Jimmy's elbow.

Jimmy popped him full on jaw. The guy tumbled back like a carnival prize, limbs tangling on the way down.

Jimmy turned. Headed back the way he came.

"Nobody's gonna see your stinking little picture," Tad shrieked from behind him. "You're finished, Jack—you're dead!

Another voice, female: "Hey, wait a sec."

Without glasses, Jimmy couldn't see clearly, but she appeared young and attractive.

"What?"

"I'm with a guy who's more interested in talking to some boy than to me," Jill Parnell told him.

Jimmy smiled. "Wanna go for a ride?"

＊

Jimmy swung north onto PCH, glow of city at their backs. He glanced at Jill, who appeared to be studying the ocean. "Did you see that?" Jimmy asked.

"What?"

"That road lamp went out when we drove by it."

"That's never happened to you?"

"Sure, but always alone, never with anybody else."

"It happens to me all the time." Jill laughed. "I wonder which of us was responsible."

In the probing headlights, a coyote loped across the highway. Jimmy had it at eighty-five, as he swung the wheel left. They swept by the animal, close enough to brush its tail.

"Quite a driver," she said.

Jimmy lit a cigarette. "So what's your story—you an actress or something?"

"Not exactly."

"Wanna smoke?"

"I don't . . ."

"Not a prude, are you?"

"It isn't much of a vice, is it—smoking?"

"I started out as an actor," said Jimmy.

"Started out?"

"It's a long story . . . I'm doing a picture now. In fact, that's where we're headed, the set. I gotta shoot one final scene, then let's you and I go have some kicks somewhere."

"I know about the scene," Jill told him.

Jimmy gave a sideways look.

"I'm one of the cattle they roped in to fill out the gang, so my duties are done." Added: "But I'm no actress."

Now Jimmy grinned. "You're telling me we're in the same picture and we haven't met until now—that's something, all right."

Streaking north. Jimmy hit ninety, a hundred.

"I'm running early for a change," he said. "Thought I'd be spending more time at Tad's goofy party. What say we cruise down closer to the water?"

*

Parked near the beach, shadows and wind. Jimmy smiled, pulled her to him. Their mouths met—lips, breath, tongues.

"It's pretty tight in this car," Jill whispered, as she pulled her mouth away.

"It's perfect," said Jimmy, kissing her neck.

His fingers loosened the buttons at the back of her cotton dress. Jill reached between her shoulder blades and undid the clasp. She tossed her bra onto the hood. They laughed. Jimmy pulled her closer and his fingertips caressed her right breast as their mouths met again.

"Shouldn't we go someplace else?" Jill breathed.

"No, right here," Jimmy said, breath in her ear. "We got the sky, the stars, everything."

He opened the driver's side, placed his left foot on the ground. Pulled Jill to him and now she was facing him, straddled across his legs. His hand moved down to her thigh and, after a moment, was inside her silk panties.

Jimmy's left arm was draped around her neck, their chests and bellies and legs, pressed together. His right hand eased her panties downward. She reached down and helped him, took them in her hand, then raised herself up before tossing them.

Jimmy unbuckled his belt, freed the snap on his jeans, and Jill helped them down. "Do you have one of those rubber thingies?" she breathed.

"It's okay, it's okay, don't worry."

They kissed even deeper and Jill rose up and opened her legs. She thrust downward, crying out as all of him slid into her. She moved on top, deep sounds rising from both of them. Jill's head rolled with the motion of her body. Rubbing, grasping, thrusting—more heat, more friction. Jimmy rocked beneath; each moment more intense. Time stretched until they feverishly reached the same place.

What they'd just experienced was, for Jill, startling and profound. Being so close to another, to the one she truly and deeply loved, was even more than she'd imagined. For a long while, she kept her arms locked around Jimmy's neck, breathing him in, until he was totally out of her. She rolled sideways across the passenger seat.

"Oh my God," Jill said, finally. "Tell me you've never felt like that before."

Jimmy leaned back and put his arms behind his head as his eyes fixed upon a spot in the sky. After a moment, he reached over and pulled a Pall Mall from its crumpled red and white pack. Fired up his Zippo.

Jill stroked his cheek, drifting back to the moment. "Things sure happen fast with you."

"Things should happen fast."

They kissed.

"Are you coming with me?"

Jill giggled. "Isn't that what just happened?"

"To the set."

"Harley made everyone promise to stay away."

"Why the hell did he do that?"

"Look, I should go back to Tad's. We can meet up tomorrow night."

Jimmy positioned himself behind the wheel. Fired up the

engine. "You can't always count on tomorrow." Then he turned and handed Jill his Zippo. "Here, take this."

Jill smiled. "What for? I don't even smoke."

"You'll give it back to me next time we see each other. But until then, just hold onto it. You know, like a promise."

✽

Hollywood precinct, LAPD. "Let me put it another way," Sergeant Montoya was saying. "Do you know anybody who *thought* they had reason to kill you?"

Specs, sipping tepid coffee from a paper cup. "Look, Sarge. This Glover character who stole my car, must have done something to somebody else—the wrong person, obviously."

"One last time," said Hancock, the other cop in the room. "You're running down Sunset, chasing the guy. It's still light out. There's car lights, streetlights—yet you don't actually see what happened?"

"I told you—I stumbled. Heard some pops and thought it was the tailpipe backfiring. The other car swung around the corner. I only glimpsed the aftermath."

"C'mon, Pelham," said Montoya, "you had to have seen *something*."

Hancock leaned closer. "And there's nobody who might have thought *you* were driving?"

"Sorry, gentlemen. I'm as in the dark as you are."

"All right," groaned Montoya. "We'll be keeping your car as evidence. You'll get it back, soon as we're done. Your date left a half hour ago. Got a ride home?"

"I'm covered," Specs told them.

TWENTY

Jimmy and Harley, standing on the cliff, facing the ocean, getting ready for the chickie run. Harley, wearing a black leather motorcycle jacket; Jimmy's, scarlet nylon. Nobody else up there. Off behind them, a pair of junk heap cars. Jimmy tossed a clod of dirt. "That's it," he declared. "That's the edge."

Harley, gazing at the blackness, a quiver in his voice. "Why are we doing this?"

Jimmy turned and headed toward the cars. "Because we have to."

Harley, shadowing him: "I'll meet you someplace, flick around knives or whatever you want. But I'm not doing this. It's crazy. It's crazy."

Wait a minute. Jimmy had expected Harley to be shaky, he was shaky himself, but was unprepared for a total, withering cop-out.

Beside one of the cars now, Jimmy's consternation was broken by the wholly unexpected arrival of Specs. "What are you doing here?" he demanded.

Catching his breath, Specs said, "I need to talk to you."

Jimmy, not believing any of this: "Not now."

"I gotta stay at your place tonight. Something happened."

"Not now, I said."

Specs, so wound up he didn't even hear him. "I hitchhiked all the way from Hollywood. Moss Levan had some guys try to kill me, but they killed some other guy by mistake. I gotta lay low. Man, this is as serious as it gets."

Taking this in, Jimmy shook his head.

Harley stood there, staring at him. Jimmy could barely contain his rage. "Listen, you pussy. Our movie needs this shot. They're all set up, down on the beach. So pull yourself together and get behind the wheel."

Harley, choking. "I can't, man, I just can't."

Jimmy was about to grab Harley and shove him in the other car, when he turned to Specs. "Will you do it—will *you* drive?" Specs gazed beyond Jimmy's shoulder for a moment. Said nothing.

"Look, it's just kicks. I explained it all, right? It'll be over before you know it."

Specs, softly, "I dunno, Jimmy."

"C'mon, man, I've seen you; I coached you, you're a natural. We'll do this and laugh our asses off. Then we'll go back to my place and play your tape and drink some beers."

Jimmy, to Harley: "Take your jacket off and give it to my friend. But you're gonna stand here and watch. And when it's over, you're gonna tell Nick and everybody else that you caved in. Got it?"

Harley, sniveling, nodded his head. Peeled off the leather jacket and tossed it to Specs, who slipped out of his sport coat, stepped over and handed it to Harley. "Be careful with it; my wallet's in the breast pocket."

Harley drifted off to the side, as Jimmy and Specs got behind the wheels of their respective cars. Jimmy: "Try the door."

Specs didn't get it at first.

Jimmy: "The roll, try it."

Specs dove out, shoulder first. Tumbled a few feet. Got up.

"Rub some dirt on your hands to grip the wheel better. Don't worry, you're gonna be fine. You trust me, don't you?"

"I trust you, Jimmy." But his voice quivered when he said it.

"You'll take all your cues from me. Watch me as we pick up speed. I'll stay even with you, but when I pull ahead, that's when you bail out."

They fired up the engines. Turned on the headlights.

Tires squealing, grass and dust flying as the cars accelerated. Speeding close together; forty, forty-five. The bluff was looming, dropping off hundreds of feet into the waves. Jimmy and Specs traded feverish glances across the darkness. Jimmy nodded vigorously at Specs, then gunned it before looking ahead out his windshield, the ground rushing toward him.

＊

On the sand below, Ray and his DP stood, tracking the play of headlights hurtling toward the edge. The cars careened off. The one that was closest hurled end-over-end. It didn't make the water but crashed on the shore, the impact causing the fuel line to ignite into a mass of flame. The other car sailed smoothly off the cliff, sailing into the ocean. An incredible shot, far beyond what Ray was hoping for when he conceived the sequence. This wide angle, intercut with the close-ups he'd already filmed, would make a magnificent climax to his picture.

"Cut!" yelled Ray, excitement in his throat.

＊

Jimmy, up on the bluff, absorbing the scene with spreading terror. *Specs never jumped from that car.*

Harley rushed up from behind. "What happened, Jimmy; something went wrong, didn't it?"

Jimmy stared at the black ocean. Tears, hot in his eyes, stinging his cheeks. Blinking through his tears, he then froze, a white beam cutting through the terror and rage. "Give me that sport coat." He grabbed it from Harley. "You stay put until Nick gets up here."

"The guy's *dead*, Jimmy. I don't even know his name."

Something had snapped and Jimmy was consumed purely by instinct. "You're gonna tell Nick it was me . . . I was driving and didn't get out."

Already stunned, Harley clearly couldn't believe what he was hearing. "But where are you going, Jimmy?"

"Just do like I told you."

Jimmy loped over to where the Spyder was parked, sleek and ghostly in the moonlight. He leaned over and kissed the hood, ran his hand all the way across it, then bolted off into the night.

*

Jimmy sat in the cab of the rumbling semi. He was in his body, yet he wasn't; aware of every particle of darkness and sensation, while taking in the scene with a kind of detached fascination. Thankfully, the driver wasn't talkative; God knows why he'd even pulled over at the sight of Jimmy with his thumb out. Up ahead, the exit for Van Nuys Boulevard. "I'll hop out here," Jimmy told him.

Jimmy felt light-headed and almost giddy as he walk-ran the few blocks to his cabin.

He'd been there less than an hour when he found himself taking one last look around. His eyes fell upon a Scotch half-inch tape box marked: *Property of Specs Pelham.* Specs's black-and-white marble notebook lay beside it. Jimmy picked it up. First page: *Lyrics and production notes, Summer 1956.*

Jimmy opened a beige canvas drum bag stuffed nearly to the brim and placed the notebook and tape box on top. Secured the drawstring. Hoisted the bag to his shoulder.

Out the door, once again, into the night and gone.

*

Jill lay sleeping in the predawn shadows, when she heard tapping on her bedroom door. She rustled, then sat up in bed. "Who is it?"

The door swung slowly open and her brother stood in the doorway. Perry barely spoke to her, much less knocked on her door at this hour.

"What's going on," Jill demanded. "What's wrong?"

Perry stepped into the room and sat down on the bed. Jill smelled beer on his breath. "Tad's party tonight," he said. "Tad invited me and told me to bring some friends. But you saw what a fruit show it was. We didn't stay long."

Jill's head was swimming. "I didn't know you were there."

Something strange, almost ominous, in her brother's demeanor.

"I saw you leave the party," Perry continued. "Saw you split with Jimmy Dean."

Jill took a moment. "I went for a drive with him." She surprised herself when she laughed. "He's a really fast driver."

Perry looked away. Silver light was oozing through the blinds. Then he turned and faced her. "I was listening to

K-FOX tonight. Dean was killed . . . in a car accident."

Jill froze. Then: "You're sick, Perry. That's a sick thing to say."

Perry stood. "I just thought you'd like to know, having hung out with him and all."

Jill remained frozen, then eased back down as Perry retreated from her room. No it wasn't possible. Then Jimmy's voice echoed in her head. *You can't always count on tomorrow.*

✱

Lower East Side apartment. Garland Alpert turned to Hiram Freeman; the two were painting the front room: "Serves him right, the punk."

"The guy got killed, Gar. You could be a little more compassionate."

"He was an arrogant asshole—a pretentious, mannered phony."

Hiram lifted his can of Rheingold from the floor and took a sip. "You make it sound personal when you talk about him."

"A phony," said Garland. "And a lot more of a square than he wanted the world to think. You saw where he came from; that town was a hayseed nightmare. I was more than happy to thwart his little charade."

Hiram took off his painter's cap. "What'd you think of that party last night?"

Garland took a moment. "Cool enough. You gonna see that chick again?"

"To whom are you referring?"

"Whom? The chick whom was practically yanking at your belt all night. You didn't dig her?"

"Not at all."

Garland turned to the wall, resumed painting. "Sometimes I don't get you, Freeman. The chick was gorgeous and obviously interested. Oona says she's really with it."

"You know what else Oona said?"

Garland stopped painting. "These fumes are starting to get to me."

"What was her name, Pam or something? The way she expressed her interest was to walk up to Oona and say, 'Who's the spade in the corner?'"

"It's just a phrase, man. It's not like she—"

"Obviously you've never been the spade at the party." Hiram drained his beer. Crushed the can. Let it fall. "You know what, Gar? Now that we've put this coat on, it doesn't really suit me after all."

Garland glared at him. "What's wrong with it?"

"I've decided I don't like off-white." Hiram turned toward his bedroom. Over his shoulder: "I'll be clearing out the end of the month."

*

**From California Coast Guard report,
filed Monday, 10/15/56**

. . . Witnesses on-site revealed that the deceased (Dean, James, resident of Sherman Oaks, Cal.) intended to exit the vehicle. While the result of the impact was total bodily immolation, determination is that a strap of leather (motorcycle) jacket became lodged on door handle, preventing deceased from removing himself as planned . . .

*

Lying on a rock-hard bed in a Lysol-scented room, *Damn you,* Jill kept thinking. *Goddamn you, Jimmy Dean.*

He'd told her not to worry when they were in his goddamn car. She didn't tell anybody it was him she'd been with. Not her old man, not child bride Stephanie, not blabbermouth Kim—not anybody. Told them it was some boy she met at a Johnny Otis sock hop, whose name she didn't know and who she never saw again. Of course, they all—especially her father—considered her a pathetic slut.

Stephanie was all set to line up a doctor in Mexico, but Saint Glenn wouldn't hear of it. Meanwhile he'd only come to visit once and had phoned only twice. It was his idea to pull Jill out of high school, telling everyone he was sending her off to Europe for a special arts program. Some program. The St. Boniface Home for Unwed Mothers.

Sister Louise wanted to know why Jill was a fallen-away Catholic. Jill's mother chose to end her own life. The Church taught that because of that, she couldn't be in heaven. Her mother was the sweetest, warmest person Jill ever knew. She did nothing wrong; in fact, she was wronged herself: Glenn should have gotten a divorce before he started messing around with Stephanie.

The nuns wanted Jill, all the young women, to admit to their "mistake." All Jill did was fall in love with Jimmy Dean. Maybe it was silly, maybe even stupid, but it wasn't a mistake. Jill wasn't convinced she wanted to hand this baby over to anybody.

Another contraction.

Sometimes she'd picture a girl, golden-brown hair, favoring her more than Jimmy. Sometimes she'd see a boy, blonde and smooth, but with a glint that, if you got too close, could slice you neatly and cleanly without even intending to.

An interesting word, *labor*. She'd heard the shrieks and moans from the maternity room, and there was work involved, all right.

Oh, that hurt. The kicking was accelerating.

She lifted the plastic call button and summoned the nurse.

REEL THREE

MAY 1958–
OCTOBER 1964

TWENTY-ONE

"You've been tuned to the *American Hour*, where we focus on the many great things about this great nation of ours. If you want to respond concerning some of the topics we touched on today—keeping Red China out of the UN, the creeping socialism in our national institutions—write to me at Campus Box 65, University of Illinois, Urbana, Illinois. Thanks again to my guest, retired Major Allen Davotney. Tune your radio dial right here—and I do mean right—for my farewell show, same time next week."

Cross-fading into a commercial, Zeke Mallory, twenty-two, could pass for sixteen. Everything else about him—crew cut, build, features—was unremarkable. Pin-striped shirt, thin tie. The room was sterile, and Zeke looked as though he could effortlessly blend in with the colorless walls.

Beside him, his guest smoked a cigarette. He too appeared unremarkable except that, at forty-five, he looked ten years older.

"Terrific interview, sir."

"Easy as pie, thanks to you. You're about to graduate, I take it."

"Yes, sir."

"I assume you've already given a lot of thought as to what you'll do once you're out in the world."

"Well, sir, I inquired about my enlistment prospects, but the preliminary response about my disability was not encouraging."

"What's the nature of your disability?"

"Rheumatic fever, eight years ago. The recruiting officer said they'd never take me."

Davotney stubbed his Viceroy into the ashtray. "I sense your disappointment. How much you'd love to serve your country."

"And quite frankly, sir, I'm concerned about the future."

"Your future?"

"The future of America."

Davotney pulled out a fresh one but did not light it. "Let's take a little stroll."

In a moment they were among the open grass and decorative trees of the quadrangle. The first flush of spring. Badminton. Whiffle ball. Transistor waves in the air.

"I started out in psych, then switched to poli-sci," Zeke was saying. "But most of the professors here are to the left of Adlai Stevenson, who I feel is much further left than this country should be allowed to drift."

"A pinko," said Davotney.

"You said it."

A moment. Music. Voices. "You know, son, there are many ways to serve your country besides traditional military service."

Zeke didn't respond, but was keenly tuned in.

Davotney smiled. "I wish to God I was your age, just starting out. The most important service I've performed—and continue to perform—is out of uniform. I assume your memory is sharp."

"It is."

"Call Chicago directory information the Monday morning after graduation." Carefully. "Ask for the listing of Northern Individual Mausoleum. I've had an instinct about you, Zeke, ever since I first tuned in to your program. Enough to go out on a limb." Davotney extended his hand. "I'll walk from here."

Zeke shook it. "Thank you, sir." He watched the older man go, consumed with a feeling he'd never had. Something was coming, and he felt ready.

✦

Central Park. Garland and Oona sat on the grass. In the distance, a sandlot softball game was in progress and a group of children was taking turns with a red Hula-Hoop. Garland ate from a bag of peanuts, breaking the shells and dropping them to the ground.

"I'm glad I'm moving while it's summer," said Oona. "Once I get to LA, it'll stay warm and bright, like summer never ended." Oona looked out, seemingly caught up in the ball game. "I'm gonna miss the park, though. Take it away and New York's just another city."

"It would take more than that," Garland replied, "to make New York *just another city*. You're just trying to convince yourself you're making the right move."

Oona looked at him. "This is a big step for me, Garland. If you were truly a friend, you'd be more supportive."

Garland popped a peanut into his mouth, then chewed a moment. "I am being supportive. I'm doing the thinking about this that you should be doing yourself."

Oona turned back toward the ball game.

"So Gail McKinney offers you this job in LA. But think

about what you're actually going to be doing; writing about movie stars and teen idols for a bunch of twelve-year-olds. You're in New York, Oona. The literature is here and the intelligence. Out there . . ." He waved his hand like he was brushing aside a gnat.

Oona let out a big breath. "Don't you get tired of being right all the time? What was it Kerouac said about intellectuals: 'So *knowing* and *perceptive* and *blank*'?"

Garland set his peanuts aside, then awkwardly took hold of her hand. "Look, you're on the way up on the fastest track there is. Choice assignments; top publications. You haven't had the Cameron Duffs of the world put the word out that you're unreliable." His face reddened and his voice broke with emotion. "But you know what? I'm proud of what I did. I got to show the world what a phony, lowlife Dean was. I'm a writer, goddammit, I'm not going to be a press agent for anybody, and you shouldn't either, long as you've still got a brain in your head."

Oona stood. "I need to go, Garland." She started away, then turned back. "Are you coming or staying here?"

Garland picked up his bag of peanuts. His eyes were glassy as he simply shook his head.

Oona offered an awkward wave, then hurried away, headed west, out of the park.

✦

Crowded though it was, New York was an easy place to be anonymous. On occasion, Jimmy glimpsed some shadow from the past, like the other day in the grocery when the stage manager from a play he'd been in, *See the Jaguar*, got behind him in line. Or that time in the Strand, when Gadge Kazan was crouched down the aisle from him, thumbing through a paperback. Or the Metropolitan Museum, when he saw a sculptress he used to sleep with—*Sarah, Susan*—gazing at a Turner.

Jimmy felt confident that no one was going to recognize him. Darkened hair and goatee and shades, with his voice pitched higher and softer. Plus, everyone who ever knew him believed him to be dead. But he knew he'd been putting off what he'd come to New York to do: fulfilling the dream of Specs Pelham. Jimmy owed it to him.

Doing so would put him in peril with the very real enemies that Specs had managed to accrue. If he became as successful as he knew Specs wanted to be, there were sure to be consequences. But not doing so was a cop-out, dooming Jimmy to more purgatorial drifting.

He got up. Went to the desk, switched on the lamp; opened the top drawer, took out Specs's marble notebook:

Lyrics and production notes, Summer of 1956

Jimmy flipped to page one, printed meticulously by hand.

Why Don't They Let Us Alone?

My dad doesn't like you
My mom says you're bad
But you're the only love
This girl's ever had
I never dreamed I'd have a love of my own
So why don't they let us
Oh, why don't they let us
Why don't they let us alone?

Next page:

Diddy Diddy Doo

Spoken: *I've got a secret locked deep in my heart.*
I knew you were The One, right from the start.
Sung: *When my friends ask me*
What I see in you
All that I tell them
Is diddy diddy doo
Diddy diddy doo
It's me and it's you
We're all that we need
So diddy diddy doo

Following page:

Little Blue Star

There's a star that shines
Just for you
It's bright and it's clear
And it's oh so true
And when you're far away
It feels a bit blue
But no matter where you are
I'll be that little blue star

Later in the book:

These songs (copyright 1956, published by my company,
Phantom Music, BMI) should be sung by teenage artists.

A young unknown voice will prove to be more valid to a teen audience.

They should not be committed to tape until they have been rigorously rehearsed, preferably right in the studio while reverb, electronic effects, and multing (recording parts more than once) are being refined.

Basic tracks recorded all at once with no concern about mic separation or track bleeding. Such blending will only enhance the sound, not undermine it.

Multi-guitars (as many as five) playing basic chord changes in unison. Trio of pianos (or piano parts) covering different octaves. Trio of basses (double bass, electric and trebled electric). As much varied percussion as possible to underscore various compositional elements. Drum kit, accent on toms, not snare, with sparing use of cymbals. Multi-tracked background vocals. Solo lead vocal, once all other pieces are in place, with the goal in mind of passion and emotion.

The final tracks should ideally be mixed, not on studio monitors, but on a single tiny speaker that best exemplifies a transistor or car radio; that is how the kids will be listening, in bedrooms and back seats.

TWENTY-TWO

Next morning, Jimmy dialed the phone. Woman with a French accent answered.

Jimmy: "May I speak to Mr. Kampeteris?"

"Who is calling?"

"Specs Pelham."

"Regarding?"

"I'm a songwriter and record prod—"

"One moment."

Ten seconds. Twenty. Half a minute. Jimmy was about to hang up when he heard a not very tuneful baritone: *Because I knew you, my life will never be the same. Because I knew you, I know I'll never love again.*

"Mr. Kampeteris?"

"A good song, but a great record. White bread but peppered with soul. I almost cut it with Betty Everett. So, you planted in town, or just blowing through?"

"Well, sir—I, ah—been kind of gearing up for my next project and—"

"I'm all ears. Tomorrow, at two-thirty. Got the address?"

*

Gulf Port Records, in a brownstone on East Sixty-Fourth. Jimmy checked in at the reception desk and, invited to look around, scoped out the gleaming lobby and the muted central corridor. The gold discs on every wall said it all, not to mention the pictures. The Greek and Nat King Cole. The Greek and Sinatra. He and Judy Garland. He and Leonard Bernstein. He and Lady Day.

A door opened. The Greek, glistening bald pate atop an ebony suit and maroon silk tie. Impeccable. "Come in, Specs."

Jimmy floated into the dark, elegant room. A dazzling canvas covered a wall on the left. Jimmy nearly gasped, having seen it reproduced in a book on Picasso. "What should I call you—Mr. Kampeteris?"

"Just Alex. Anything to drink?"

"No thank you."

"That's something my father taught me about a first meeting: 'Never accept a drink and don't ask to use the toilet.'"

The Greek laughed. Jimmy laughed with him, taking an armchair.

"One thing about me—while I like to have a good time, I don't like to waste *any* time. Specs, I'm looking for somebody to cut a single—just one side, I'm not promising anything beyond that—on one of my acts. You up for it?"

Jimmy: "Sure am."

"Everything about it's gotta sound like a hit. If you're the producer I suspect you are, you'll deliver exactly that."

"I appreciate that vote of—"

"They copied your demo, right? If anybody associated with your song had made a record that sounded anything like it, they would have done it before then." Out came a Kool from its pewter case. "There's a session tomorrow night with the Essentials."

Never heard of them. "One of my favorites."

"I wanna cut a Brill Building tune called 'Street Life.' Got smash written all over it."

Jimmy took this in.

"That all right with you, Specs?"

"I was hoping to record my own songs."

"I'm in the market for a producer at the moment. This works, we can take a look at your book later. And mind you, we're just trollin'. I ain't gonna release it unless we pull a big sweet fish into the boat."

A moment. "Thank you, sir."

"For what?"

"Giving me a shot like this."

The Greek beamed. "Just remember, baby. The first one's easy to get. It's the second that can be elusive."

✱

Jimmy was in his pad, listening to an acetate of the piano-vocal demo of "Street Life."

> *When I walk on the street, there's the world at my feet,*
> *Swarming with people, and covered in concrete.*
> *Everything you want is here, pulling you close, drawing you*
>   *near.*
> *Never thought I'd feel alive as this,*
> *Like I can open my arms and give the world a kiss.*
> *This street life is the sweet life to me.*

Specs's marble notebook was open on Jimmy's lap. *How the hell am I going to pull this off?* Specs had provided him with a blueprint, but he was going to be dealing with studio pros, telling them how to do things any one of them knew more about than he did. And then Jimmy thought that maybe he was looking at this all wrong. He needed to tap into his skills as an actor, play the role of a record producer who knew exactly what he was doing. As far as he could tell, record producing was much the same as directing, and he had been directed by the best in the business.

✦

Jimmy stepped into the small studio the Greek had booked on West Forty-Seventh. An engineer named Michael, quiet and preoccupied. Rhythm section—piano, bass, drums—the Greek booked them, too. The Greek himself was there with Zouzou, his Creole secretary. Michael asked him how the tracks should be configured. The Greek pointed at Jimmy. "That's the boss man right there. I'm just here to be amazed."

The engineer looked at Jimmy, who droned: "I'm not here to do your job for you, Michael. You run the board. I've got enough to be concerned with."

The Essentials showed up all at once, a gospel-turned-R & B quartet, built around Reginald Davis—Reggie D to those in the biz. The Greek greeted the group while simultaneously settling them into session like everyone knew each other and they'd been working together for years. Jimmy handed Michael the demo.

"Sweet tune," Jackie, one of the singers said, after it spun.

"Catchy melody," said another.

Reggie D, not a word.

The players ran down the basic track while Jimmy listened.

After two run-throughs, the piano player said: "We're

ready for a take."

"The hell you are," said Jimmy. "Keep running it and I'll tell you when you're ready."

Seeing that this would take some time, the singers retired to a lounge adjacent to the studio. Two hours later, as the track was still being rehearsed, Jimmy leaned into Michael's ear—sharper on the bass drum; more echo on the voices.

"Why put the reverb on? We can add it later in the mix."

"I want to hear what we've got now—not when everybody's gone and we can't recreate it."

Michael shook his head.

An hour later, the red light finally went on, and the band, weary but freed up after so many run-throughs, nailed it in a single take.

"Okay, that's a good start," Jimmy said.

"A start?" asked Michael.

"This has to get bigger."

"You want me to mix all the instruments down to one basic track? That's the only way to have room for overdubs."

"That's exactly what I want."

Jimmy augmented what they had with tripled piano, bowed bass. Tambourine and maracas, which he played himself. It was coming together, he could feel it. He dismissed the musicians, then told Michael to get the singers.

"Now let's do the background vocals. I want you guys to hum whole notes to reinforce the chord changes."

After they nailed it, Jimmy told them, "Thanks, fellows. You can go home now." To Reggie D: "Your turn," he said.

"It's after midnight," he grumbled. "About fucking time."

Only the Greek and Zouzou remained as spectators. Jimmy felt he was finally in territory he knew something about. After a few run-throughs, he stepped into the main room and walked up to Reggie D. "I want you to take off your shirt."

"Beg your pardon?"

"You're hiding, getting by on the strength of your voice. I want you to feel these lyrics, reveal yourself through them."

"And taking my fucking shirt off for you is going to accomplish that?"

"I don't know, let's see."

Reggie D peered through the glass at the Greek, who was clearly not about to offer support. The singer defiantly peeled off his jacket and tie, then stripped his shirt and stood barechested.

"Dim the lights," Jimmy ordered.

Michael dimmed them just enough so that Reggie D could read the lyrics on the music stand. After the first verse, the singer had undergone a shift.

> *"When the man gives the word, like I've always heard,*
> *I wish I could be free as a bird,*
> *But I know there'll come a time,*
> *When every last word's gonna rhyme*
> *And you know I'm gonna smile on that day*
> *When I make my own way and you'll hear me say,*
> *This street life is the sweet life for me."*

Reggie D was pissed off and fed up, you could hear it in every note. Exactly what was needed—seething, determined anger. He viscerally ad-libbed over the final chorus.

Jimmy leaned forward, pressed talk-back. "Thank you, Reginald. Now you can go home, too."

Again, Jimmy had Michael mix the instruments, vocals—every element of the sonic presentation—down to one monaural track. It was one in the morning; they'd been at it six hours. Jimmy felt great, but something was missing. He floated around. In a corner of the control room was a beige guitar case. He leaned down, flipped the steel latches. A solid-body electric; honey-shaded, with a gleaming black pickguard. "Who owns this instrument?"

"It's mine," Michael replied.

"We need a solo on top of that piano figure. How about if you play it?"

"There's just one guitar amp here with a blown speaker. It'll sound like a mess."

"Let's try it anyway."

Michael reluctantly plugged the guitar in. The amplifier crackled like it was being incinerated.

"Let's hear it with the track," Jimmy insisted.

The track was pristine; piano sparkling, the overdubs filling everything out.

At the solo, Michael—angry, frustrated, an instrumental manifestation of Reggie D's attitude—cut loose with frantic, seemingly disconnected figures. The distortion sent the needles into red.

When they listened back, Michael said, "This is awful, man. Everybody who plays this is gonna think there's something wrong with the recording. Gonna say I screwed it up."

"Look," said Jimmy. "Get the picture in your head. This guy is walking down the street and everything is flowing. But inside, he's got this garble and squawk. That's how it's gonna hit anybody who listens. And sorry to say, Michael. Nobody's gonna give you a glimmer of thought."

Michael, to the Greek. "Help me out here, Alex."

The Greek beamed. "Never heard anything like it. Theater for the ear."

＊

Lunch, the following day. The Greek, to Jimmy: "You can spin this shit into gold, baby, no doubt about it."

Jimmy, chewing lettuce, didn't respond.

"I'm gonna let you in on a secret, Specs."

Jimmy put his fork aside.

The Greek leaned forward. "I've got this condition. Six months, a year maybe, then, it's stone time—I'll be totally deaf."

A moment. "I don't know what to say, Alex."

"Don't say anything; I'll only hear half of it anyway." The Greek chuckled, opening his pewter case as he pulled out a Kool. "Every Friday I cab it down to the waterfront where a chopper takes me to my weekend home in Sag Harbor. Even before this hearing thing came down, I was clock-watching until the end of the workweek. I need to turn the reins over to somebody who has the juice."

"You saying what I think you're saying?"

"Two and a half points on everything you produce. Three if it goes top five. The only stipulation, you gotta cut the songs on which I own the publishing. Don't worry, there's some undeniable hits in the pool."

Jimmy looked out the window. A woman was staring in from the sidewalk; toothless, eating a sandwich she had likely fished out of a trash can. Then he heard the Greek say: "You notice anything funny last night?"

Jimmy looked at him.

The Greek was smiling. "You didn't introduce yourself to anybody, and I didn't introduce you either. Not to Michael, not to Reggie D, not to any of the players. Now, maybe you felt shy or preoccupied or something, but why would a gracious individual such as I, be so careless?"

Jimmy kept looking. "I don't know Alex. You tell me."

The Greek leaned forward. "Because, like you, I was being cautious; I'm not looking to get us killed."

And then he spun it. Specs Pelham had written a big hit song, three years before; in pop music, a lifetime ago. But although Moss Levan had been unsuccessful at rubbing Specs out, the man still had a very sharp memory.

"You'll be under contract to me, and my name will remain on the records," the Greek concluded. "The bread will be what it's about."

"Will I ever get to cut my own songs?"

"Down the road, if we're making hits. Right now, it's a producer I'm looking for." The Greek lifted his wineglass and took a sip. "You'll be on salary. Not huge, but steady. Royalties will flow with the rest of Gulf Port's stream—in a Frankfurt account. I've always sold a ton of product in Europe, and all of my finances are kept in trust over there. It tends to confound the Treasury Department. Besides, a young cat like you shouldn't have too much gumbo in his bowl. Better to stay hungry. When you cash out, you'll be like me, set for the haul And by the way, Specs can't be your real first name, so what is it?

"Stephen."

"Pick a last name for the sessions so I won't be so rude as to not introduce you to the people we're working with."

Jimmy shrugged. "How about James?"

"Stephen James it is."

Now Jimmy leaned forward. "Since the bread is what it's about, and it's kept over in Germany, I want an accounting of my salary, as well as royalties, every two weeks. You know as well as I do that any man who can't take care of his money deserves what he gets."

The Greek appeared thrown for a second, then beamed. "Not only an artist, but a businessman. You're gonna do great, baby. *We're* gonna do great."

TWENTY-THREE

A s Jill performed her minimum-wage duties in the gift shop at the LA County Museum, she was usually thinking of one of three things. The first was travel, second was her own artwork, and third was the infant son she'd handed over to be adopted.

The first two, she loved thinking about, helping her through the placid and utterly predictable days. The third she actively resisted and would push back whenever it threatened to take form. Getting better at doing so, Jill hoped it would someday be a memory so vague and hazy that it seemed to belong to somebody else.

She sat behind the cash register, pleasantly lost in a guide to Italy. A woman was approaching. Wild-eyed, hair like steel wool, paint-splattered T-shirt and jeans. Engineer boots, paint on them too. She banged her fist on the counter as she glared at Jill, who glanced up. "Is there a problem?"

"You're the problem," the woman declared.

"What are you—"

"This is the biggest museum in LA, right? And Los Angeles is the third largest city in the US, right?"

"If you say—"

"So why the hell are the books on LA artists—California artists—in the section designated as regional—while all the books on New York artists are considered national, and even international?"

"I didn't arrange the display."

"Of course not. You just sit on your ass and read about Europe—a dead civilization, by the way—while the only true artists in this town are ghettoized as locals."

"Why don't you write a letter or something?"

"The Italians are fascists—you know that, don't you?"

The phone rang. "Excuse me." Jill sighed, lifted the receiver. "Gift shop."

The woman leaned across the counter. "While you take your stupid call, I'm going to take all the American artists—regardless of where they stretch their canvases—and arrange them according to importance."

On the other end of the line, a male voice: "Jill, your dad agrees with me. At least read the script. It's got to be more interesting than the museum."

Jill said into the receiver: "One second, Tad." She watched as the woman pulled books from the shelves and tossed them to the floor. "I'm calling the security guard."

"Better hurry. I'm thinking about putting a match to these."

Jill kept an eye on her as she said into the phone. "I'm dealing with a situation here, Tad. Give me a call at home tonight."

*

Jill, dressed in jeans, tennis shoes and pin-striped blouse, stepped onto a soundstage at ABC television. In the house were half a dozen executives, all men, all in suits, and a pair of well-dressed women secretaries, notepads in hand. "Thank you for coming, Miss Parnell," said one of the men.

Jill smiled. An empty chair was onstage and she stood beside it.

Another suit: "I'm Herb Foy, creator and head writer for the show. I see you're empty-handed. Did you bring the pages we sent?"

Jill smiled faintly. "I left them at home."

Pause. The exec beside Foy: "Let's start with the scene where Traci meets Brandon at the beach. Alice, would you give her those sides please?"

As the secretary brought the script pages to the stage, Foy said, "Out of curiosity, Miss Parnell, why would you turn up without the essential materials? Certainly, you've auditioned before."

"Thank you," Jill said, as she accepted the pages. To the house: "Actually, I never have. I came here at the suggestion of a friend who just opened a talent agency."

Foy turned to the other suits. "I don't care whose kid she is. This is a waste of time. The girl's going to subject us to a cold reading. Let's bring in the next actress."

A different voice, from behind Foy. "Miss Parnell, what about telling us a story, just off the top of your head."

"What kind of story?"

"Something that might reveal a bit about yourself. Whatever comes to mind."

Jill looked like she was about to walk offstage when she said: "I was at the Norton Simon, out in Pasadena. They were having a Degas exhibition. I'd never seen a Degas, much less a whole collection. It was crowded. Margaret Dodd was there that day, looking at the paintings. I'm sure you remember her. She played the part of Millie, the housekeeper on the NBC comedy the *Months of May*. She's also a very serious visual artist, mostly in the impressionistic mode. While I was standing there, surrounded by Degas's genius, I heard this undercurrent. 'That's Millie. Do you see Millie standing over there?' I looked at Margaret, who had been off that show for a few years. Her face was red as she slinked out of the gallery . . . I don't know what I'm doing here. I'm really a painter myself; at least I'm trying to be. So you're right, Mr. Foy. Let's not waste each other's time."

❋

Jill's kitchen. Her agent, former teen heartthrob but no longer platinum-haired Tad Harbor, sat across from her. As Jill was pouring him a glass of orange juice, she said, "Why would they want me for a callback? I all but told them to stuff themselves."

"They didn't see one actress who made an impression. At least you did that."

Jill, quiet for a moment. "Tell them this. If they want to see me again, they need to offer me the part. And whatever they're offering needs to be three times the usual. That's what it will take for me to sell my soul."

"Jill, what you're talking about, only stars get that."

Jill gingerly lifted her tea bag out of its cup. "Didn't you say that whoever gets this part is sure to become a star? If it's a fait accompli, they should be willing to pay for it at the top."

❋

Jill, at the counter in the gift shop, listlessly working on a pen-and-ink sketch, answered the ringing phone. "Oh, hi, Tad."

"Bad news, kid. They want you for Traci."

Jill closed her sketch pad. "They tripled the quote?"

"Doubled it."

"Not enough, Tad."

TWENTY-FOUR

The Berghoff, Chicago's Loop. Table in the corner. Agents Davotney and Mallory.

Davotney took a sip from his stein. "They make their own beer here. You ought to try one."

"I don't drink, sir."

"Never once—college or anything?"

"Never."

"I'm getting a little worried about you, Zeke. There doesn't seem to be any fun in your life." A moment. Sounds from the lunch crowd. "So what was it you wanted to discuss?"

Zeke set his soup spoon on the table, then dabbed his lips with the cloth napkin. "I'm not convinced that what I'm doing—the surveillance tasks—are very effective."

"Everybody's happy with your work, Zeke."

"Nothing ever happens at their meetings."

Davotney fired up a Viceroy. "Communism is the biggest threat to our American way of life."

"I agree with you, sir, that Russia is and that China is. But these pinkos I'm monitoring couldn't organize lunch."

Davotney smiled. "Those lefties could fuck up a wet dream, we used to say."

Zeke grimaced. "I feel there's a genuine domestic threat that has yet to be identified—at least by our agency." He leaned forward. "I was in radio, sir. I understand it—its powers of persuasion. A lot of the music being broadcast is performed by Negroes and encourages loose morals and race mixing. The biggest Negro names—Charles Berry from St. Louis and Richard Penniman, are sexual deviants. Presley, Jerry Lee Lewis, who sing Negro bop, are known fornicators. The people profiting from all of this, many of whom come from the world of jukeboxes and nightclubs, have direct ties to organized crime. I'd like to throw out a net from here in Chicago and see how far it spreads."

Davotney drew hard on his cigarette. "Write up a report and I'll see what I can do. You sure you won't have a beer? You don't know what you're missing."

✱

Zeke stepped into the conference room. Davotney and another man were seated at a long table. "Agent Mallory," said Davotney, "this gentleman is from Washington. At the national level, we don't usually reveal identities unless it's essential to a specific action."

"Understood, sir," said Zeke.

The man, Davotney's age, even a bit older, took over. "Leadership is very interested in supporting your action regarding a nationwide network of organized crime, specifically as it relates to the radio and recording businesses."

Zeke almost expressed appreciation. Thought better of it.

"The Chicago connection you identified, Salvatore Vinetta. We're going to authorize a wiretap on his home in River Forest as well as his office on Dearborn. Determine if, as you suspect, he's engaged in paying for favors to get music played by certain disc jockeys and program directors. You will have a budget as well as administrative support."

Zeke couldn't help smiling. "Thank you, sir."

The fellow nodded but didn't smile. "Have at it, agent Mallory."

*

Transcript of Audio Surveillance

The following conversation was monitored July 2, 1959, between the home (kitchen) telephone of Salvatore "Skip" Vinetta (River Forest, Ill.) and coin-operated (Pacific Bell) telephone registered to the Brown Derby restaurant, Los Angeles, Cal. First part of conversation was unrecorded due to equipment malfunction. Recording commenced approximately forty-five seconds into conversation. Participants identified as Salvatore Vinetta himself, alias Sal the Barber, alias Solly Sparks, alias Sal Soretti; and Moishe Lidman, named changed legally to Moss Levan, of Sherman Oaks, California, 1948. *Note: elements of conversation suspected to be in code.*

ML:—gonna need a little help on that.

SV: Too bad it ain't in the grooves.

ML: You got that right. That's why we gotta—

SV: You sure this is the market—break it here?

ML: Don't matter what the fuck. Your yard, Detroit. Just cuff that goofball PD on FLC. What's-his-fuck—

SV: Barney?

ML: —always got his hand out.

SV: He runs his mouth, Mossy.

ML: Ah, give him some grease. Nobody listens to him anyway. Not off-air.

SV: All right, I'll set up a goody box. What I hear, he likes dark chocolate.

ML: Did you lay that bet down for me, our friend in the desert?

SV: It's down, Mossy. Hey, anything lately about the vanishing act?

ML: Going on three and not a glimpse.

SV: He's out there somewhere. Not good for us.

ML: (unintelligible) . . . as he don't make any noise, he's a nonissue. I put the word out. Anybody works with him is going pine.

SV: (laughing) As in a box, right?

ML: You got it . . . (unintelligible) . . . so far off the screen he might as well be fucking dead.

SV: Like that other poor bastard.

ML: Unlucky, unlucky. What the fuck.

SV: I'll call you once I've got Barney in the rack.

ML: He's in already.

SV: I mean for that piece of shit record that (unintelligible) . . . Should stick to making bowling balls. Something somebody wants.

ML: You got that, Skipper. Barney's gonna have to—

(connection lost)

✱

The Greek's office. Jimmy. Sitting across from the Greek, lit a cigarette. "You said you wanted to talk."

"You know the game, baby. I need a hit."

"You think I'm not aware of that?" Jimmy replied, trailing a plume of smoke.

"'Street Life' got to thirty-seven, but with all the federal heat on the industry, I couldn't give it the kind of boost that was called for. The last two have taken the gas pipe, not even denting the Hot One Hundred. The next will have to go at least Top Ten."

"I'm working with the material you're giving me."

"Some great songs."

"As far as you and I are concerned."

The Greek, sphinxlike.

"What about *them*?" Jimmy said.

"Them?"

Jimmy leaned forward. "You know as well as anybody, Alex, the biggest audience for 45 rpms are twelve-year-olds, especially twelve-year-old girls. That's who we're selling to."

The Greek sulked.

Jimmy, not about to let go. "We gotta be dumber somehow. Dumb, but real. Dumb, but sincere."

The Greek laughed. "When you work that one out, baby, be sure to let me know."

Jimmy scowled. "I have worked it out. I'm sitting on at least a dozen hits."

"And who's gonna sing these songs of yours. None of my acts are kids."

"We can find somebody to sing them, young artists we can make into stars. But it's the songs that count."

The Greek looked away. "This is the part of being the boss that I've never enjoyed." A moment. "Reggie D's going solo, and I don't think you're the cat to produce. Sorry, Specs, I gotta cut you loose."

✽

In a high-rise apartment overlooking Chicago's Loop, Zeke Mallory sat on the sofa, his TV dinner on a plastic tray-top table in front of him. Knock on the door. Zeke, surprised, put his fork aside, then rose to answer. Eased the door open.

Davotney there, a topcoat over his suit and tie.

"Hello, sir. How did you get past the doorman?"

Davotney smiled with the flush of a man who's had a few. "If I couldn't slip by a civilian, I'd be losing my touch."

Zeke, uncomfortable. "Well, come in."

Davotney, as he was stepping inside. "No, agent Mallory, the point is for you to come out. I left Sandra and some other people in the Cape Cod Room at the Drake. I want you to celebrate with us."

"Celebrate what?"

"The new year. The new decade. The terrific work you've done with the radio campaign."

"Thanks, but I just planned to be here."

"On New Year's Eve—what the hell kind of a plan is that?"

Zeke stood awkwardly. "You know, sir, the radio investigation, I don't feel it's going as well as you seem to think."

"We've got a House Committee involved. Our first court case is coming up. Truckloads of press. Leadership couldn't be more pleased."

"Respectfully, sir, so much of that is window dressing. A bunch of goofy disc jockeys, while the big fish in organized crime remain at large."

"Let's not talk shop tonight, Zeke. For Chrissake, grab your coat. There's a young lady over there, a good friend of Sandra's, who's looking forward to meeting you. I told everybody if you wouldn't come willingly, I was going to drag you out."

"I followed up on a reference in the surveillance transcripts. A botched contract job a few years ago on Sunset Boulevard in Los Angeles. A petty thief named Brendan Mark Glover got killed, but that's not who they were gunning for. The intended victim, Stephen "Specs" Pelham, was suing Moss Levan and company. Apparently, he went underground. If we were to find him before the mob does, we could not only save his life, but turn him into a valuable witness."

"This is your last chance, Zeke. Are you going to ring in the New Year, or sit here by your lonesome?"

"I made dinner, sir. I'd prefer to stay here and finish it."

Davotney, now in the doorway, glanced down at Zeke's tray-top table. "You call that dinner? See you Monday, agent Mallory."

"Happy New Year, sir."

TWENTY-FIVE

Hollywood Recorder: July 1, 1960

'Rebel' Finds its Cause

"Rebel Without a Cause," the never-released-here pic during whose filming star-crossed actor James Dean lost his life, has been experiencing a rebirth in the UK. A series of midnight screenings, plus a rave by Keith R. Nashley of the London Daily Express, have brought the teddy boys (and girls) out in droves. British censors would not permit the actual moment when Dean's car explodes short of the Pacific but have approved footage right up to that point. "Save yourself, Jimmy," and "Hit your brake, Jimmy," are frequently heard as the ghastly scene unfolds. Tragically, Dean did neither.

Not everyone is so enamored of what has all the makings of a cult. Cambridge psychologist George Allington states: "The way the teenagers, not to mention the cinema owners, are treating this film is absolutely ghoulish. Will a sequel include young Dean's ashes and his incinerated coffin?"

The Archbishop of Canterbury expressed similar disapproval: "British youth should be about the business of celebrating life and not allow themselves to be titillated by destructive acts in some gloomy cinema."

Many young theatergoers are seeing it more than once. "Jimmy was true," remarked Thelma Cross after her seventh viewing at a Richmond cinema. "For what he believed in, he offered up his life."

Nicholas Ray, who produced and directed, told the London Daily Observer: "It's ironic that a classic like "Rebel" had to come all the way to England to find its audience."

*

Sign behind lectern: *Waterford Welcomes Ronald Reagan*

Reagan stood at the podium, facing about a hundred fifty after-dinner guests.

"My favorite guest star?" He laughed. "That's easy. My wife, Nancy.

A few in the crowd expressed surprise. "No, Nancy was a splendid actress. She starred in *The Next Voice You Hear*; some of you must have seen it. A terrific picture about an ordinary housewife who hears the voice of God coming through the radio."

When a few laughed, he added. "It's wonderful, and Nancy was wonderful in it. James Whitmore was her costar. Nineteen-fifty. Then she gave it all up for me." He smiled. "I think we have time for one last question." Pointed. "Yes, in the back there."

A middle-aged woman stood. "I just read in *Photoplay* that James Dean, the young man who . . . assaulted you, is becoming something of a star in Great Britain."

Reagan smiled. "It's a shame he's not around to enjoy it."

Ripple of laughter.

Reagan, suddenly serious. "Let's hope that no one gets the bright idea of promoting him over here, as he seems to have a lousy effect on teenagers, and we already have enough of those problems." Smile returned. "I've had a wonderful time here in your community, a wonderful time here tonight. Good night to you all."

As he started to go, a man, in a clear voice, called out: "Where do you stand in the upcoming presidential race?"

Reagan looked around. His genial manner faded like a set

of blinds had just been drawn.

"I've been asked by management not to get into such matters. To do so might be taken as . . . divisive."

A few in the crowd expressed lighthearted disapproval. Reagan looked as though he was again about to bid goodnight, then gripped both sides of the podium.

"I have spent most of my life as a Democrat. But I have a growing sense that a Republican ticket headed by Vice President Nixon, who hails from my adopted state of California, will not be cowed by the specter of communism. I don't feel that assurance when I look at some of the liberal apologists on the Democratic side of the aisle."

A smatter of applause.

Encouraged, Reagan's voice gained resonance: "We need to ask ourselves: Are we going to uphold, or are we going to abandon the vision held by our forefathers when they conceived the dream that is America? Does a coterie of eggheads in the District of Columbia know better than we do how to manage our lives? And when it comes to government handouts, we need to bear in mind that when somebody builds you a house, they are also building you a prison."

The wave of applause was clearly beyond what Reagan anticipated. He took a step back as the ovation swelled, seeming unlikely to diminish, as table after table rose to their feet. He looked surprised, but pleased. Very pleased, indeed.

*

Outdoor set of a Warner Brothers Western. A trio of sleepy horses tied to a hitching post. Clint Walker, in buckskin, signing autographs off to the side. Studio exec Stan was alongside Jack Warner himself, strolling through. Warner, speaking:

"I had to pay Nick Ray a fortune to get that picture back. It damn well better do some business."

"I don't think it can miss, Mr. Warner."

"I dunno. I'm used to having the star promote it. I understand you were buddies with Dean."

Stan took a moment. "I babysat him through *Eden*. A pain in the ass, may he rest in peace."

Warner: "Let him fill some seats for us. Then he can rest." He popped gum into his mouth, then stuck the wrappings in his pocket. "We'll stoke the fires all year, then make a big splash next summer when all the delinquents are out of school. If we sell enough tickets, we'll take *Eden* out of mothballs for a Christmas release."

*

From the moment television writer-producer Herb Foy read the galleys of *Breakfast at Tiffany's*, he'd planned his version. Traci is a small-town girl on her own in Los Angeles. Unconventional, but appealing. Wacky, but levelheaded. High-spirited, but vulnerable. Every man she meets falls for her. So Jill could be seen smiling and acting *absentminded but with a wealth of common sense* every Wednesday at eight o'clock.

Is America ready for Traci? was the question *Newsweek* posed when the show premiered in the fall of '59. By the end of the first season, a poll was published in *Parade* magazine, which listed Jill Parnell as one of America's ten most influential women.

Since Traci, Jill's life had not been the same. For example, she took her Studebaker to the same garage who'd been servicing it for the past three years. Jill hadn't watched the first episode of the show, had gone out to dinner by herself, and the next morning at seven-thirty, her phone rang. It was Charley the garage owner, telling her that her car was ready. Not only that but they had washed and waxed and detailed the exterior, as well as replaced the floor mats, free of charge. Jill uttered thanks, confused by the awareness that nothing like it had ever happened before. She'd always had to call and sometimes it would be ready and sometimes it wouldn't, but they did a good job and were cheap and it was surprising that they'd call to let her know the work was completed. "We'll send a car over for you," Charley said, practically chirping. "By the way, my wife and I thought you were terrific last night. Never knew you were so funny, Miss Parnell." Then he added, "If I was you, I'd think about getting something flashier to drive."

And then she understood. Like it or not, she was a TV star now. Like it or not, she was wacky but levelheaded. Like it or not, she was Traci.

*

Nate 'n Al's delicatessen, Beverly Hills. Jill was winding up lunch with Stephanie, her father's wife.

Stephanie, smiling, "We don't see enough of you these days, Jillsy."

"It's tough to get away from the set."

"I've got a little favor to ask."

As Jill lit up a Newport, using the Zippo Jimmy had given her, Stephanie pressed on. "It's all very hush-hush. But your father is going to host an industry fundraiser for the Vice President next month."

"Host, where?"

"At the house. An evening, cocktail-type event. No more

than a hundred people but they'll all be writing checks."

"Richard Nixon, at the house?"

"The trouble is, my mother and I will be on a cruise. Your dad needs someone to serve as hostess. I know you don't like that kind of thing, but it would mean so much to him."

An older woman appeared at Jill's elbow. "Would you sign this napkin for my granddaughter?"

"What's her name?" asked Jill, as she set her cigarette in the ashtray.

"Wendy."

Jill scrawled and handed it to the woman. The woman glanced at it, then put it in her purse. "I'm surprised to find that Traci's a smoker."

Jill smiled with effort. "Traci doesn't smoke. I do."

"I won't tell my granddaughter. She thinks you're an angel."

Jill turned back to Stephanie. "Where were we?"

*

"Garland Alpert, please come to TWA passenger pickup."

Garland strolled through the LA terminal carrying a duffel bag, over two thousand miles further west than he'd ever been. He spotted the face he was looking for, beside the glass doors, and vigorously waved.

Oona smiled, but stayed put. As Garland approached, she said, "You look incredibly out of place. Come on, the car's idling at the curb."

Minutes later, they were headed north on Centinela in Oona's orange VW bug.

"Where'd you learn to drive?" asked Garland.

"Back in high school. Comes in handy out here."

"Another of Oona's secrets." He gazed out, taking in the palm trees and vivid colors. "It's a change of scene, all right. I still don't see why you split from New York for beefcake and beach bunnies."

"Excuse me, Hemingway, but aren't you on assignment for *TV Weekly*?"

"Don't tell me you think that *Pop Diary* means anything. Interviewing young-adult morons for a bunch of teenage morons."

"Rock 'n' roll? Teen flicks? They're pop art. Ask Warhol. If I thought it didn't mean anything to anyone, I couldn't do it." Headed east, Oona asked, "What hotel are you at?"

"The Del Capri in Westwood." Garland looked over. "Unless you've changed your mind about me staying with you."

Oona, looking straight ahead. "Forget it, Gar, we played that scene already."

*

Knock, knock. In her dressing room, Jill put out her cigarette, answered the door, a smile spreading across her face.

"Hi, Jill. I'm Garland Alpert."

"Right. From *TV Weekly*."

"I'm not on the masthead, I just freelance for them sometimes."

"Well, thanks for coming," said Jill, on her way to the sofa.

Garland took the chair facing her. His notebook came out. "Did your father have anything to do with your landing the part of Traci?"

Jill laughed. "Are you sure you're with *TVW*? I thought this was gonna be a soft piece."

"Don't worry. It's just something I was wondering myself."

Jill went to her cigarette case on the dressing table. "You want one?"

"Not my brand. You have a brother, don't you?"

Jill nodded, lighting up with the Zippo, then taking a deep drag.

"Think he'll go into the Industry?"

"No, Perry's more interested in . . . I don't know what he's interested in. I don't like to talk about my family."

"Let me look at the questions my editor suggested. What about you and Brandon? Any truth to the whispers that the two of you are an item off-screen?"

"We're just friends."

"From what I hear, your leading man might be a little light in the loafers."

"You don't watch the show, do you?"

"I'm aware of the show. Can't say I watch it."

"Look, I've been here all day and I could use a drink. Let's go someplace and you can ask me whatever you need to know about Traci."

"You'll have to drive. I took a taxi here."

"Everything else is off the record. Deal?"

Garland was smiling as Jill grabbed her handbag

＊

Jill drove to Barney's Beanery where, even if she were recognized, the clientele was committed to keeping their cool and would not approach her.

"Some of the Ferus Gallery crowd hang out here," she told Garland. "I've heard that Kienholz is practically a regular, although I've never seen him. Why don't you roll out whatever questions you have, so we can eventually have a conversation?"

"I've got all I need from the PR people at the network. Truth is, there's another article I want to write, although I'm sure no editor will touch it. I want to find out all of what Kennedy was up to when he was in LA for the Democratic convention." Garland leaned forward like he was taking Jill further into his confidence. "I wanna call it: 'Will JFK be Our First Movie Star President?'"

Jill's expression took an inquisitive turn. "Kennedy's a movie star?"

Garland took a sip of his draft, his mouth twisting slightly as though it didn't quite agree with him. "You've heard of RKO Pictures?"

Jill nodded.

"Did you know that the K in there stands for Kennedy? They've been playing out here since the thirties. The old man had Gloria Swanson as his mistress and our boy Jack nearly married Gene Tierney." He took another sip, which didn't appear to agree with him any more than the one before it. "The only reason that didn't happen was that Tierney was a divorcee and it wouldn't look good for Catholic Jack to go against the faith. I'm the furthest thing from a Catholic, but I'm as devout as that guy." He chuckled. "Kennedy's old man probably put it best: 'It's not what you are, it's what people think you are.'"

Jill, with a slight laugh. "It sounds like you're carrying some kind of grudge."

"I'm just sick of all the phonies in Washington; in Hollywood. Kennedy's a lightweight and a philanderer, and it's not just starlets. Secretaries, stewardesses, hat-check girls.

The press know it, but nobody will put it into print because they're charmed by him."

"Maybe they're not enamored of the alternative."

"Nixon? A disaster, but at least you know what you're up against. Come November, I'll be sitting this one out. I gather you'll be voting for Jack."

"Call me old-fashioned. I don't believe people should reveal what goes on in the voting booth, or the bedroom."

Neither said anything for a moment. A pool game was clicking near them. Jill's double vodka tonic was nearly empty.

Finally, Garland asked: "Why do you do it?"

Jill, a bit thrown. "What?"

"That silly-ass television show. You clearly aren't into it."

"We're done with our interview, I thought."

"The money, right? It's gotta be the money."

Garland was staring with a can't-wait-to-hear-this expression.

At last, Jill said: "The truth is, my life wasn't going anywhere and I didn't have anything else to do." She laughed, as though the admission surprised even her.

"Hey, I've got an idea for you . . . for us," said Garland, abruptly shifting gears.

"I'll write this girl-next-door article for *TV Weekly*, making you sound like the *Song of Bernadette*. Then I'll talk to a friend of mine who publishes *Ciao* magazine. Kind of a *Playboy* knockoff. You could be the centerfold for, say, the Valentine issue."

Jill looked at him curiously. "You're not serious, are you?"

"I kind of am."

She drained her glass. "First of all, *Playboy* itself is ridiculous. Think of what they call the young women in there.

Bunnies . . . Playmates. Toys, not to be taken seriously. No different from the cars and the hi-fis and the aftershave. Guys who read *Playboy* are playing, all right. With themselves. If they had a real woman in bed with them, they'd piss the sheets."

"And second of all?"

"What?"

"You said there were two things. What's second?"

Jill laughed. "Second is, I can't stand anybody looking at me, even with my clothes on. Putting myself out there like that, would be my idea of a nightmare."

*

Two weeks later, Jill was in bed when the phone rang.

"Hello."

"What the hell were you thinking?"

Her father.

"What are you talking—"

"*TV Weekly.*"

Jill sat up, reached for her Newports on the bedside table.

"Since when are you interested in politics?"

"Just relax, Dad."

"You endorsed Kennedy for Chrissake. Have you forgotten I'm hosting the Vice President at my house next weekend?"

"I won't come if it's going to embarrass you."

"You *can't* come, unless you're going to help me explain to Mr. Nixon why my daughter, who never took an interest in national affairs, is stumping for the opposing candidate?"

"It was a casual conversation. Plus, I never endorsed anybody, Dad. If it says that, the writer just assumed it."

"You've never forgiven me for that business back in high

school, when you nearly screwed up your life for good. It's because of who I am that you got the lead in that ridiculous, dreck-ridden sitcom, and this is the thanks—"

Jill slammed down the phone.

TWENTY-SIX

Jimmy's suite, the Gramercy Park Hotel. He'd moved there while working with the Greek and now, living off his savings, was thinking about finding a less expensive domicile. Not that the place was extravagant, all it had besides a sleeping room and tiny bath was a living room and a tight, open kitchen. But it was nice having housekeeping turn down the bed every day.

Stir-crazy, he rose from the couch and turned off *The Untouchables* with an aggressive twist. Jimmy enjoyed the show but it was a summer rerun, one he'd seen before. He stepped over to the closet and pulled out his brown leather bomber jacket. As he went to the door, he glanced down at his snub-nosed .38 on the table; he stared at it, like he was about to tell it something. He grabbed it and shoved it into his jacket pocket.

Down the elevator, through the lobby and into the balmy July evening. He headed uptown. Blocks, minutes. Found himself in Central Park. That was handy, as he suddenly needed to piss, was looking for a set of bushes as he passed a low building and his eyes fell on a sign: "Restrooms."

Inside, a pair of young guys stood, facing each other. Jimmy stepped around them to reach the row of urinals along the far wall. Sidled up, unzipped; proceeded to do his business. A strident voice from behind. "Yeah, well, you've owed me for over a month, and every day you don't pay me, I'm tacking on five more bucks. And you know what'll happen if you don't make good."

Jimmy glanced over his shoulder. Big guy; pale, pockmarked; sandy hair greased back, said: "What are you lookin' at, you fuckin' fairy?"

Jimmy turned back, faced the wall. Guy growled: "Get outa here, Emmett. But be back tomorrow night at eight sharp with every cent you owe. I don't care if you gotta turn out your old lady to get it. Don't make me come to your shithole and smoke you out."

Emmett scurried. Just Jimmy and the goon. Jimmy finished, zipped up. Looked around. No way out of there that didn't include confronting the bastard. And now Jimmy noted something he hadn't before. The guy had on a scarlet nylon jacket that zipped up the front; the exact style of the one he'd worn in *Rebel*. For some reason, it made him laugh.

"What's so fucking funny?" said the goon, a wild glint in his eyes. Reached into his pocket, came up with a flick knife.

Jimmy's eyes went to all eight inches of the blade. "What do you want?"

Goon looked dreamy, crazed. "I don't know yet. I need to think about it."

A pair of collegiate types stepped in, caught the tableau, knife included, then turned and hustled out.

Goon chuckled: "You'd think people would be better citizens."

"What do you *want*?" Jimmy repeated.

"Get in that stall over there."

Jimmy glanced behind, but stayed where he was. One of

the chipped, gray doors was partially open.

"What are you waiting for, for Chrissake?"

Jimmy yanked out his gun. The goon's eyes widened. Jimmy leveled it at his chest. "Drop the blade, you piece of shit."

"You ain't gonna fire that off in here."

"Drop it."

The knife clinked to floor.

"Now slowly kick it over to me."

The goon moved his filthy tennis shoe carefully. Eased the blade across the cement. Jimmy leaned forward, picked it up. Closed it up and pocketed it.

"Can I go now?" the goon said.

Some part of Jimmy was enjoying this. "Get down on your knees."

"What?"

"You heard me. On your knees."

The goon obeyed; lower lip quivering, face pale as the porcelain sink.

Jimmy strode over. "Take off your jacket."

"Why?"

"Take it *off.*"

"Aw, man, I just spent good money for this. I was just kidding around with you."

Jimmy raised the gun so it was pointed at the left eye.

The goon slowly, carefully, slipped out of the jacket.

"Now hand it to me."

The guy shoved it toward him.

"Open your mouth," Jimmy ordered, stepping closer.

"Why?"

"Stop whining and say *ah.*"

The goon's lips parted.

Jimmy pushed the two-inch barrel forward until it was nestled between the goon's yellow teeth. Pulled back the hammer and it clicked into place. "Now close your eyes, stay on your knees and count out loud to a hundred."

He painstakingly withdrew the barrel, the goon counting as Jimmy left the restroom.

As he stepped outside, he wadded up the scarlet jacket, then shoved it into a nearly full trash can.

＊

Jimmy, in the nighttime neon of Times Square. At a little stand where a vendor was selling Italian ices and hot pretzels, Jimmy bought one of each; took a bite, then followed with a sip. His eyes fell on a glowing marquee and what he saw caused him to drop both pretzel and cup on the sidewalk. *James Dean . . . Natalie Wood . . . Rebel Without a Cause.*

＊

The theater was packed with teenagers, many of whom had clearly seen it more than once, as they joined in on the dialogue and addressed the characters in anticipation of their actions. Jimmy had only seen his performance on the big screen while viewing dailies, so this was a revelation. His gigantic image was mesmerizing. Midway through the third viewing, he bolted from the theater and rushed out into the glaring neon.

Hands in his pockets, head down, he began walking, in a daze. *Man, I was good in that thing; no wonder the kids are going nuts for it.* A flawless performance he can't share with anybody, tell anybody it's him.

＊

Pop Diary, September 1961

Jimmy's Gang

by Oona Stickney

Jimmy understands, which is why we send him letters, addressed to Warner Brothers, Hollywood. Of course, he's not about to answer. But all the answers are right up there on the screen. We see "Rebel" again and again and are holding our breath until "Eden" appears. With each viewing, some new revelation is dispensed. "You're tearing me apart!" screams Jimmy. And we scream right along with him. We know how it ends. In tragedy. In a burst of flame. But such a fabulous flash.

Some have taken it too far, have gone to join him. Sylvia Karris of Hampton Roads, Virginia, wrists slashed after watching "Rebel." Michael Cray and Betsy Loder of Seaside, Oregon, holding hands as they leaped off a cliff into the vast and unforgiving ocean, after seeing the film for the seventeenth time. Dale Bartholomew of Pentwater, Michigan, mangled to death in a version of chickie run. Rowan Leroy Morrissey, Louisville, Kentucky, mortally stabbed by a switchblade, mirroring the knife fight outside the Griffith Observatory, but with a lethal outcome.

And parents have not been immune. Harold Harper of McLean, Texas, perished in the emergency room, rushed there after his son Gilbert pounced on him, the way Jimmy attacked his father in "Rebel." And so many others, both here and overseas, with less dramatic consequences. Not to mention the hundreds of séances for Jimmy; the thousands of sessions at the Ouija board. The countless flickering candles; the thousands of copies of "The Little Prince," Jimmy's favorite book. So cool of Jimmy to have stayed up there on the screen, digging us, as much as we're digging him.

✱

Jimmy Dean, who was still mesmerizing armies of teenagers in darkened movie houses, was sick of seeing all those scarlet jackets slinking on the streets and in the subways. *Rebel* was just a melodrama about a bunch of punks who either ruin their lives or lose them; who'd want to imitate that? And how could his performance cause teenagers all over the globe to stab each other or slit their wrists or strangle their parents or drive off a cliff? It wasn't his responsibility, he'd tell himself, but still, it troubled him. Life couldn't be any stranger.

Since the day after Thanksgiving, *East of Eden* had been running in Times Square. Jimmy resisted it all through the holidays, but finally bought a ticket and took a seat.

Once the picture faded out, he drifted into the neon, feeling like his body was made of particles and light, same as that image on the screen. Watching himself was like a ringside seat in the afterlife. If it hadn't been for that thing with Reagan, he'd be on his tenth or twelfth film by now, having left Brando in the dust. Instead, he'd returned to New York to live out a dream that belonged to a man who was dead for real and he'd even made a mess of that.

Wait a minute, *what the hell.*

Music, coming out of . . . a radio, a jukebox? A female voice, haunting and beckoning, curling out from some Forty-Second Street bar.

> *Because I knew you, I know I'll never be the same.*
> *Because I knew you, I know I'll never love again.*

Jimmy felt gooseflesh on his arms, the hair on his head standing on end. A message, dropped like a letter from the other side.

> *Because I knew you, I'll never be at rest.*

He rushed back to his suite at the Gramercy Park, peeled off his clothes and curled up in bed. Sleep didn't come until well after it was light, and when it did take him over, he was trembling and was still trembling when he awakened, yet he knew what he needed to do.

TWENTY-SEVEN

"**Y**ou don't get second chances in this business, Specs," the Greek was telling Jimmy, as they sat in his office. "You've only got one face to fall flat on."

"You can say that," Jimmy declared. "But nobody could have made real hits out of the material you were handing me."

The Greek looked at him as though he were vaguely familiar and was trying to place him.

Jimmy, pacing like there was no seat on earth that could contain his pent-up energy. "You hired me to make hits and I'm sitting on a whole batch of them. You've gotta let me have my head, Alex. No more aiming for the middle."

The Greek smiled tightly but was nonetheless intrigued; Jimmy's fire, undeniable.

"I want to come back, but not on salary. I won't take a dime unless the record's a smash. But for what I produce, I want fifteen percent off the top of all sales and half of all publishing royalties."

"Fifteen percent? No producer gets that. How would I take care of the artists?"

"I'll pay them a flat fee out of my end of the take. This isn't about the artists, it's about the material."

The Greek's smile was back. "You seem pretty damn sure of yourself. When do you want to hit the studio?"

❋

NIM regional headquarters; Davotney's office, overlooking Lake Michigan. Gloomy out there, chilled and drizzling. Zeke Mallory, facing his boss across the major's expansive desk. The older man was smiling. "Zeke, you and I are going to California. Some Republican businessmen out there are backing Richard Nixon for governor. They want our perspective as to how he let Illinois slip through his fingers in his failed run for president."

"We know how that happened. The mob stole it for Kennedy."

"It's the same crowd who bankrolled Nixon when he first ran for Congress. Cowboy money. Oil, aerospace, B of A. They view this as the way to get their man back on track."

Zeke, looking uncomfortable, nodded his head.

❋

Cabana, Beverly Hills Hotel. Davotney and Zeke were with a trio of prosperous looking men: one old, one middle-aged, one in his twenties. The old guy, financer Sanford Butterfield: "We need Nixon ready for the White House in '68 at the latest. Being governor of California will reposition him for that. There were a lot of plans underway that Kennedy has already bungled. That Cuba disaster last spring. A lot of us made a big investment in Nixon and we need him looking out for our interests."

Davotney: "The California Democrats aren't the kind of well-oiled machine that Daley has in Chicago. Nixon remains a national figure. You can expect him to win the governorship by at least six points."

Butterfield glanced at his two associates, then stood: "We appreciate your counsel today, gentlemen. A pleasure to meet you both."

Handshakes, except for Zeke. "I have to say something."

Everyone stared. The first words out of his mouth.

Davotney: "By all means, Mallory."

"You're making an enormous mistake, promoting Nixon. He may be a national, even international figure, but he's damaged goods."

Middle-aged guy. "Not here in his home state."

"When Nixon went back to Whittier for his high school reunion, there were two separate receiving lines; those who would shake his hand, and those who wouldn't. You need somebody fresh, whose image isn't tarnished and set in stone. In other words, you need to create someone."

Davotney was glaring at Zeke. Butterfield laughed. "Out of thin air, you're saying?"

"This is Hollywood, Mr. Butterfield. What you need is a star."

✳

Ronald Reagan stepped off the elevator at the Manhattan headquarters of BBD&O, his gray suit matching his mood. Looking like a pallbearer, he pulled open the glass doors. A couple of office workers on a cigarette break clearly recognized his famous face, then swiftly returned to their conversation. Reagan long ago determined that New Yorkers were as impressed with celebrity as anyone else; they just worked harder at not showing it. At the massive desk, a silver-haired receptionist: "Hello, Fran."

"Mr. Reagan," she replied. "Mr. Ridley and the others are

in the conference room. Down the corridor. Second door on the left. Care for some coffee?"

"No thanks."

Resolute, Reagan headed down the hall.

✱

Conference room, an hour later. Ridley, Larry Beckman of Revue Productions, and a younger guy Reagan had never met until today.

Reagan, agitated. "The only scripts I want to follow are the ones on the show. What I say out on the mashed potato circuit should be of my own choosing."

Ridley, clearly not enjoying this. "Frankly, Ron, your views are further to the right than most people are willing to embrace."

"There's nothing I'm saying that isn't the truth."

Ridley, leaning forward, looked down at his notes. "Does this sound familiar? It's you being quoted in the Des Moines Register. 'The government tells us that nearly twenty million people go to bed hungry each night. But, let's face it; that could mean that a lot of those people had an early dinner and were merely craving a bedtime snack.'"

Beckman: "There are a plenty of viewers who disagree with you. It's affecting the show."

Ridley glanced over at the younger man. "Hal, do you have that letter we got from Kenosha?"

Hal pulled it from its folder. "You referenced the present administration as 'creeping socialism.' Our plant manager there was head of the Vote for Kennedy Committee in southern Wisconsin." Set it aside. "Maybe this would have flown during Eisenhower, but there's a new spirit in the country.

People are thinking forward."

"It's a sexier time," said Ridley.

"Bigger government, smaller lives," muttered Reagan.

Ridley: "We can only go with our research, Ron."

Reagan leaned back. "Gentlemen, I'm going to need to think about this. Talk it over with Nancy and with MCA."

"To determine what?"

"Whether I want to keep going out, if it means watering down my presentation. I've worked hard, honing these points. I might prefer to not say anything at all."

Ridley stared at him. "Well, that's for you to decide, Ron, how to represent these views of yours. I suggest you contact a speaker's bureau and have them start handling the arrangements."

Looking troubled, Reagan turned to Beckman. "Larry, we haven't even discussed the show."

"We're canceling," said Beckman.

Reagan sat a little higher in his chair. "Canceling? The show?"

"It just isn't delivering any longer," Beckman told him.

Ridley turned again to Hal, who produced a sheaf of papers. "We have a dissolution agreement, freeing you from your responsibilities to Revue Productions and the *General Electric Theater*. MCA will receive a copy this afternoon."

Reagan, stunned. "Because of what I've been saying?"

Ridley: "Because of the ratings."

Beckman: "We had a good run, Ron. It's time to move forward."

Reagan, deflated, looked around the table. "I guess I should have expected as much from a group like this."

"A group like what?" said Ridley.

"A bunch of New Yorkers."

"New Yorkers?" said Beckman.

"Democrats," said Reagan.

Ridley smiled tightly. "I thought *you* were a Democrat, Ron."

TWENTY-EIGHT

When the Greek hired him back, Jimmy started attending teen talent shows in Brooklyn and the Bronx, signing up performers who caught his ear and forming acts. The Candies were a mixed-race quartet of girls, ages fifteen to seventeen. The Ebonies were a black trio, nineteen-year-old tenor Nate Adderly, backed by the sixteen-year-old Dawkins twins, Lil and Lorna. And the Borough Brothers, five Italian guys from Flatbush, all under twenty. Jimmy would hang out, chow down on burgers and slices, slurp Cokes and malts, listen to their dreams, then get them and their guardians on paper.

One night in his suite in the Gramercy Park, while listening to Wagner's *Ring Cycle*, he had a revelation. Specs was right in his goal to make a big sound. But even he wasn't thinking big enough. With these dumb, romantic songs, what was called for was Technicolor.

So, when Jimmy finally hit the studio, he didn't only hire the hottest pop studio cats. He tapped members of the New York Philharmonic—violins, violas, cellos, double basses; oboes and clarinets, bassoons and double bassoons. Timpani. Trumpets—sections at a time, many of which he'd double and triple. The parts weren't complicated; Jimmy would hum them to the arranger who would dutifully notate them on music paper. Strings restated the melody. Horns blew whole notes to accentuate the chord changes, providing even more surging motion behind the wash of sound.

As Specs envisioned, Jimmy cut with no isolation or separation, bathing everything in echo ("it's like garlic," he'd say, "you can't use too much"), bouncing tracks, generating a monaural tidal wave. "You've got to make these records sound huge to the kids, like the world could end with a broken heart, because for them, it does."

Jimmy acquired, as it was called in the music biz, a studio tan. A kind of alabaster sheen, the result of working around the clock. Day or night made little difference to him, as he donned jet-black wraparound shades every waking hour.

His sessions were strictly Fort Knox; even the Greek was banned, although he was writing the checks. A tenor man was fired because his wife called the studio to find out when they might be wrapping. Unlike most producers who fretted over the clock, Jimmy would lock the place out for days on end. Everyone who worked with him signed a confidentiality agreement; what went down in his sessions was nobody-but-nobody's business. An armed guard stood sentinel by the door. The Greek still insisted that none but his own name could go on the label and Jimmy saw the wisdom in that.

This rigorous campaign paid off beautifully. A pair of number ones and a number two, that one only missing the top of the charts because the first two refused to drop, trading places for six weeks before reluctantly giving way to some piece-of-shit, Looney Tunes instrumental from a Saturday morning cartoon.

Came time to cut the follow-ups, each of the three acts wanted to renegotiate their contract; one showing up with parents, two with lawyers. Jimmy sat down with them respectively, not in an office, but in the studio where he played a demo of their next potential hit.

"Sounds great, when do we start recording?"

To which Jimmy replied: "The money you're making at all those sock hops and roller rinks and TV dance parties, that's all yours. But the songs are mine. The records are mine. If you don't want to sing them, there are hundreds of kids within ten miles of here who'd get down on their knees to do just that. The contract stands. The deal stands. You want another smash, or shall I find somebody else?"

✱

Richard Nixon's image, on black-and-white TV. The man looked harried, crazed, defeated. "You won't have Nixon to kick around anymore. Gentlemen, this is my last press conference."

Zeke, perched on a barstool, alongside Davotney.

The bartender, to Zeke: "Another lime 7 Up?"

"No thank you," Zeke replied.

Davotney nodded at the screen: "I admit I wasn't pleased when you contradicted me in that meeting, but you sure as hell called that one right." A sip of Ballantine's. "In fact, you're always right, Zeke. That's what I keep telling leadership."

✱

Greek's office. As Jimmy entered, the boss was drinking Piper with a man in a maroon velvet suit. Silk fedora. The Greek started talking, Jimmy figuring they were into the second bottle. "The kids can't get enough of your records. Biggest year Gulf Port ever had. This windfall has necessitated a change of direction. Want some champagne?"

"No thanks."

"I'm going to release your product exclusively. Stop trying to push those other tired horses up the hill. Which is why I've called in the legendary Fontaine Lee."

Fontaine stood. "So the genius does exist. I always wondered when I'd meet the man behind 'Because I Knew You.' I've had to listen all afternoon to Alexander the Great, how he discovered you and all."

Alex laughed. "Shut up, Fon."

Fontaine extended his hand. "The pleasure's all mine, Specs."

Jimmy shook hands without cracking a smile.

"Fontaine's one of the good guys," said the Greek. "Owns Vi-Count Records, out of Chicago. A unique operation. He takes the runoff from other companies, records that didn't shake up the charts, and rereleases them. Unlike us," the Greek explained, "Vi-Count doesn't invest in artists or recording costs. He breathes new life into records by introducing them to an untainted and highly focused market."

"What market is that?"

Fontaine set down his glass. "My market. R & B. R being race, B being black."

The Greek: "Exclusively pressing and distribution. Doesn't have to move that many units to make a profit, the cheap bastard."

Fontaine: "At least cats like you end up making a little instead of losing a lot. Pour me some more of those bubbles."

The Greek, as he poured, "Anyway, Fontaine's going to free us up to only push those kiddie concertos you keep spinning." Lifted his glass. "To the future."

TWENTY-NINE

St. Theresa Hotel, Harlem. In the lobby, Garland Alpert was lounging on a sofa, casual as ever. Hiram Freeman strolled in, camera bag over his shoulder. Garland: "Wow, they'll let anybody in here."

Hiram stopped, looked at Garland, not sure how to take his remark. Garland was smiling. Hiram smiled back. "You're the one out of his element, Alpert."

"Naw, my ticket's punched. I'm here to interview Malcolm X."

Hiram, not sure how he felt about this. "Well, I'm here to photograph Malcolm."

"A tag team, just like old times. Why don't you sit?"

"Doesn't it strike you as odd," Hiram said, "that Malcolm would agree to a feature in something so semi-trashy as *Ciao* magazine?"

"Not a feature, strictly Q and A. But anything to get the message out, right? It's good to see you, Freeman."

Hiram eased himself down. "That last conversation we had, you were right, I hate to admit. Been in the city all this time and I'm not on staff anywhere. Still taking the assignments the editors consider me right for, which is to say the ones involving a black personage. That's the only reason I'm here."

"Tell me about it. I've been pimping for *TV Weekly* and hustling jokes to *Mad* magazine. Everybody sees me as some kind of pop art, showbiz writer. The only substantial stuff I get is like this, what they consider beyond the reach of the old guard. I'd give anything to be able to call my own shots."

"We better haul up to the suite. I've heard Malcolm is a stickler for time. Won't work with anybody, doesn't wear a watch."

*

Michael had called, asking Jimmy to come over. It wasn't unusual that something had gone awry in the studio; dealing with equipment and electricity, things went wrong all the time. When Jimmy arrived, Michael appeared discomfited as he led Jimmy into the main room. "Sorry, man. They kind of made me get you here."

The Baldoni brothers from LA. Dark suits, all muscle. Jimmy was inwardly kicking himself for getting careless, not packing his .38. Sergio, the brains of the family, held a .22 in his mitt. As he was frisking Jimmy, he chimed, "You think you could make the kinda noise you're making and not draw attention? Then when the Greek palmed all his old acts off to Fontaine Lee, that cinched it. Mr. Lee, by the way, is presently in some alley on South Michigan having his thumbs realigned." To his brother, Dominic: "Clean-ola."

Jimmy hadn't met these guys, but obviously Specs had. He needed to come up with something, fast as he could. "Where's Alex?"

"He retired," Sergio told Jimmy. "We had his pilot take us all for a ride in his whirlybird. I had a gun shoved into the pilot's neck while my brother and a friend of ours dangled the

Greek headfirst over the harbor. It was only for old times' sake that we didn't let go. Later in the day, he sold the company for a very modest price."

"Sold it to Moss Levan." Jimmy's voice quaked as he spoke. He seemed to be withering but was frantically opening the drawers of his sense-memories, trying to summon everything the moment required.

"There are three contracts, Pelham," Sergio droned. "The one you signed with Hermosa in '56 entitles us to everything you produced for Gulf Port. By the way, I hope you haven't spent the bread the Greek's been paying you, because most of that belongs to us. We'll all be taking a little trip to wherever-the-fuck you've been keeping it, to make a major withdrawal. As for our new arrangement, you'll get a quarter point on what you produce. The company is now called Coast to Coast Records. Try to work with anybody else—no fucking around next time."

Dominic pulled a set of papers out of his coat, shoved them at Jimmy. "Sign on the dotted."

Jimmy, trembling miserably, but it was rising inside of him; spreading, he nearly had hold of it. "You said three. What's the other contract?"

Sergio laughed. "The one on your head if you're not working with us and you step into a recording studio in the next ten years."

"Moss don't like to be contra-dicked around," said Dominic.

Sergio pulled a ballpoint pen from his coat, clicking it as he handed it over.

Jimmy tried to sign, but his hand was shaking. He had it; it was there, he just needed to go with it. Bent over the papers, he collapsed, looking like he might dissolve as he spread out on the wooden floor. His body convulsed with gut wrenching sobs. "I knew this day would come . . . I knew it would."

The brothers looked at each other. Sergio stepped forward. "Just sign the fucking paper so we can all get on with our lives."

Jimmy's moans were replaced by a retching that seemed to rise up from somewhere even deeper than his gut. He gasped for air, then vomited bile coming from his mouth and onto Sergio's gleaming Florsheims.

"For Chrissake, look where you're puking!"

Jimmy twisted himself into a fetal ball. Dominic barked: "Get him to sign so we can get the fuck outa here."

Sergio set his pistol on top of a speaker cabinet, then yanked out a handkerchief and set about squeamishly brushing the vomit from his shoe. Once he was done, he looked hard at Jimmy. "There's something not right here."

In a blink, Jimmy was coiling upward. Grabbed the .22 off the speaker. CRACK! A shot to Sergio's kneecap.

Dominic, stunned and then shocked, as Jimmy blasted him in the thigh, sending him onto his back. "Jesus—sweet Jesus!"

Michael gaped at the scene, white as linen.

Jimmy appeared calm on his way out the door.

❋

To the Management and Staff of the Gramercy Park Hotel:

Recent events have caused me to check out tonight. I left (in a sealed envelope) some cash for the maid staff. I also left some for the desk personnel. If anyone calls for me—by phone, mail, or in person—tell them I'm gone and have provided no for-warding address.

Your (former) guest,
Room 310

Zeke Mallory finished reading the note, handwritten on hotel stationery. He looked up. "May I have this?"

The Gramercy Park manager, an anxious fellow with shiny spectacles, shifted in his chair. "We were planning on keeping that for our records."

"Let me put it a different way," said Zeke, folding the paper, fitting it into its envelope, before securing it in his inside breast pocket. "I'll be taking this with me."

❋

Hospital room, Zeke at Sergio Baldoni's bedside.

"Your brother indicated that you'd been after Specs Pelham since he left Los Angeles."

"My brother didn't indicate jack. I'm the one does the talking. Been that way since the fourth grade."

"We'll all get a lot further if you cooperate."

"The asshole didn't like that we bought the company fair and square, and he went cowboy on us."

Zeke sighed. When he was almost at the door, he heard Sergio add: "It wasn't the same guy."

Zeke stopped. A slow turn. "I beg your pardon."

"I'd met Pelham in Los Angeles. This guy's hands were dif-ferent, a few other things. A similar look, but nobody changes the way he did. When you find out what the hell's going on, I'd love to know."

THIRTY

In Hamburg's infamous Reeperbahn, Dolph's Amazing Feats was a shabby, garish arcade. Its features included Sausage Man, a family of pinheads, a weightlifting dwarf, and a grainy, eight-millimeter film that depicted the birth of triplets.

Jimmy stood in the pit, head shaved to his skull. He glanced at his Elgin wristwatch, then strapped on a helmet and pulled on a pair of gloves. Almost midnight, the last ride of the shift. The pit was a worn, wood-paneled circle tucked into the ground.

Jimmy climbed onto a war-era BMW motorcycle, turned the engine over, revved it and accelerated. The tires, cracked and bald, hugged the wooden wall, whirling round and round at ever higher speeds and precarious angles, while the crowd, a dozen leering faces, looked down in anticipation, then surprise, then indifference.

After five minutes, Jimmy eased up on the accelerator, rolled down to a halt. He tugged off the gloves and tossed them in a basket. Dolph appeared, top of the pit. Customers had vanished. Dolph lowered a set of rusted iron rings attached to a pulley. Jimmy grabbed hold and was hoisted out. He and Dolph exchanged not a word, nor a glance.

Jimmy stepped into a tiny hut, checked himself in the grimy mirror and threw on his brown leather flight jacket. Then he was off, floating into the urban glow.

The Reeperbahn embraced gambling, stripping, hooking, female mud wrestling, female impersonating, dogfighting, beer guzzling, pill popping—and that was what was out in the open. Vaguely concealed were live sex acts that involved humans and nonhumans, as well as the occasional amateur fight to the death. The area was actually gated to separate it from the rest of Hamburg. The Bangkok of Europe, Jimmy had been immersed in it ever since he left the States.

He was working in order to keep from being bored but was growing restless. Money wasn't a problem. He had beaten Moss Levan and company to Frankfurt, and his salary and royalties from Gulf Port and BMI were secure in a Hamburg bank. When he's needed to use a name it's been Byron Krats, and he had a complete set of black-market papers to go with it. Birth certificate, driver's license, passport; even a library card.

Byron was his middle name, and the Krats part, his own invention, was a reconfiguration of Trask, as in Cal Trask of *Eden*, and Stark, as in Jim Stark of *Rebel*. He's adopted a slight German accent, subtle enough to fit in; his voice pitched lower than its natural timbre.

Striding through the Reeperbahn, Jimmy wondered if his time here was up, whether he needed to finally embrace what he'd come to Germany for besides his money. Was it time to try out his new self on an old friend?

He paused at the entrance to The Star Club, deciding whether or not to go in. Sometimes it was crowded and sometimes it wasn't, depending on what act was there. For the most part, they booked British combos, who bashed out their version of American rock 'n' roll. "Talented mimics," Alex would have called them.

One thing Jimmy liked about them was that their hair was, more often than not, longer and combed forward, covering their foreheads and even ears, falling below the collar. With the long hair came Edwardian jackets and sharkskin pants and Cuban heels, a whole new look that Jimmy appreciated. Besides its boldness, it seemed to be canceling out the leather and red nylon jackets, jeans and motorcycle boots so many of the groups favored previously. This garb went along, of course, with the swept back duck's ass hairstyle that Jimmy himself had been so instrumental in popularizing throughout the world. It had gone on too long, the Dean cult.

Entering the club, Jimmy noted that tonight's band, warbling in English, was a mix of French haircuts (three of them) and a pair of Dean replicas, one wearing Ray-Bans in the pitch-dark club, who was stepping up to the microphone. A familiar-sounding chord pattern unfolded and then the Jimmy look-alike began warbling:

Because I knew you, my life will never be the same
Because I knew you, I know I'll never love again

*

At the Porsche factory, Stuttgart, Jimmy was sporting a pair of wraparound sunglasses on his shaved skull. He stood outside a garage with Rudi, who looked prosperous in his suit and tie. His old friend hadn't caught on yet, and Jimmy wasn't giving off any clues. "If you are permanently hired, Mr. Krats, you will be driving on your own. But for the first two weeks, all test drivers are accompanied and assessed, so I will be coming with you." Rudi handed over the keys.

Jimmy smiled. Opened the door. Climbed behind the wheel.

*

Autobahn, German countryside, lush and green, the bronze Porsche was gliding through it. Inside, Jimmy was gripping the wheel, with Rudi in the passenger seat. A hundred ten . . . twenty . . . thirty-five.

"That is fast enough, Mr. Krats. I no longer need to be convinced that you are an expert driver." Rudi eased back in his seat. At just below eighty-five, he said, "So you were born here but raised in America. Do you speak German?"

"Not really. Being German was not something you wanted to broadcast during my early years in the States."

Rudi smiled. "I used to live there as well."

Jimmy smiled, then purposefully said: "Did your father bring you straight to California? Santa Monica, where he knew some people?"

A curious expression crossed Rudi's face.

Jimmy smiled, half turning toward him. "Remember that time on the way to Salinas? Some idiot in a black-and-white Ford swung out in front of us. If I'd been driving something other than the Spyder, it never would have responded like it did. We'd have been goners."

Rudi's mouth dropped and his eyes widened. "*Jimmy?*" He was smiling; this was not a joke, not a hallucination, it really was his presumed-dead friend. But how? Why?

As the Porsche sailed over the crest of a hill, Merino sheep, at least twenty, were spread chaotically. No way around them. Jimmy didn't brake but tried to maneuver, swerving left, right, left again; almost clear when one panicked and bounded in front of the car. The impact sent it against the windshield, smashing the glass. Jimmy lost control and the Porsche veered off the road, rolling five, six times, finishing on its side in a bean field.

In the ghostly aftermath, Jimmy felt wetness in his eyes and ears. *This can't be happening. Not now, not when everything was about to go so beautifully. Where's Rudi?*

He heard a low, agonized groaning, and then there was nothing but huge, surging pain and terrible darkness.

*

Throughout that hideous four days, Jill left the sofa only to go to the bathroom or duck into the kitchen to heat up some food. She slept on the sofa, refused to answer the phone, kept switching from Cronkite to Huntley and Brinkley, then back again; the first time she'd encountered round-the-clock coverage of an event. Rather than being bored by images and reports they'd shown before, the repetition was mesmerizing. She would drift off to sleep only to awaken to the ongoing nightmare.

At one point, they were interviewing some dressmaker from Dallas who had apparently filmed the entire event. "As I was shooting, the President was coming down the street . . . and I just kept shooting." In her haze, Jill thought he was the gunman, confessing to the crime.

They offered quite a bit of coverage about the accused assassin. Curiously, Jill couldn't keep his name in her head. There seemed no doubt he'd been the one. A nobody, who wanted his annoying, smirking image in the history books.

She was watching on Sunday morning when the Dallas police led him out before the cameras, looking arrogant with his pasty face and dark sweater, when some stocky guy wearing a dark suit and hat lunged forward and shot him. At first Jill thought he'd only been punched in the stomach, but the reporter kept saying: 'He's been shot—he's been shot!' She almost felt bad when they announced an hour or so later that he'd died in Parkland Hospital, the same place where they'd rushed the President, but couldn't save him.

Jill would never forget the flag-draped casket inside the Capitol rotunda, the riderless black stallion, the mournful military drums, the eternal flame at Arlington—no other programs, not even commercials. While the casket was rolling through Washington, the procession passed a theater showing John Wayne's latest movie. What was occurring was so much more momentous than some Hollywood fantasy.

She finally went to bed on Monday night. Didn't wake until Tuesday evening. The world was different. Jill was different, and what was the point to anything?

✸

Jimmy lay in the hospital, hooked up to a morphine drip. An executive from Porsche had come to communicate what Jimmy already knew. Rudi was dead. That they would cover Jimmy's hospital bills, as well as his months of rehabilitation, was a dim consolation. He was left for an endless chain of days, his brain fuzzy, a bitter taste in his mouth that never went away. *First Specs and now Rudi. Everything I touch turns to ashes, turns to dust.*

The only thing that sustained him, kept his spirit afloat, was the movie that kept running through his head. Jimmy wasn't sure how or when it started. It was an image of a lone guy on a motorcycle, not an English Triumph or an Italian

Ducati, but a chopped-up Milwaukee-made Harley, gliding along the highways of America.

Sometimes there would be flat green fields on either side, suggesting Indiana; sometimes there would be distant mountains, indicating Colorado or Utah. Always out in the open, a visual manifestation of that Woody Guthrie song "This Land is Your Land."

Whenever Jimmy beheld this image, even though he was watching some other, younger guy behind the handlebars, he could feel the wind on his own face and the powerful thrust of the engine between his thighs. There was no story, no real character, only an overpowering rush of feeling, an undeniable sense of freedom.

One morning, a male voice, German accent: "Are you ready, sir? It will feel like the skin is ripping, but do not worry, you will be good as new once the bandages and gauze are removed."

Jimmy lay still. It hurt like hell and took forever. But he was getting all too accustomed to pain and distorted time.

Once it was done: "I will leave you to yourself. Move carefully. The mirror is on the wall to your left."

Jimmy rose agonizingly to a sitting position. Felt dizzy, got his bearings. Looked down at his legs, probing through the flannel gown. They were pale and thinner but had been working well enough in his inch-by-inch trips from the bed to the bathroom; upper body, adjusting to trauma. *What am I going to look like?* Standing now, he shuffled, precariously gripping the balance pole with his weakened right hand. Eyes on the beige wall as he was working up the nerve to look. Scalp, lacerated, like he was wearing a knitted cap. Forehead, smooth and free of scars. Cheekbones lifted slightly. Nose wider, having smashed against the dashboard. Both sides of his face riddled from glass shards, some of which were still embedded. Chin rebuilt along with the jawbone. Face resembled a caricature rendering of what it used to be. Overall impression was still there, but not the details. Features much more pronounced. No longer pretty. Severe looking. Gazing back, eyes haunted. Given what shape he'd been in, the surgeon served him well. Jimmy cocked his head and smiled. "Hello, Mr. Krats."

THIRTY-ONE

"Quiet on the set!" shouted Philip, the director. "Let's nail this last pickup so we can wrap the season. All right, action."

Jill, as Traci, sat in a booth in, of all things, a malt shop. She'd been saying for the last two seasons that Traci was getting too old for the malt shop, but Vincent Clydell, a close friend of writer-producer Herb Foy, played the part of Paul, malt shop owner, and Jill would find herself slurping a strawberry shake (Traci's favorite) in every other episode. Brandon, Traci's sweater-clad boyfriend, sat across from her. There were two straws in the tall, frosty glass and Brandon leaned forward and pursed his lips around the one closest to him.

"Brandon," Jill-as-Traci said, "I can't cape—"

"Cut," said Philip, among a smattering of laughter. "Jill, the word is *cope*. I can't cope. Okay, action."

Brandon tipped forward and once again encircled the straw with his lips.

"Brandon," Jill repeated, "I can't . . . what's the word?"

This time, not Philip, but Herb Foy's voice boomed across the soundstage. "Cope, for Chrissake! Just deliver the line so we can all get out of here. Keep rolling."

Once again, Brandon leaned closer. As he was drawing on the straw, Jill uttered: "Brandon, I can't . . . keep doing this stupid scene . . . doing this stupid show. It's not good, it's not funny and I can't . . . keep . . . doing it. Can't . . ." She formed the word carefully. "*Cape*. Not another year, not another day, not another minute."

*

Booker's, a Midtown watering hole. Garland and Hiram were at a table. Garland lifted his bottle of Rheingold and clinked it against Hiram's. "Here's to *Ciao*."

Hiram, taken aback. "*Ciao?*"

"Handleman named me editor-in-chief of *Ciao* magazine."

"Congratulations."

Garland smiled. "I want you as my photo editor."

Hiram, stunned. "I don't know."

"Handleman started with *Playboy*. He's gonna do a similar thing here in New York, but a more international publication. It's the opportunity of a lifetime."

"It's a skin mag. Would I have to shoot a bunch of center-folds?"

"I'll get other guys to shoot them. There'll be plenty of content." Garland smiled. "Freeman. It's time to grow up and sell out."

*

On the tarmac, waiting for luggage to come off her Alitalia flight, Jill Parnell stood outside the Florence air terminal. Dawn. She felt exhausted, yet wide awake. Light tan raincoat and peach-shaded silk scarf. A stout woman appeared at her side. "Excuse me, but we—my husband and I—couldn't help but notice you at Kennedy International."

Jill looked at her. Not unfriendly, but not welcoming.

"Aren't you that girl on television—aren't you Traci?"

Jill smiled, hard and soft in the same expression. "Not anymore."

✱

Jimmy was sitting beside the room's only window. Not much of a view; a yard, a tree, a quiet stretch of street. He'd been in the clinic seven months and was preparing to spend the next month as an outpatient as a prelude to reentering the world. *But what will that world be like?* Besides a face that didn't resemble the one he was born with, he can no longer do so many of the things that he felt defined him. He can't drive; his left leg, the one that would operate the clutch of any competition vehicle, was all but useless below the knee. His right hand, the one that would manipulate a shift and steering wheel, could barely grip a pencil. For the first time in his postpubescent life, he was unable to achieve, much less sustain, an erection. Not that he hadn't tried, lying in bed, conjuring up images of girls he'd known, boys he'd known; men, women. All kinds of bodies and body parts. Back-seat sex on Indiana country roads; memories and fantasies of New York bedrooms, trailers on the back lots of Hollywood, the neon shadows of Hamburg's Reeperbahn. Nothing doing.

His only solace was the movie, the one of the lone biker, celebrating the breathtaking openness of the American highway. It would still his thoughts before falling asleep and fill his dreams as he slept at night.

"May we have a word, Mr. Krats?"

Jimmy turned from the window. A trim guy with a buzz cut stood there, a half smile on his face. He was already pulling up the only free chair in the room and opening his briefcase. "You prefer to speak English, that is my understanding."

Jimmy nodded.

My name is Henrik Ehrenmann, with the Office of National Inquiry. We have been conducting an investigation into your accident."

Jimmy looked at him: "The people from Porsche have been here and I went through it all with them."

"Yes, but this is a matter of governmental concern. A German citizen with a substantial position inside one of our most prestigious companies was killed in an accident in which you were driving."

"It wasn't my fault, that's been established." Jimmy bit his lip realizing that, with that last line, his German accent had slipped a bit.

"According to your statements, you were born here but raised in Scotland since 1937. The problem we are having is that there is no birth record of Byron Krats anywhere in Germany."

"I have a birth certificate," Jimmy said.

"We are sure that you do. The problem remains that we cannot locate substantiation of your citizenship."

Jimmy's mind was spinning. "Were not a lot of records destroyed in the war?"

The questions continued in an amiable but distressing fashion for the next forty minutes. Finally, the government man closed his briefcase and got to his feet.

"We will continue this conversation as soon as you are relocated for rehabilitation. If you are who you say you are, of course we will do everything we can to help you get your life started once again. If you are not . . ." He didn't finish the sentence but merely shrugged, although Jimmy knew damn well what he meant. *If you are not, you may be in more trouble than you can ever imagine.*

Jimmy watched him leave the room, then watched from his window as he strode out of the clinic and walked to a Mercedes parked at the curb. And although he didn't feel ready, Jimmy knew he needed to do the same: leave the clinic, leave Germany, leave that very night. But to go where?

THIRTY-TWO

Hollywood Recorder, June 6, 1964

Reagan Switches Parties, Returns to Big Screen

Last week, politically outspoken Ronald Reagan issued the following statement: "After being a lifelong Democrat, I am formally declaring a commitment to the Republican Party; its platforms and principles." The former SAG Treasurer and General Electric pitchman toured the country for several years on behalf of the company, ultimately developing a speech which came to be regarded in many circles as politically provocative due to its conservative focus. Since the cancellation of the "General Electric Theater," he has been cast in "The Killers," a feature film from Universal, scheduled to commence principal photography next week.

In his office, Zeke Mallory set the publication aside and picked up the phone. "Butterfield and Associates," came a chirping voice from two thousand miles west.

"Sanford Butterfield, please."

"May I ask what this is regarding?"

"No, you may not."

＊

Set of *The Killers,* outdoor location at Universal Studios. Ronald Reagan stood facing Angie Dickinson. She was looking at him, waiting. Realizing that nothing more was coming from her costar, she turned and walked out of the scene.

"Cut!" shouted director Don Siegel. He left his spot, headed toward Reagan. "For God's sake. You know you're supposed to belt her—it's in the script."

Reagan looked sheepish. "I just don't feel comfortable, hitting a woman like that."

"It's called acting."

"But it's unsympathetic."

"You're playing a bad guy. C'mon, Ron. You know the game."

"Can we break?" asked Reagan.

"By all means. Let's take ten and remember what we're doing here."

Reagan walked off, tense, dejected. A pair of suits approached, Sanford Butterfield and a younger man. "Good afternoon, Mr. Reagan."

"What can I do for you?"

Offering his hand. "Sanford Butterfield. This is Ted Sazrac. Our focus group is called Golden State Executives. We understand you have quite a speech in your pocket, the one you were giving before GE's ad agency stifled you. How would you feel about delivering it at the Ambassador for some major Republican donors?"

Now Reagan smiled. "I've been wanting to get my teeth into something more real than making horse operas."

Butterfield smiled back. "We were hoping you'd say that. And you're right. Hitting a woman would be very unsympathetic."

*

"You said you wanted privacy, Mr. Krats," Lyle, the realtor was saying. "One of the great things about this place, you can only get to it by what is effectively a private road."

Jimmy was in the front passenger seat of Lyle's Ford Galaxie. The road was narrow, bushes pushing out from either side, nearly brushing the car. Lyle jerked the wheel and swerved, and they were in front of ten-foot-high iron gates. He hopped out, produced some keys, shouldered the gate open, then hustled back to the driver's seat. Parked in a circular drive. The fountain out front looked dismal from neglect. "Install some colored lights," Lyle said, "you could watch it for hours."

They were out of the car now, Laurel Canyon spread out around them. He led Jimmy up a set of steps. Jimmy leaned on his cane as he counted them. Twenty-seven. Dressed in a turtleneck and fitted with a black hairpiece, he took in the scene behind aviator shades. Lyle worked his keys, pushed open the massive oak door. Dark foyer, Mediterranean tile.

"Spacious living room. Formal dining. Kitchen with a cozy breakfast nook. Laundry at the back entrance. You won't believe the den. Game room downstairs. The upstairs master bedroom is sensational, gold fixtures in the bath. C'mon through, Mr. Krats, you gotta see the backyard. Avocado trees and practically an orange grove. Massive pool with a cabana."

Jimmy just stood, taking it in. Lyle kept vamping. "An acre and a half out there. Besides being on a ridge, the property in back drops off hundreds of feet. Might as well have a moat around it, all for four fifty a month, with an option to buy." Looked at Jimmy, who hadn't moved. "Don't you wanna see the back yard? The upstairs?"

"No need to," Jimmy told him, in his subtle German accent. "I will take it."

*

Reagan, at the podium, confident and in control. The audience was rapt, beholding a man totally in his element. "When I was young, I had an ant farm. Of course, I didn't realize it at the time, but looking back, I realize that's how big government views us. Not as individuals, but as a nameless and faceless collective. With individualism, each face is different, each voice unique. In a collective, each story is the same. A mass. The *masses*, as big government refers to us. And right now, we have a window of opportunity; a season of choice. And not just for us, but for our children and for our children's children. We, as individuals, must make a choice *for* individuals."

*

Jimmy sat in a deep leather armchair, watching the television in disquieted fascination.

"Freedom isn't granted," Reagan was saying, "It is a hard-fought, ongoing battle. And it can be lost in increments. A compromise here; a concession there. Until you look around and you wonder where it's gone, and then it's too late. Once you lose it, there's no guarantee you'll get it back. Make no mistake, no one is going to return it to you. And if you don't look after yourself, who are you capable of looking after? It may not be a popular sentiment these days, but in this world, in nature and in human affairs, it's every man for himself. To the swiftest, go the spoils."

Jimmy rose, stepped over to the television and shut it off. He'd come to where his life had been derailed, hoping he could somehow find a sense of purpose. All of that seemed suddenly pointless and he felt tricked. Reagan. *Reagan again.*

Jimmy sat pensively in his new home, gazing out the window at the lights of Los Angeles.

REEL
FOUR

NOVEMBER 1964—
NOVEMBER 1966

THIRTY-THREE

In a sprawling house on Canyon Road, in the foothills outside Boulder, Colorado, fifteen-year-old Grace Hobson's eyes were locked onto the televised image of James Dean brandishing a switchblade at the Griffith Observatory. Grace, smooth red hair and fair skin, did not notice when her mother appeared in the doorway.

"Come, Grace, it's time to wash up for dinner."

Male announcer: "Join us tonight for Channel Nine's Late Show at eleven p.m. when we will be presenting James Dean, Natalie Wood, and Sal Mineo in *Rebel Without a Cause*, a classic tragedy of mixed-up youth."

Dean's image was gone, replaced by a Sanka commercial. Now Grace looked at her mother. "Can I stay up late tonight? There's no school tomorrow."

"You can stay up until ten."

"But I need to stay up late—"

"Why would that be?"

"—to watch a movie."

"Then of course you can't."

"But I really need to watch it."

"Everyone's sitting down for Thanksgiving dinner. Go wash your hands. You're between your two cousins."

"My cousins smell funny."

"Keep your voice down."

"I really need to watch it."

*

Grace snuck out of bed that night. Watching James Dean felt like looking into a mirror. It wasn't romantic on her part, although it was profound adoration. He was a lifeline, something Grace needed to grab hold of.

Next morning at breakfast, she was in a daze, wishing she had someone she could tell how she felt. How watching him had touched her. But it was also nice, holding onto a secret like that. For out there in the world was finally someone she understood; someone who would understand and listen to her. She took some of the allowance money she'd been stashing in her drawer and rode the bus to the department store.

It was packed that day after Thanksgiving. After looking around, she approached a male clerk who looked like he might be working his way through CU.

"I hope you can help me. I'm trying to find a dark red nylon jacket that zips up the front."

"This way." Started leading her toward a rack in the corner.

"I've looked at those already. They all have hoods on them."

"Well, those aren't jackets, they're parkas. We don't have any light jackets now, they're not in season."

"Could I order one?"

"Why would you want to; you won't be able to wear it until April or May. I'd wait if I were you."

Grace couldn't help smiling. "I saw a movie last night.

James Dean was wearing a red nylon jacket. Do you know that cool actor James Dean?"

"Must have been an *old* movie. Isn't he the one who drove his car off a cliff?"

"He did that in the movie."

"He did in real life, too."

Grace felt a chill all the way through her. "Are you telling me he's dead?"

*

Living room, Laurel Canyon. Guy seated across from Jimmy. Mid-forties. Huge head, bristly hair, more salt than pepper; massive chest and shoulders. Looked like he was perpetually disgruntled or ill-at-ease.

"So, Gus, why were you kicked off the police department?" Jimmy delivered this in the voice he'd adopted, lower-registered that held a trace of German.

Gus shrugged, redistributing his weight. "Some worm from Internal Affairs claimed my partner and I looked the other way on a protection racket."

"Did you?"

Scowling harder. "Did I what?"

"Do what he said you did."

"They shouldn't have fired us for it."

"What about family?"

"My ex is a secretary for the LAPD. She filed for divorce the day after I was off the force."

"Kids?"

Gus shook his head.

"Shall I ring for more coffee?"

"No thanks."

Jimmy rose from his seat. "You met Blanca, who prepares three meals a day, and Yamoto takes care of the grounds. Do you shoot pool?"

"Not lately."

"Start practicing during your downtime. I need to play to help with my coordination. We will get you your own cue. You will be doing the driving. Every Friday at two p.m. you will take me down to Century City for a meeting with my broker, who sees to it that I make money while I sleep, even though I do not sleep. You are licensed to carry in California?"

"Nevada and Arizona, too. All up-to-date."

That was crucial. Jimmy felt secure enough in his altered look and identity that he wouldn't need to pack any heat himself, but vulnerable enough to still want some protection. Jimmy stood, leaning on the ornate walking stick he now perpetually relied upon. Put his hand out. "You will be calling me Mr. Krats. Can you move in tomorrow?"

*

Communique, National Internal Monitoring

Regarding the recent report from NIM leadership, the clear assumption is that President Johnson will seek reelection in 1968. Leadership is promoting Richard Nixon to oppose him, although this agent remains on record that Nixon is an unimaginative selection, not the kind of candidate to secure America's future. While he (Nixon) considers himself an international statesman, what we need to develop is a populist star. I have identified Ronald Reagan as such a figure (evidenced by his impeccable nationally televised performance in support of Senator Goldwater's unsuccessful presidential bid), and that is why it is imperative that he be put forth for the California governorship in 1966. While 1968 would be too soon for a presidential run, we need a candidate for 1972, as it is far from assured that Nixon's bid will be successful. The California state campaign commences less than a year from now. What I am proposing should be regarded as a viable contingency to the current course of national action which (respectfully but vigorously) this agent considers to be flawed.

Filed 2/6/65 by E. (Zeke) Mallory

✷

Sidewalk café, Florence. Jill and a young woman were sharing espressos. Jill: "I'm not sure what I expected, but the instruction isn't all that challenging so far."

Dutch accent: "My understanding is that they break it down to the basics, then allow us to progress from there. Your work is not representational?"

"Mixed media. I like to incorporate images from films and advertising."

"You know something of those mediums?"

Jill smiled. "I grew up near Los Angeles. You know; Hollywood and all. You couldn't help but take some of it in."

✷

Dear Byron Krats,

I saw your advertisement in the "Recorder" soliciting a screenwriter for what sounds like a biker pic. I'm the perpetrator of "Road Map" (a flick in precisely that genre) produced & directed by the infamous (and infamously cheap) Karl Logan. You may not have seen it or even heard of it as it played almost exclusively on outdoor screens, although I'm told it raked in plenty. (I grew up in the biz, my father being the producer Glenn Parnell, and know the creativity is in the accounting). I'm not bitter, though, as I see that kind of success as a death blow to old, bloated, artery-hardened Hollywood. Since I've never heard of you, I figure you to be a newcomer who isn't jaded (yet) by the workings of this town. Want to stick them with something new and different? I'm your boy. If you wish to be pursuant, please write or call at the address or number provided.

> All most sincerely,
> Perry Parnell

*

Gus picked up Perry Parnell in Jimmy's new black Lincoln Continental, drove him from West Hollywood to Laurel Canyon, and deposited him in Jimmy's amber-lit living room. An elegant decanter of red wine, two crystal glasses, and a pair of linen napkins were poised on the coffee table. Perry sat waiting, sporting a sleek Italian leather jacket and round, red-tinted shades, each lens like the bottom of a cough-syrup bottle.

Jimmy, impeccable black hairpiece, descended the staircase and sank into one of the velvet-covered chairs. He greeted Perry in his vaguely Germanic voice.

"Why all the formality, man, picking me up and all?" was Perry's response.

"I figured you would want to be relaxed, not concerned about finding the house. Would you like a glass of wine? There is bread and cheese to go with it."

"It's a control thing, right? Not only do I have to come to you, I don't even get to decide when I want to leave. Don't get me wrong, it's cool and all; I just get what the game is."

Jimmy smiled. "Do you want to leave now?"

"Since I wrote a biker pic already, I assume that's why I'm here. Can you shed any more light than what you told me on the phone?"

Jimmy said nothing, poured them each a glass of wine.

"So, a road picture," Perry went on. "But what happens? What's the jeopardy?"

Jimmy smiled again. "That is where you are supposed to come in."

"You want me to pitch you your own movie?"

"I would like to hear how you might go about developing that kind of premise."

Perry stood. He seemed distressed yet somehow enthusiastic. "We're talking about a film—and that's a capital *F*—that should define where America is, where it's been and where it's going. How it's all doomed because . . ." His cadence increased. "Because of what we did to the Indians, the whole Duke Wayne karmic trip. It should be a buddy picture but with mystical undertones."

Jimmy shook his head. "No, just one man against . . . whatever he is up against."

Perry fired up a Marlboro. "Okay, so maybe he's a fish out of water, like you, man. He's always been intrigued by the American West. We'll set out on the ultimate highway, seat of our jeans, Kerouac-style, forging our own reverse manifest destiny."

"Reverse?"

Perry waved his arms, directing invisible traffic. "You see, man, this country has always pushed westward, but now it's all settled and leveled, suburbs and skyscrapers and trailer parks and Dairy Queens and drive-in restaurants. Nobody realizes it's over. We need to wake people up."

"What about the story; how does it start?"

Heaviness in the room, then Perry said, "Our two guys—"

"*One* guy."

"—finances his trip by selling a load of Mary Jane. We see the deal go down, then he buys a new chopper and hits the open road." Perry reclaimed his chair. "I'll come up with a treatment first. Character backgrounds, motivations, every beat."

There was silence, clearly nothing more was coming. Jimmy stood and put his hand out. "Thank you, my friend. You have given me a lot to think about. I will be in touch."

THIRTY-FOUR

H iram had prepared himself, but still it was a shock to see his mother like this; eyes shut and hands folded on her dark blue church dress. He leaned over and tenderly kissed her forehead; it felt like the wax of an unlit candle. Yet he had to take the picture. People had drifted up and spoken to him—his sister Cora, his brother Floyd, the Robinsons, who ran the parlor—but Hiram scarcely heard anything. His eyes kept darting back to her. Motionless. Lifeless. He discreetly snapped the shot, then took his place in the reception line and dimly greeted acquaintances and strangers and relatives, many of whom had to explain how they were related. His breath got shallow and his forehead damp; hands cold and warm at the same time. "I need some air," he told his wife, Marlene, who was seven months pregnant with their first.

He stepped out into the waning light of that August evening. Hiram's life had begun on these streets in Watts. Those first days when he'd gotten his hands on a camera seemed a lifetime before.

As he walked toward 118th Place, there was crowd, a hundred or so. He got closer, and the scene came more into focus. A black man, early twenties, was cursing at a white cop. A tow truck was hooking up the man's car, the man not taking it quietly. "What you wanna haul me in for? What you wanna go and tow my car for? Why you wanna do us like that?"

The crowd was buzzing and humming, and the cop tried to mollify him. "Now, c'mon, Marquette. You know the rules. You shouldn't have gotten behind the wheel in the condition you're in."

"What condition, you cracker asshole? The only condition I know is that I'm a block away from my fuckin' house." He gestured. "That's my mama, right over there. She'll vouch for me, just like my brother's been vouchin' for me. Hell, I don't even drink. That's just aftershave lotion, I'll swear to that on my grave."

The cop took a step toward him, and the young man swung. The cop leaned back, dodged it easily. Wildly, half-heartedly, Marquette swung again, the way a kid would swing in a playground fight he doesn't want any part of. This blow didn't land either, but another cop—stocky, red-faced, grimacing, baton in hand—sent a blow to Marquette's midsection, which sounded like a ball bat thudding into a mattress. The crowd oohed, and then another young black man rushed forward and he too received a blow to the ribs. Marquette swung for real this time, but the club knocked back his arm, then slammed against the side of his skull. He staggered backward, legs wobbling. The cop grabbed him around the neck, dragging him to the squad car. The other young man, subdued by the first cop, was also dragged to the car and flung into the back seat.

The crowd surged forward. A woman who Hiram figured to be the mother of both men, leapt onto the second cop's back, riding him for a moment, dress hiked up, bare legs exposed. The cop got her to the car where his partner opened the back door. She was shoved inside with her sons.

The first cop said, "Let's get the hell out of here," and the squad car sped away.

"Chickenshits! Motherfucking cowards!"

Another pair of cops stood, keeping the crowd at bay. As the two made their way toward their car, several people followed, taunting. Hiram glanced around. The crowd had swollen, one hundred fifty or so. Kids and older people too; none of them happy about what they'd witnessed.

"They didn't have to take Mrs. Frye away like that—she was just looking out for her boys."

"Big bad cops. Picking on a defenseless woman."

The cops were almost to their car when a young girl, a teenager, rushed out of the crowd and spat at the one who was closest. His hand went to his neck as he wheeled around, a mass of fury. "That bitch spit on me!"

"C'mon, it's not worth it," said his partner.

But the cop rushed into the crowd until he reached the laughing girl, flinging his arm around her neck.

"Let go of me—I didn't do anything."

He dragged her toward the car. The other cop had the door open and the girl was flung into the back seat. BANG, the door closed. BANG, the other door. The driver cop fired up the engine as the crowd buzzed furiously.

The cops pulled away; the crowd gesturing, waving fists. A young kid stepped into the street, a half-filled bottle of pop in hand. Hiram aimed his camera, the gesture automatic, perfectly in sync as the kid flung the bottle at the fleeing police car. CRASH! It hit the fender as the cops sped toward safety.

The shattering glass ignited the crowd, a flame to a pool of gas. The tow truck, Marquette's car held to it by a thick hook and chain, was pelted with rocks, dirt clods, cinders.

Backed-up traffic began to crawl, and those few cars that contained white occupants were pelted with debris, accompanied by cries of contempt.

*

Pacific Palisades, bedroom, Ron and Nancy in bed. She was reading Jeane Dixon's biography, *A Gift of Prophesy*, as he was glued to the eleven o'clock news. From Watts—flames, looting. Nancy looked up from her book: "Look at those criminals, making off with TV sets and stereos. It's disgraceful."

Reagan, half smiling. "Yes, but it will help."

Nancy looked over. "What are you talking about?"

"Governor Brown is vacationing in Greece while all hell is breaking loose. Don't think I'm not going to use this when I take him on next year."

Nancy put her book aside.

"Butterfield and Sazrac and that Republican group of theirs want to back me for governor in sixty-six."

"You're going to say yes, aren't you, Ronnie?"

Reagan smiled and pulled her to him. "I already have."

*

Hiram was on a TWA flight, high over Kansas or Nebraska—it looked flat as hell anyway—on his way back to New York, needing to change planes in Chicago. He felt bone-tired, had sent Marlene back home the day after his mother's funeral, while he stayed on and kept shooting around the clock. The Watts uprising had left thirty-four dead, a thousand injured, four hundred arrested, and two hundred million in damages.

With that image he'd captured, the kid hurling the pop bottle, Hiram sensed that the world had shifted. Malcolm had been slain six months before by what struck Hiram as a highly planned operation, and nobody seemed at all eager to get to the bottom of it. To the degree the government was tracking Malcolm, there was no way they didn't, at the very least, know it was coming.

Yes, the world felt different now, and Hiram felt different in it; he wasn't going to let this moment go unseen.

At Chicago's O'Hare, he passed a magazine rack. A red banner with white letters, similar to the *Life* logo, caught his eye. *Ebony* was published in Chicago, by blacks and for a black audience. He opened the glossy pages. *Johnson Publications, South Michigan Avenue.* When Hiram left the terminal, he didn't go to catch his connecting flight, but climbed in back of a taxi and gave *Ebony*'s address to the driver.

THIRTY-FIVE

J immy, in the back seat of his gleaming black Continental, was reading beneath the overheard light. Gus at the wheel, gliding around the midnight streets of LA, headed east on Santa Monica. When he felt restless, which he was experiencing with mounting regularity, Jimmy would have Gus drive him around.

Jimmy was rereading Perry Parnell's twelve-page treatment, and a second go-through didn't make it any better. He liked the guy; although Perry was full of beans, Jimmy enjoyed his energy. But he'd paid good money and waited six long months for *this*?

"Any stop you want to make tonight, Mr. Krats?"

"No, let's head home."

Jimmy sighed, leaned back in his seat. He missed driving, missed the Spyder, wondered what became of it, experiencing a pang of guilt for having abandoned it the way he did.

*

Jimmy's dining room. Jimmy and Perry were sitting across from each other at the long wooden table. Wagner booming from some other part of the house. Pizza and salad spread out between them, and they each had a Coors going. It was apparent from the cans strewn about the table that they'd arrived at some level of inebriation.

Jimmy, his German accent slipping a bit: "You're telling me you think the picture should be shot without a script?"

Perry, leaning forward, slice in hand. "Docu-style. No sets or costumes. Rural locations. Tight crew. No extras or traffic or municipal pigs to pay off, man. No goddamn unions. Artistic control. Final cut. Some head from one of the studios owes me a solid. He'll score us a camera and miles of film. Sneak us in so we can edit after hours. I know a lotta groovy musicians who'll make us a heavy soundtrack."

Jimmy smiled mischievously. "If there is no script, what do I need you for?"

Perry, a moment. "Fuck it. I'll be your producing partner, Byron. That'll free you up more to direct."

Jimmy held his smile but didn't really respond.

Perry, back in his rhythm. "Hollywood deals in still lifes. Sunbaked Dynaflow should be like an action painting. The kind of picture you'd see once, then go back and see again, and have a totally new experience."

"Sunbaked Dynaflow?"

Perry beamed, leaning back in his chair. "Great title isn't it? Just came to me."

"Dynaflow is a Buick engine. It has nothing to do with a bike."

A moment, then, "You know that, and I know that, but the kids who see this won't know it. It's impressionistic, it sounds good."

Jimmy popped open a fresh can. "But what the hell does it mean?"

"Sunbaked, because we'll be filming a lot in the desert. Like America's becoming a desert, you dig? And Dynaflow because, like I said, it sounds groovy. It suggests Dionysus, the god of wine."

"I know who Dionysus is, Perry."

"And Sunbaked is like Apollo, the sun god. Only this time he's destructive. Dionysus is who we want them to root for."

"But Dionysus loses?"

"Of course he loses. That's what makes it a tragedy. Anti-Hollywood."

*

Italian Country Road, outside Florence. Jill, on a scooter, turned onto a long, dirt-covered drive, leading to a farmhouse. She killed the engine, dismounted, then approached the barn behind the main structure. A dark-haired young man appeared. In Italian: "May I be of help?"

Jill unfastened the strap on her helmet. Also in Italian: "I am here to see Guiseppe Tellio."

Young man, in English: "The accent. You are American?"

"I am."

"These are working hours. Guiseppe is working."

Jill reached into the pocket of her madras windbreaker. "I have an invitation for him." Handed it over. "An opening at the Kiere Gallery. A showing of my work. Well, I'm part of the show."

Looking at it: "Guiseppe does not attend openings."

Voice, from off behind: "Antonio."

Guiseppe Tellio stood in the doorway of the barn, looking even more intense than any photo Jill had ever seen of him; piercing glare, silver beard, oil paint on his overalls, brush in hand.

Young man, to Jill: "I must go."

To Tellio, Jill offered a slight wave. The master stared at her, then turned and faded back inside.

✳

Dark bar in Florence. Guiseppe Tellio and Antonio, the young assistant, across from Jill.

"Tell him," she said, "I am so honored that he came."

Antonio translated. The master nodded, saying nothing.

"I was hoping that he would see enough in the work to allow me to apprentice with him."

Antonio translated. Again, no response.

"Guiseppe Tellio is one of the main reasons I came to Florence."

As Antonio imparted this, the old man sipped his grappa, then set his drink aside. He gave his reply to Antonio, who delivered it to Jill: "The work, your work, is infantile and of no consequence. The idea of becoming an artist is a waste of your time. It would be a waste of mine, as well as that of anyone who is subjected to it."

Jill stared at the old man, who smiled at her. He added something to Antonio, who told her: "I am, however, in need of someone to cook and clean throughout the day and to be a mistress throughout the night. You appear amply suited for such duties."

Jill started to say something, then rose in a shot and rushed from the table.

✳

Ciao magazine, hallway. Hiram Freeman was walking one direction; Garland Alpert, the other. Garland held a magazine in his hand. "Freeman, what the hell is this?"

"Looks like the current issue of *Ebony*."

"What is your photo—a photo that some people are saying might win the Pulitzer—doing on the cover?"

"I submitted it to them."

"Why the hell would you do that? You're *Ciao's* photo editor, for God's sake."

"You would have never led with that."

"We certainly would have run it."

Hiram's heart was beating and his mind was tumbling. *Ciao* guaranteed a healthy income. Marlene was pregnant. "Look, Gar, what we're talking about here is a once-in-a-life-time shot. I didn't want it stuck between a Schlitz ad and Girls of the South of France."

Red-faced and indignant, Garland turned on his heel and stormed back down the hallway.

Hiram thought about it for hours, not just his dustup with Garland, but everything that had played out during the riot. Yes, the ground had shifted, the game had changed, and Hiram knew which side he was on.

Before leaving that day, he turned in his resignation.

*

Davotney stood behind his desk, beaming. To Zeke, who was sitting, he said, "I called you up here to have a drink, agent Mallory."

"You know I don't drink, sir."

Davotney went to his cabinet and began pouring. "Well, today's an exception."

Zeke, waiting.

Davotney handed him a glass. "We need to drink to your new assignment."

Zeke clutched the glass, said nothing.

"Leadership is transferring you to Los Angeles. One of the things you'll be doing is pulling strings to help ensure that Reagan is elected governor."

Davotney's glass touched his. Zeke took a tentative, thoughtful sip. It tasted harsh but he swallowed every drop.

THIRTY-SIX

J ill, in Venice. She'd come here after dropping out of the
visual arts program in Florence. Since her harsh dismissal
by Guiseppe Tellio, she hadn't stretched a canvas, hadn't
picked up a brush; didn't know if she ever would again. She
felt like one of the characters in that O'Neill play *The Iceman
Cometh*. Her lifelong dream of being a visual artist had been a
dream all right; a pipe dream.

She'd just finished her waitressing shift in the pesce trat-
toria and was having a late drink with the two owners, brothers Renato and Luigi, enjoying Renato's impressive collection
of American jazz and blues. Chet Baker was on the system.

"Miles is better than Chet," she insisted, sharing Prosecco
with the boys.

"Miles Davis is this." Renato tapped his temple with his
index finger. "Chet Baker lives here." He thumped his chest
with his fist.

Luigi put Nat King Cole on the turntable. The trio, not the
pop stuff he crooned on television until the cigarettes caught
up with him; his sponsor, Chesterfield, effectively killing
him. A man and woman were lingering in the restaurant; the
woman dark-haired, twenties; the man dressed mod, around
thirty. They seemed to be enjoying the music.

As Jill was leaving, the guy got up from his table and stepped out the door, not far behind her. Outside, she could hear him, bootheels scuffling over the paved stones. *Dammit.* She improvised a circuitous route, crossing over a canal, doubling back. But he stayed with her, thirty yards behind. She decided to quit playing mouse to his cat and get home the swiftest way possible.

Jill passed the tobacconist, then the mask shop, hollow eyes glaring at her. She turned down her street. It seemed narrower than the others, not as well lit; neighbors asleep. Her place, last door on the left. She passed through the hundred feet of blind alley and reached the thick wooden door. The lock was rusty and tight. She had to maneuver it to get the teeth just right. Maddening, maddening. Footsteps again. Quickening, closing in as she fumbled. Steady, steady, she told herself as she worked the key. It wasn't catching. She pulled it out for another attempt and it slipped from her fingers, the sound ringing as it hit the pavement in the stillness.

Jill stooped frantically to pick it up, beset with a wave of—what? She spun around as he came closer in his long coat, an insipid smirk on his face.

"What do you want?" Jill snapped.

"No need to be so jumpy, luv." An Englishmen, not what she was expecting. "I want to meet with you tomorrow."

"For what?"

He performed an awkward bow, not wholly without charm. "Trevor Trilby. I'm a film director, scouting locations here. You are the most compelling woman I have seen in years, and I am going to turn you into one of the world's greatest stars. Have you acted before?

"Never."

Stepping closer, he handed her a card. "Meet me at this address, not far from the Guggenheim collection. I have a suite that serves as my temporary production office." He turned and strolled toward the opening at the end of the street.

✦

Jill showed up, looking casually elegant. Trevor Trilby introduced the woman from the night before as "Maria, my assistant." A young Italian guy was "my production designer" and an older Brit "my director of photography." A third guy sat in the corner. Unruly, rust-shaded curly hair, pale, and not-so-great skin. Trevor didn't introduce him and Garland Alpert didn't introduce himself.

"You look right for the role," said Trevor, "but I'd still like to conduct an audition."

He pressed a half dozen pages of script toward her, which she waved aside.

"If you want me for the part, you'll have to offer it to me. Then I'll read the script and let you know whether I accept."

The phone rang and Maria went to answer it.

"Look," said Trevor, "this role will make you an international star. It's *Taming of the Shrew* with a sci-fi take, set on Venus. You would be in nearly every frame. Of course you look smashing, but I need to know whether you can handle dialogue."

"Isn't that your job, to coax a performance out of me? You know what you want, right?"

Trevor, visibly thrown, took a few pages and set them back on the table. "Just one scene, luv. Merely to get a sense of things. For all I know, you've never so much as been in a grammar school production."

Garland piped up: "For Chrisssake, Trilby, this is Jill Parnell. She carried a major American television comedy for several seasons." He looked at Jill. "Garland Alpert. I interviewed you for *TV Weekly*."

Jill, a thin smile. "Oh yes. The conversation that was supposed to be off the record."

Garland shrugged as everyone else looked at Jill.

"So I have the part?"

*

One night, Jimmy's phone rang. He set aside the latest issue of *Esquire* and lifted the receiver. "Hello."

"Great news, Byron. I hope you're sitting down." Perry sounded amped-up, but then he always sounded amped-up. "I ran into Karl Logan of Double W Pictures. Loves our concept; he's offered us seed money to go out and shoot a sequence."

A moment. "Perry, we do not even have a script."

"I thought we decided on an experimental approach."

"Logan screwed you, you told me. Why would you get involved with him again?"

"I'll read the fine print this time. Look, Logan's pictures never lose money but he's never had a blockbuster. With SD, there'll be enough to feed everybody for a long, long time."

"SD?"

"Sunbaked Dynaflow."

Jimmy thought a moment. "Call me in the morning when you are sober."

"I haven't had a drop; swear on my mother."

"Then call when you are not high."

"And we'll talk about it?"

"Yes. We will talk about it."

*

Jill and Trevor were locked in an embrace as Trevor groaned in ecstasy. They remained still for a time, then Jill eased herself from beneath him. It was dawn; silver light peeking through the curtains of Trevor's suite. Trevor reached for his Gauloises. Lit one. Took a drag. Handed it over.

Jill: "When did you know?"

"That you'd be my lover?" A moment. "I knew you were perfect for the film. I suppose the rest came later. But it's all the same, love and work. Without one, the other doesn't amount to much."

Smoke, quiet. "I think," said Jill, "that film work is over-rated."

"That's because growing up with it, you got to peek behind the curtain. What hooked me was a Nicholas Ray film. The one where James Dean loses his life. I saw it when I was at Cambridge."

Jill stiffened. "I was in that picture," she said, practically to herself.

Trevor, up on one elbow. "You're joking."

"Just one of the gang kids. The only thing I'd ever done before that stupid TV show."

Trevor took the cigarette. "What was Dean like?"

Jill said nothing.

"Was he as intense off screen as on?"

Jill, quietly. "I never really got to know him." She eased the cigarette from Trevor's fingers. "Why are you giving Garland Alpert so much access?"

"*Ciao* magazine, we need it to promote the film."

"Well, you can't trust him."

In the front room, the phone started ringing.

"Oh, God, that's got to be Brent. I'm bloody well not answering."

"Who's Brent?"

"Peter Brent, the bloody producer. He's threatening to pull the plug if I don't toss some sex into the script. The man made a fortune on blue movies, and it's all he knows."

"Sounds serious."

"Brent doesn't know the first thing about art." Trevor grabbed the cigarette from Jill. "Hiring me has put the wanker out of his depth."

✱

Indoor set, made to look like the interior of a spacecraft. Jill sat, wearing a skintight, lime-shaded plastic suit, with Trevor and the crew spread among lights and cables and a massive camera. Trevor approached Jill and spoke to her, just above a whisper. "How are you feeling, darling?"

"Beat," she answered.

"I'd like to try one more scene."

Jill looked at him wearily.

"You've just woken up from the dream, right? You're still in that netherworld, half in and half out of reality. The dream was about Revotrad, the man you're longing for. I want you to return to the cot and lean back and slowly let your hands caress your body. Where it's going to take you is, well, you know, she begins to pleasure herself."

"Pleasure myself?"

"Well, Cressida does. You'll be in character."

"There's nothing of the kind in the script."

"But it's completely in keeping with what Cressida is feeling at the moment." Trevor stepped forward and nuzzled her neck. "If it doesn't work, we won't use it. Come on, one final scene."

"Trevor, I know why you're doing this."

"I'll clear the set, once you've slipped out of your costume."

In a daze, Jill heard Trevor telling the crew they were done for the day. Then there was just him, the lights and the camera operator in that sterile space. The camera op was a stout and sturdy woman, Nina, from whom Jill had not heard one word since the start of the production.

With the numbness of a diver who had just emerged from freezing water, Jill peeled her costume, a latex jumpsuit that came off easily. She was naked as Trevor instructed her to recline on a plastic settee and lean back with her legs parted.

"That's splendid, darling. Now drop your right hand, and with two fingers, just rub yourself gently, you know how to do it. And close your eyes, like this is the best you've ever felt, the best you're ever going to feel. That's right, now lick your lips; let's see that lovely tongue of yours. Spread those fingers, so we can see a bit of pink. That's marvelous, that's smashing, luv."

And now Jill could feel something; the camera, probing her. She felt the scream rising up inside of her. But she blocked it, kept silent, feeling the fury, hot but lifeless in her gut.

✱

Jill sat waiting to be called for her Alitalia flight, her mind racing. She wished she could sleep, wanting to just black out until she got to LA. She'd love to take another pill but was beyond the required dosage. *Why did I do it?* She should have told Trevor to take *his* clothes off, but that wouldn't excite anybody. Staircase wit, wasn't that what the French called it, when you think of what you should have said as you're leaving the party? Jill wished she could have seen his stupid phony face when he rolled out of bed this morning and read her note, telling him what he could do with his lousy cartoon of a movie.

"What a coincidence."

She looked up and Garland Alpert was standing there, smiling.

"Looks like we're on the same flight. You'll be changing planes at Kennedy, I take it."

Jill looked away, feeling defensive.

"How goes it, Jill, isn't there still a lot of shooting left?"

"I'm done with all that," she declared.

"You and Trevor had a falling out?"

"You could say so."

"Personal or professional?"

"Excuse me?"

"Your disagreement; was it over the film?"

"Look, Alpert—"

"Garland."

"The one and only time you and I spoke caused quite a bit of trouble for me. Having been burned once, I don't feel inclined to offer up any insights."

At that moment, they announced the flight in English.

"Boy, you can really hold a grudge. It'd be nice if you and I could be friends or something."

Jill scooped up her bag. "Screw yourself, Alpert. You should have thought about that a long time ago."

THIRTY-SEVEN

A rizona highway, dusk. Jimmy, in the back seat of his Continental, Gus at the wheel. The car was slowing, pulling off to the side.

Jimmy: "What the hell is going on?"

"Looks like Perry wants something."

Perry was standing in the middle of the road, waving his arms, the production van pulled over, the small crew standing off to the side. As the Continental stopped, he rushed over.

Jimmy lowered the rear window and asked wearily: "What is it this time?"

"Didn't you see that image on the mountain we just passed?"

"What?"

"Looked like the face of an Indian brave. No, fuck that, it *was* the face of an Indian brave. It'll make a statement about the enduring corruption of America."

"We have enough statements, Perry."

"You've been in a shitty mood all day, Byron. If you didn't want to shoot, you should have just told me."

"Coming here has only confirmed my misgivings."

"Misgivings?"

"We do not have a script. We do not have a story. Not even one character. Unless we were to cast some incredible—I will not even say actor. Some incredible performer, all we're looking at is landscapes, suitable for a magazine, but not a feature-length motion picture. I am sorry, Perry. This approach is not going to work."

✱

Zeke sat at his desk among stacks of cardboard boxes, filled with pristine files. Middle of the night, the Chicago skyline glowing out the window. Taking a break from clearing out his office for his move to Los Angeles, he was reading with only the aid of a green-shaded lawyer's lamp, reviewing the file on Stephen "Specs" Pelham, part of Zeke's first national action. The missing person's case that originated in Los Angeles had never stopped haunting him. He recalled how Sergio Baldoni put it that day in his hospital room: *It wasn't the same guy.* Zeke's gut told him that was true. Plus, the Specs Pelham the Baldoni brothers encountered had been violent. The profile he'd worked up on Pelham suggested nothing of the kind.

Besides Pelham's lawsuit against Moss Levan, the file noted that he'd been a court reporter during the James Dean trial and apparently associated with Dean after the hung jury. Strange, Zeke thought, that Pelham became friendly with the man who shot Ronald Reagan.

Exhausted, Zeke sighed and leaned back. He glanced once again at the file, the unsolved case fluttering like a moth in the dimly lit room; small and remote, yet too troublesome to ignore.

✱

Los Angeles International Airport, Zeke Mallory, landing in his new home base, striding through the terminal, briefcase in hand. As he passed a newsstand, he stopped cold. He marched toward the magazine rack, eyes on the cover of *Time*, blood red letters on black background: *Is God Dead?* He grabbed the magazine and snapped at the vendor behind the counter: "How long has this been in circulation?"

"What?"

"This." He thrust it forward.

"*Time?* We got it this morning."

Zeke stepped toward him. "I'm taking this with me, but I won't be paying for it."

"We sell papers here, mister. We don't give them away."

Zeke, through his teeth. "What you should do is put a match to them. I'm taking this—confiscating it—and don't try to stop me."

✱

Ronald Reagan, speaking to a crowd outdoors. The banner behind him:

TIIIIMMMMMMMBBERRRR!
The Western Wood Cutters Association for Reagan

"Our great state, particularly this part of it, is known for its towering redwoods. But when it comes to preserving them, some can't see the trees for the forest. Trees are a natural resource, and resources are meant to be used, or what good are they? Do we just want to look at a hundred thousand acres or so of trees? That's just navel-gazing. Where's the progress in that?"

Some chuckles, several claps, as Reagan beamed.

*

Jill was driving along Sunset, coming from breakfast at Du-par's a place she'd enjoyed since back in high school. Having rained the night before, it was one of those LA days when everything was wrapped in a glow. She had the radio on, the Supremes cooing and oohing as she glided in her convertible. The boulevard, as always, was lined with billboards, primarily lauding the films currently in release. One of the images caught her eye, a woman from the waist up, leaning back, lips glistening and parted, eyes dreamy. Across where her breasts would be exposed it said: *Traci Takes It Off—in this month's issue of* Ciao!

Jill felt a click as her brain locked into place. Trevor's film—that scene he'd talked her into shooting. She, who'd never wanted to be looked at to begin with, was posing like some ludicrous slut as she gazed lustily down upon the never-ending stream of traffic on Sunset Boulevard. *Ciao* magazine, thousands of copies. Hundreds of men touching themselves, leering at her in bedrooms, bathrooms, dorm rooms. Someone was honking. Her hands unsteady on the wheel, she jerked it to the right and pulled over to the curb, another horn blaring as she eased to a stop. Feeling a wave pressing upwards from her gut, Jill opened the door and leaned over, violently heaving, but nothing would come up.

THIRTY-EIGHT

Jimmy, as scarlet-jacketed Jim Stark, stands outside the Griffith Observatory, hands atop his head. "Okay," he yells to the cops, squinting in response to the probing spotlights. "We're coming out."

He walks forward cautiously, baby-faced Sal Mineo, in the role of Plato, a step and a half behind. In a flash, Plato streaks toward the spotlights. "Watch it, he's armed!" shouts a rough voice from off-screen. A trio of sharp reports and Plato collapses face down on the cement. Jimmy has rushed after him, but not soon enough. The agony on his face is heart-wrenching and he screams: "I've got the gun; I've got the gun!"

✱

Seventeen-year-old high school junior Grace Hobson, eyes filling with tears, sat in the blue darkness of the University of Colorado's Old Main Auditorium. As the neoclassical soundtrack swelled and the credits rolled, Grace remained frozen. The lights came on; a pair of student ushers strode along each aisle. One of them, at Grace's row: "We need to clear the auditorium."

Grace, as though aroused from a grief-consumed sleep. "Are you really going to show it again tomorrow night?"

*

After the film, which she'd sat through twice, Grace walked to downtown Boulder. The clock outside the Wells Fargo told her it was eleven forty-seven. She passed the bus station; fluorescent lights, a few people. She went in and stretched out on one of the benches, then fell asleep.

When she opened her eyes, it was dawn. She stumbled out, stiff and weary, and drifted back to campus. Went to the gymnasium and took a shower, then to the student union for eggs and pancakes. The library opened at nine, and she was the first to be let in. She'd used it for school projects; her mother had told her it was the best in the region and she would always find whatever she needed.

There weren't many people inside. It was a football weekend, everyone gearing up for the game. Grace hated football, especially since everybody made such a big noise about it.

She knew where they kept the old newspapers and periodicals, some of them bound, some on microfilm, for which you had to turn a heavy crank and peer through a magnifying lens. She found what she was looking for, and more. Articles from the *New York Times*, about Jimmy in his two films. *Life* magazine, him back in Indiana. The *Los Angeles Times*: Jimmy on trial for shooting Ronald Reagan, then getting killed while making *Rebel Without a Cause*. Some of the articles made it sound like Jimmy had shot Reagan on purpose. If that were the case, Grace was certain that Jimmy had a reason, like Reagan had been a jerk to him. Grace could completely understand that. She had a gym teacher she wouldn't mind shooting.

In the *Reader's Guide to Periodical Literature*, she found

more obscure pieces, her favorites being the ones written as Jimmy's fame spread around the globe a few years after his death. She stayed until the library closed at six and ended up having just enough time to go to the Sink and elbow her way through the football crowd to get a cheeseburger, fries, and a Coke. Grace had plenty of money, having raided her bottom drawer where she stashed her weekly allowance. She never did anything to earn it, but her parents kept giving it to her anyway. And she never spent it, just stashed it in her drawer or put it into the bank account she'd opened, having told them she was saving for college. Fat chance. Jimmy dropped out of UCLA. College was for the football dummies and their stupid-ass fans.

*

Hobson living room, Boulder, Colorado, Sunday afternoon. Grace sat facing her parents; her mother, talking: "Of course we filed a missing person report, Grace. You were missing."

Her father: "Where were you all weekend, dear? You still haven't told us."

"We missed church this morning because of you."

Grace took a sip of hot chocolate. "I was at the movies."

Father: "Movies don't run around the clock, Grace. Where did you sleep?"

"I didn't. I walked around all night. Then I went back to the library, as soon as they opened in the morning."

"What were you doing there?" her mother demanded.

"A project for school."

"What kind of project?"

"I'm . . . building a telescope."

"Well, I'm calling your teacher to verify this," Grace's

father told her.

"Don't," said Grace.

"Don't, because you're lying?"

"Of course she's lying," said Grace's mother. "Look at her."

Her father leaned forward, wagging his finger. "You need to start making sense, young lady, or else we're going to have you talk to a—"

Grace erupted: "You're tearing me *ap-aaaaaarrtt!*"

✳

Dear Norris and Helen,

I would say "dear Dad and Mom" but I no longer consider you as such. Since I'm on my own and always have been, I might as well be shoving off sooner rather than later. Away from this tomb of a house, that graveyard of a school, this smoking disaster of a town. You'll be upset I'm sure, but it will be just another opportunity for you to feel sorry for yourselves. I'm beginning to find myself, who I really am and what I really am. So goodbye, whoever you were.

> Your eSTRANGEd offspring,
> Grace

✳

Union Station, Denver. Train arrivals and departures being called. Grace sat on a wooden bench. Across the way, a young woman was sifting through a set of receipts, lime green wallet lying on the bench next to her purse; she looked up, hearing something related to her departure. Sandy hair; eighteen, nineteen years old. The young woman stood; five foot four, about the same height as Grace. Slight frame, as well. She rushed toward one of the ticket windows at the far end of the station. Grace's eyes fixed on the exposed wallet. She glanced around—nobody looking.

*

The train reached Los Angeles at midday. Grace got in a taxi and told the driver to take her to the Griffith Observatory, not caring how much it cost. She wandered around there, seeing the auditorium used in *Rebel*, trying to determine which seat Jimmy may have sat in, then going out to the observation deck where the knife fight took place. She dropped dimes into a huge telescope and gazed out at the smog-tinted LA basin. Grace breathed in, hoping some of the very air Jimmy had exhaled was still present.

Around five o'clock she left, walking this time, drifting aimlessly. She wasn't tired but knew she needed a place to stay. The wallet she'd lifted came in handy, not just for the hundred eighty dollars inside, but for the Utah driver's license and University of Denver student ID, all in the name of Wanda Lynne Felks, eighteen, of Provo, Utah. That cash, along with the traveler's checks she'd converted from her stored-up allowance and savings account, set her up pretty well.

When Grace checked into the Citrus Motel on Melrose just west of Vermont, the creep at the desk, complete with pancake makeup, didn't even raise an eyebrow as he checked her in at a weekly rate.

The room was done in startling shades of orange, green, and yellow, and reeked of antiseptic and cigarette smoke. Smoking was a habit Grace hadn't adopted. She'd tried it after seeing *Rebel* that first time; Camels, then Marlboros, then

Salems; but filtered or not, mentholated or not, they still made her gag. *What had Jimmy seen in them?*

She had dinner at a neighborhood taco stand. The only food she'd ever tried besides regular American was from a Chinese restaurant in Boulder, so she wasn't sure what she'd be getting when she ordered tamales. They were really spicy, had to order an extra bottle of Coke to cool her mouth.

Back at the motel, a Tony Curtis movie was on TV, and she watched it until her eyes fluttered shut. She woke up to somebody yelling out in the parking lot. "Come out here, Laurie. Come out, you bitch, or I'll break that door down. Come out, or I'll drag you out." This went on half the night, but Grace didn't open the door to tell the guy to shut up. It was a big voice that sounded crazy.

Grace rode the buses all the next day. She didn't much care where she was going, an open-ended sightseeing tour. Some woman who sat next to her told her there were a lot of movie theaters in Westwood. She made her way there and found one on practically every block. Made a double feature of it, albeit at two different theaters: *Thunderball*, the James Bond flick she'd seen before, and *Appaloosa*, a Western she'd never seen, starring Marlon Brando. A lot of writers compared Jimmy to Brando. To Grace, Brando seemed like some distant uncle, while Jimmy was an older brother, right there with you.

THIRTY-NINE

P erry Parnell called Jimmy, wanting to get together. Jimmy
didn't feel like going out, and suggested he come to the
house in Laurel Canyon.

As usual, Perry was late. He had on a fringe jacket and
beat-up Stetson. Jimmy glanced down and, sure enough, there
were the cowboy boots. Perry had clearly entered his wrangler
period.

"Great news, Byron," Perry said with his usual enthu-
siasm. "Logan loved our footage. He wants to set a meeting
with the three of us. My guess, he's considering funding the
whole picture."

"We have talked about this, Perry," Jimmy said, assuming
his Germanic accent. "Besides not having a script, we do not
have the actor who can handle your free-form approach."

"Double W Pictures has incredible distribution, especially
overseas."

"But we need to have something to distribute."

"We just need to make a film, man. It's like the new
music. None of these old Hollywood cats understand it but
they know there's millions to rake in. The soundtrack alone
will put us in the black."

Perry kept jabbering, but Jimmy wasn't taking much of it
in, feeling he must have a lot more in common with the old

Hollywood that Perry so despised. *Who made movies without scripts or actors?*

Then Perry said something that made Jimmy sit up in his leather upholstered armchair. "I wish Harley was still around. He could carry the whole thing."

"What did you say?"

"Harley Dale, the star of *Road Map*. I wrote the story, but he came up with all his lines and got the other actors into it as well. If we had him here, we'd have a movie."

A long silence. "You said you wished he *was still around*. What happened to him?"

"You knew Harley?"

Jimmy shook his head no.

"He went into his garage one night and stuck a hose in the gas pipe. Harley was a deep cat. It was him who rolled out of his car the night Jimmy Dean drove off the cliff. My theory is Harley never got over losing Jimmy like that. Jimmy was his mentor. Too bad old Harl's not around. He would have been part of this thing that's coming up, Jimmy Trip."

"What the hell is that?"

"Nick Ray is putting it together. A whole weekend of screenings and panels commemorating the tenth anniversary of Jimmy's death. They've asked my sister to be on one but there's no way she'll accept. She hardly goes out anymore. Not since that spread—and I mean *spread*—in *Ciao* magazine."

"Why would your sister be part of Jimmy Trip?"

"Before she was a TV star, she had a bit part in *Rebel*."

*

After resigning from *Ciao*, Hiram felt the urge to head back west. Marlene didn't need much convincing, and next thing he knew they and baby Taryn were packed up and leaving for Los Angeles.

Now Hiram was in the El Coyote restaurant on Santa Monica Boulevard, sipping Carta Blanca, munching chips and salsa, waiting for Oona Stickney. When he reached out to people he knew in LA, he kept hearing about *Spoonful*, largely funded behind the scenes by a set of record labels and producers. His old friend Oona was features editor. How many years ago was it that she introduced him to Garland—ten? No, going on twelve.

Here she was now, dayglow and beaming as she approached the table. Hiram got to his feet and they embraced; she took the chair across from him.

"Look at you," he said, "all breezy and casual."

"You're looking pretty casual yourself, man. It's been way too long."

"That it has."

As they set about catching up, the waiter appeared and took their order. When he left the table, Hiram said: "This publication you're with, I want to hear more about it."

"Readership is exploding. The focus is on rock music and that's a good thing, since there's a hot new band every week. But we dip into politics too. I was thinking that for more of the weighty stuff, you'd be the perfect photographer. Freelance at first, but steady, I promise."

Hiram smiled. "Any assignments on the horizon?"

"Ronald Reagan. Neck and neck for the governorship. Have you heard his speeches? Free enterprise, as long as you're rich, white, and corporate. I thought Nixon was the worst this state could produce."

"Have you got an interview set up?"

"Hell no. Reagan won't talk to *Spoonful*. But he's got a speech coming up at the Beverly Wilshire. Addressing a bunch of clergymen, so he should be in good form. You snap the event, and I'll provide the coverage."

❋

Grace stood at a bus stop, near the motel, on her way to get her hair cut. Her LA pilgrimage hadn't come to much. How many times could she float around the Griffith Observatory?

The nights out here, even the evenings, were getting chilly. The heat wasn't working in her room, but she didn't want to bring it up because the staff at the motel, the desk clerks especially, were starting to give her weird looks.

She was running through her money. Grace had never had a job, didn't know what kind of job she could handle anyway, and the thought of easing back in at Boulder High, something she never thought she'd consider, suddenly didn't seem like such a terrible thing. She'd have a lot of explaining to do, but Norris and Helen would take her in because that was what they felt they were supposed to do.

Grace was thinking all this, vaguely wondering when the bus would come. They were really spotty; yesterday she'd waited over an hour.

The bus stop was in front of a bookstore. A poster in the front window caught her eye: She stepped over, drinking in the words: *Nouveau Theater, Santa Monica . . . Friday and Saturday, October 28th and 29th . . . Jimmy Trip, a Tribute to James Dean . . . 10th Anniversary . . . Screenings . . . Panels . . . Special Guests . . . Celebration.*

Grace was reaching into her handbag for pen and paper when a guy appeared beside her. He hadn't shaved in days and, as he drew even closer, was clearly in need of a bath.

"Staying at the Citrus, huh, kid? I saw you coming out of there."

Grace took a step back, doing her best to still stand her ground. "Never mind where I'm staying, mister."

The guy smiled. What teeth he had were predictably discolored. "I'm not the enemy, little girl, I'm trying to help. Gets crazy around here. Anybody messes with you, you're gonna need a little something to even things out. Look what I got."

Grace glanced down and spotted the silver, snub-nosed revolver filling the guy's open palm.

"Twenty-five bucks, loaded and ready."

She took a moment. "How about twenty?"

*

Jill stood looking in the bathroom mirror. In her bathrobe, the only clothing she'd worn in days, she stared at her pallid face, eyes with dark greenish-blue pouches underneath. Her hair was a matted mess. *Ciao* magazine, with its ten-page spread "Traci Takes It Off" was open on the counter, each frame more lurid than the next. Her father had called and berated her: "Whatever career you had is ruined for good. How could you be so dumb?"

She'd called Tad Harbor who'd contacted a lawyer for her. Nothing doing. The film had been shot in Italy and any litigation would include *Ciao* hiding behind international precedents. Plus, no one had put a gun to her head. She called *Ciao's* offices in New York and a female with an English accent answered and Garland Alpert, the little worm, refused to take Jill's call.

How could she drive around, sit in restaurants, be among

people? Everyone would be undressing her, knowing what she looked like down to every detail; a human mannequin, every part of her exposed.

It was a man's world, all right, a rigged game run by masters and patriarchs. Guiseppe Tellio had mocked her as an artist, had even mocked her ambition to *become* an artist. Yet he was probably right, the horny old goat. What did Jill Parnell have to express, to contribute? Her only success, her flimsy, vacuous gesture, had been portraying a bubblehead on a nationally televised comedy. And now the joke was on her, mocked in a way she'd not intended and had never anticipated. The image she'd cynically served up was now quartered and hung out as a consumable slab of meat.

She glanced at the open medicine cabinet, then at the prescription bottle of Quinalbarbitone she'd brought with her from England. Her mind started churning. Just take a handful and lie down and let darkness spread like a sheet.

She grabbed the bottle, held out her palm and turned the bottle over. Twenty maybe, more than enough. A drinking glass on the counter. Jill set down the bottle and reached for the glass. But then, as though some hand had seized her shoulder, she stopped, drew her arm back and flung the pills, which bounced off the tiled wall and the shower curtain before rolling all over the floor.

Jill turned on the faucet and leaned down, cupping her hands. Then she vigorously splashed cold water again and again on her face.

FORTY

P ouring rain, the first night of Jimmy Trip. Jimmy had Gus
drop him right in front of the theater. He had his ornate
walking stick but no umbrella, and Jimmy got pretty wet
even from the short walk from the curb. Perry had included
Byron Krats on the guest list, which was superfluous, as the
box office was shut down for the night. Jimmy had timed it
to come after the *Rebel* screening, feeling no need to see two
hours of his former self flickering in shadows and light.

The theater was packed. The house lights were up and a
long table was onstage, four men and a woman were seated,
facing the audience, microphones on small stands set in front
of each of them. Jimmy settled into an aisle seat, second row
from the back. At first, he didn't recognize the older guy on
the far left of the stage, who was wearing an eye patch. But as
the guy addressed the crowd, Jimmy realized it was Nick Ray

Nick introduced Leonard Rosenman, who had composed
the scores for both *Eden* and *Rebel*. Jimmy had taken a few
piano lessons from him during *Eden* but both of them had
become frustrated pretty fast.

Jimmy pretty much tuned Rosenman out, the guy always
was a blowhard, and then Ray was talking again.

" . . . so pleased and grateful that she consented to be with
us tonight. She was one of the gang members in *Rebel* before
she went on to bigger roles. Please welcome Jill Parnell."

To Jimmy, she appeared nervous as she spoke. Jimmy found himself tuning in.

"Most people consider me an actress, but I've never seen myself as that. I wanted to be a visual artist; that had always been my dream. But I took that role in *Rebel*, if you could really call it a role, just because I wanted to get to know Jimmy. And I did get to know him, but not until very late in the production. The last night, in fact, the night he died." Tears were streaming down her cheeks and she was visibly trembling.

Jimmy felt like a radio was on in his head and he was tuning it, trying to get rid of the static. *No mistaking it . . . seen her before.*

" . . . a secret I've been holding for the past ten years."

What's she saying?

"We conceived a child together that night."

Tad Harbor's party, I drove her down to the beach.

"And I was young and afraid and didn't know what to do, so I gave up the baby. Gave up my son, who's living out there somewhere."

I have a kid, a son.

"And I hope that somehow, I can find a way to get in touch with him and let him know that even though other people raised him, he was brought into this world with love. Because the only thing in life that I've ever been sure about is that I loved Jimmy, and I'm in no way ashamed of that."

She left the stage to a wave of applause, and Jimmy sat there feeling like the theater was some oversized pool he was swimming in.

Nick was talking again. "It's been a deeply emotional night and we'll be back again at the same time tomorrow for the screening of *Eden*, plus an entirely different panel. I'm pleased to say that tonight, we will end with something that hasn't been seen since it aired nearly twelve years ago. Don't ask me how I got it because, as they say, if I told you, I'd have to kill you. I'll shut up and let the piece speak for itself. With what time we have left, we'll have a Q and A, after."

The lights came down once more. Onscreen was Jimmy standing in what looked like a doctor's office; Ronald Reagan in a bathrobe, staring at him.

No, this can't be happening.

"I have to tell the police about the gunshot wound," declared Reagan.

"That's a very bad idea, Doc," Jimmy replied.

They're not going to show this.

Reagan now held a phone in his hand. "It's a matter of record."

"It don't need to be a matter of nothin'."

Somebody stop it, please.

Now Jimmy's hand was filled with a .32 pistol.

"So that's the way it is, after I've sewn you up and saved your life?"

There was a tableau of Jimmy staring and Reagan staring back at him.

Jimmy rose, frantically headed toward the exit. Pulling open the door, he heard the onscreen shot, then scattered reactions.

When he stepped outside, the rain had receded to a drizzle, but there was no sign of Gus. *Dammit, I need to get out of here.* Jimmy felt like he might keel over and pass out. He steadied himself on his walking stick. *Goddammit, Gus, where are you?*

Jimmy heard the glass doors of the theater being pushed open behind him, and he turned, expecting to see the first of the crowd pouring out. But it was just one kid, a teenager with swept-back platinum hair, dressed in a scarlet *Rebel* jacket, grinning like Christmas morning. Jimmy couldn't determine if it was a male or female.

"Is it over?" Jimmy asked.

"It is for me, man. Nothing could top that. Wow, that was something. Never dreamed I'd get to see it."

"You enjoyed watching that?"

"Hell yes. It was amazing."

"What did you like about it?"

"You sure ask a lot of questions." The kid stepped closer. "Jimmy wasn't acting, like he wasn't acting when that car went over the cliff. He'd take things as far as they needed to go and was ready for anything."

Jimmy heard a brief honk. Gus had glided up to the curve. Jimmy turned back to the girl, whose eyes had widened. "Wow, is that your car?"

"Need a ride?"

Hardly any conversation as they glided through the streets. Jimmy figured the kid was plenty suspicious, thinking maybe he'd ask her to come home with him. She told him she was Wanda Lynne Felks, although Jimmy felt pretty sure that wasn't her real name. He gave her a sideways glance, then said, "James Dean, what do you see in him?"

A moment. "I go to the University of Denver. I'm doing a paper on him and came out here to do research."

"Oh, I see." But his tone said he wasn't going for it.

"Why are you interested in people who are into James Dean?"

"Well," Jimmy said, "I knew him."

"I don't believe you."

"The man was flesh and blood. He lived out here. I knew him."

"Okay, what was he like?"

"Unhappy. Miserable, most of the time."

"Yeah, but he was authentic."

"What do you mean by that?"

Grace leaned toward him. "That knife scene in *Rebel*, up at the Griffith Observatory. They wanted to use fake knives and Jimmy insisted on the real thing."

"Actually, it was just the opposite. Dean got cut and was very upset about it."

"How do you know, were you there?"

Jimmy took a moment. "I heard about it from somebody who was."

"Even if you knew Jimmy, and I doubt you really did, you still don't know what you're talking about."

When they reached her crummy motel in Hollywood, Gus opened the door and the car's dome light came on. She'd zipped her jacket halfway. As she was climbing out—no thank you, nothing—Jimmy glimpsed her shoulder holster that held a small revolver. The kid must have felt she needed it and, on her own in LA, most likely did.

Jimmy thought about her all the way back to Laurel Canyon, and by Sunday morning, his thoughts had crystalized.

FORTY-ONE

"Why are you calling so early?" Perry asked. "And I gotta tell you I'm disappointed, Byron. You said you'd be at the fest this weekend."

"I was there on Friday."

"Why didn't I see you?"

"I was busy producing our film."

"I don't get it," said Perry.

"The kind of thing you have been talking about, turning an actor loose on camera, I found a girl who's perfect for it."

"A girl?"

"Put her onscreen and you will not be able to take your eyes off her."

"Can she handle a chopper?"

"There is something about her that is, like, the future."

✳

Sunday, around six in the evening. Grace was sitting in her motel room, Burger King Whopper, Coke, and fries on the table in front of her; a paperback copy of *The Little Prince* open on the bed. The television was on, Grace looking up as an in-progress news report caught her attention. She felt a jolt. It all made sense, a telescope coming into focus.

At that moment, the phone rang. Grace stared at it. She'd

only received a few calls the whole time she'd been there, always the front desk, wanting to tell her some bullshit. She lifted the receiver cautiously. "Hello," she said.

The voice on the other end, in measured Germanic cadence, delivered what sounded to her like a prepared speech. It took her a moment to realize it was the guy from the other night, the one with the fancy car. He was making a film, he explained, and would she be interested in getting together and exploring it further? "How about tomorrow, would that suit you?"

"I can't tomorrow," Grace told him.

"You have plans all day?"

"Yes, all day, I'm sure."

"Please do not think this is about anything but what I am telling you. With this picture, this role, your whole life could change. What about meeting tomorrow night?"

"There's something I need to go to, at the Beverly Wilshire. I don't know how long it's gonna last. But there's a good chance I'll be . . . tied up after that. Or I might be leaving town."

"Tuesday won't work either?"

"I don't know about Tuesday. Look, I need to go."

*

Jimmy was thrown off by the phone call. The girl, whatever her real name was, was living in a rathole, on her own in LA. Somebody reaches out who could alter her dismal existence, and she acts like she's booked from now until doomsday. The whole exchange bothered him, hanging over him through-out Sunday night, still with him when he woke up Monday morning.

At the dining table, while breakfast was being served, Jimmy glanced through the *LA Times*. The item on page six seized his attention.

. . . *Two points down in the polls, and with the gubernatorial election less than a week away, Ronald Reagan will address a luncheon crowd of ecumenical clergy today at the Beverly Wilshire.* . . .

Jimmy had a sick feeling. *Why would she be going to the Beverly Wilshire on that day, at that time?* Perhaps she wanted to see in the flesh the man Jimmy Dean had shot and nearly killed. *But she has a gun.*

✱

In the hotel ballroom, Ronald Reagan was well into his remarks. "The student protesters we're talking about seem to forget that their soapboxes are at state-funded institutions. Even though I'd love to put a gag over their mouths, am I, as governor, going to make them stop talking? No, but I, not to mention the people of California, sure as heck don't need to listen. And let's not forget that those already loud and strident voices tend to be supported by microphones and sound systems and massive speakers. Isn't that disruptive to those other students who are in school to study and not be indoctrinated?

✱

Jimmy was doing something he never thought he'd do again. He was driving a car. When he told Gus he wanted to take the Lincoln out, Gus was clearly surprised. "Don't worry," Jimmy had said. "I'm not putting you out of a job."

Good thing it was automatic transmission. Jimmy had to be concerned with only the wheel and brake. He'd never driven as slowly as he had that day and was relieved when, at last, he pulled into a parking garage.

Outside the hotel, Jimmy's eyes scanned the scene; no sight of her anywhere.

As he pressed forward, he noticed a crouching figure aiming a camera at the small crowd. The photographer snapped off a couple of shots, then rose to a standing position. Jimmy looked, sensing something familiar about him. The cameraman locked eyes with Jimmy for a moment. There was an instant where Jimmy felt he could have placed him. Then he turned, searching for the kid who called herself Wanda Lynne Felks.

He got closer to the sidewalk leading to the hotel; some guy said: "You're not with the press. How about getting back?" Jimmy ignored him, then realized he wasn't the one being addressed. He did a double take at the figure at his left elbow. How had he missed that scarlet nylon jacket?

He was trying to think of what to do when a voice chimed: "Over here, Mr. Reagan."

"Mr. Reagan, over here," someone else called out.

Ronald Reagan, in the flesh. Bluish-gray suit, scarlet tie, bronze skin and hair, clearly not about to stop and do any hand-clasping. He was half turned, smiling and waving. Somebody shouted a question and he shook his head, not like he didn't know the answer, more like he genially had no intention of answering. He kept coming, making his way toward a dark gleaming Cadillac. The door was open, an aide standing there.

Jimmy was jostled slightly, then glanced over at the girl, who had her right hand shoved into her jacket pocket.

She looked startled. "What the hell are you doing here?"

"I came here to tell you something."

"What?" she said, her eyes tracking Reagan.

"Something about Jimmy. Something nobody knows but me."

"You can tell me later," she said, never taking her eyes off Reagan, nearly past them as he moved toward the waiting car.

"Okay," said Jimmy. "But give me the gun first."

*

"It better be good, Hiram," Oona was saying. "You got me out of bed for this."

In Hiram's studio on Crenshaw Boulevard, he led her into his developing room where a set of prints were attached to a line over the sink. He took one down and handed it to Oona.

She studied it a moment. "What about it?"

"Look closer."

Squinting this time, she said. "I don't know what I'm supposed to be looking at."

"The guy with the dark hair that looks like a rug. Check out his right hand."

"Oh my God," she said. "I'm no fan of Reagan, but we need to tell somebody who can deal with it." Oona stepped out into the larger room. "I could use a shot, Hiram, the liquid kind. Do you have anything to drink in this joint?"

FORTY-TWO

Boulder, Colorado, the Hobsons' living room. Grace, in pin-striped blouse and pleated skirt, platinum hair transformed to its natural red, sat on the sofa flanked by her parents; Zeke Mallory and Allen Davotney, on chairs facing them.

"I still don't understand," Norris was saying," why you're insisting that our daughter was at some political event, when she says she was on a train coming home."

Davotney smiled. "When you reported Grace missing, she went into a national database. Her picture was on file."

"Are you saying you have a picture of her at this event?" asked Helen.

"Do we need to call an attorney?" asked Norris. "Even if Grace was there, and we believe her when she says she wasn't, there's no crime in that."

Zeke pulled a photograph from his briefcase and handed it to Grace. "We're interested in the man who was standing next to you outside the Beverly Hilton."

Grace studied the photograph, which clearly showed the gun she'd bought, although she wasn't the one holding it. She was trying to remain steady, but her voice broke: "I'd met him once before and then ran into him that day."

"What made you go to the hotel in the first place?" asked Davotney.

"I just . . . I'd been hearing about the election the whole time I was in Los Angeles. I thought I'd go see for myself."

Davotney leaned toward her. "Did you go out and see the other candidate too?"

Grace shook her head.

"Who was running against Reagan, by the way?"

Again Grace shook her head.

"So you were only interested in Ronald Reagan?"

"I guess so. You know, he'd been a movie star."

"Look, Grace," said Zeke. "You ran away and now you're back home, and we're sure you'll sort everything out with your parents. But we need to know about the man you were standing next to in that picture. Did he give you his name?"

Now she was crying. "He told me a lot of crazy things."

"His *name*, Miss Hobson."

"He said he'd put me in a movie." She looked at Zeke, then at Davotney. Then leaned back as though trying to disappear into the sofa. "Krats, I think it was. Brian, or maybe Byron Krats, but it was probably a fake."

Zeke resisted the urge to break into a grin. "What makes you say it might have been false?"

Norris awkwardly draped his arm around his daughter. "Just tell them, darling. You have nothing to hide."

"He took me to the hotel coffee shop and bought me breakfast. That's where he told me he was really James Dean, the actor who died ten years ago."

❧

Gus Pettibone was standing in the dusk on an overlook, just off Mulholland. Mallory and Davotney were facing him, the haze of Los Angeles beyond.

Zeke: "Your employer has no birth record, Social Security, Selective Service, IRS, school, health—nothing anywhere. Not a traffic ticket, nothing. The man didn't exist before setting up banking and investments near the end of 1964."

"So you're not FBI and you're not working with Internal Affairs," Gus was saying. "Who the hell are you guys?"

"We give orders to those people," said Davotney.

Gus shrugged. "What can I tell you? Byron's always been straight with me."

Davotney: "We need to make sure the man is who he says he is."

"A handwriting sample should clear everything up," Zeke said. "Do you have that grocery list I asked you to bring?"

Gus pulled a sheet of paper from his pocket and handed it to Zeke. "What kind of trouble is he in?"

*

Byron Krats's handwriting was a perfect match to Specs Pelham's farewell note to the Gramercy Park Hotel. And both matched the diagnostic essay in the LAPD files that Dean had generated before his 1954 trial.

James Byron Dean, born February 8, 1931, Fairmount, Indiana, hadn't died in a car crash after all. His buddy, Stephen "Specs" Pelham, owned Dean's original Porsche Speedster. That car was confiscated after the attempt on Pelham's life. Dean's Spyder was abandoned the same night. Harley Dale, the sole witness to the fatal crash, had killed himself in 1963. But Zeke and Davotney didn't need a witness. Not a doubt, the charred body in the Hollywood cemetery was Pelham.

When Dean assumed Pelham's identity, he inherited his enemies, who finally came after him. To become Krats, Dean must have arranged for new identification, then fled the country, or else purchased documents on the European black market.

Dean as Krats had signed on with the Conestoga Investment Corporation in Century City, who didn't trouble themselves with how he'd amassed his fortune. Dean must have accessed his music business earnings while in Europe.

Having spent all night and morning putting this together at LAPD, Zeke and Davotney were at Pink's hot dog stand on Melrose, at an outside table.

"The man could have set down his anchor anywhere in the world," Davotney was saying. "Why did he return to Los Angeles?"

"Ronald Reagan," said Zeke.

"Of course. It's unfinished business for this nutcase. He must be boiling now that Reagan has a chance at some real power. Pass that mustard, Zeke." Davotney squirted it on his hot dog, then leaned across the table. "Everything you've accomplished is on the line with this. Not to mention everything you're working toward, which you've convinced me is nothing less than the future of the country."

Zeke, utterly exhausted, didn't say anything.

Davotney laughed. "It's a hell of a lot easier to kill somebody who everyone thinks is dead."

"I've never killed anybody, Major."

"The way I'm seeing it, we won't have to."

Zeke appeared uncomfortable as he tried to wrap his mind around what Davotney was getting at.

"The man shot two mob guys in the kneecaps. One phone call and it's over. They'll be overjoyed and we won't have to get our hands dirty."

Zeke nodded, then reached into his basket. Took his first bite.

*

Jill pulled her jacket tight around her, a suede one she'd purchased in an open-air market in Florence. She walked along the dark and chilly ocean. Being autumn, it was a bit later in the year than the night she'd shared down here so many years ago with Jimmy. Was this the exact spot? It seemed to be in the vicinity.

Ever since her public disclosure, Jill felt elated. She hadn't consciously realized what a burden she was carrying, not only having given up her child, but the fact of losing Jimmy before she'd even had any time with him. Would he have fallen in love with her? She'd once convinced herself before she met him that he would if there were a real opportunity.

Jimmy was like a comet streaking across the sky; brilliant, dazzling but gone in an instant. How could someone simply dissolve like that, as if he'd been heated on a burner and vaporized? She felt she'd been tricked; should have known that Jimmy's destiny was elsewhere. Why had she let herself be taken in by someone so sure to be annihilated?

She stopped on the sand, stood beside the waves, and slipped Jimmy's Zippo from her jacket pocket. She pulled a cigarette from its pack and cupped her hands around the lighter as she ignited it. The flame flared strong and true as it always did. She flicked down the cap and inhaled deeply, the mentholated smoke blending with the bracing salt air. Then, without any hesitation, she hurled the lighter at the sea.

*

Standing on the deck behind his house, Jimmy was smoking, the soft lights from inside and the glow of the television behind him.

Gus took the night off, something about his ex-wife and some emergency. That was fine with Jimmy, who'd planned nothing more than to stay in and watch the election returns.

He had plenty of thinking to do. After leaving the Beverly Wilshire and telling that kid his story, he'd felt light, like he'd been lifted off the ground. It hadn't been that difficult, once he got going. He wondered if she believed it. No matter, he'd done it for himself as much as for her, although he'd saved the kid a world of trouble. Best for everybody that she took the bus back home.

For the first time since his own trouble started, a dozen years before, Jimmy felt linked to the future. Not just his own, but to the world somehow. He felt small but not insignificant, a detail in some huge painting that, without his little inclusion, would somehow be incomplete.

As soon as he could, he would find his son and convince whoever was raising him to allow him into the boy's life. He'd convince Jill Parnell to do the same. Jimmy had grown up knowing his mother was dead and his father cared nothing for him, and how had that turned out?

Once all that was in place, he would come forward with everything, who he was and who he'd pretended to be. No doubt he'd be arrested and retried and likely sent to prison. But he was in prison already. *Who knows, now that Reagan has been elected governor, maybe he'll pardon me.*

From the hills, there was the wail of a coyote, and then another, and Jimmy laughed under his breath. *You hear them a lot more than you see them.*

As Jimmy took a deep and final drag on his cigarette, there was another sound he didn't hear. A single shot from a high-powered rifle that echoed all over the canyon.

ACKNOWLEDGMENTS

Several years ago, the author came across a Dennis Stock photograph of James Dean brandishing a pistol at Ronald Reagan. That image was the flashpoint that became *The Cold Last Swim*.

Thanks to:

Deborah Gibson Robertson, for her skilled and meticulous editing and preparation of the manuscript.

Mary Bisbee-Beek, for enthusiastic book promotion.

Matt Wise for his early and abiding belief in the work.

Tom Leavens, for introducing Gibson House Press to it.

Also:

Lawrence Block, Tim Combs, Steve Cowan, Janet Feder, Jim Heald, Kate Kuper, Rocky Maffit, Colin Mahoney, Lisa Miller, Stuart Oken, Alan Rosen, Louis Rosen, Nina Sacco, Celia Seaton and Laney Wax, each of whom lent support in various ways at various stages.

And always:

Michele Leonard and Simone Leonard, who inspired and sustained every stage of the writing.

ABOUT THE AUTHOR

Besides *The Cold Last Swim*, Junior Burke is the author of the novels *Something Gorgeous* and *A Thousand Eyes*. He is also a songwriter and recording artist whose 2007 album *While You Were Gone* was named by New York's Bowery Poetry Club as one of the best releases of that year. Other albums include *Spot of Time* (2017) and the EP *America's a Lonely Town* (2019). He lives in rural Colorado. *Visit juniorburke.com.*

GIBSON HOUSE PRESS connects
literary fiction with curious and discerning
readers. We publish novels by musicians
and other artists who love music.

GibsonHousePress.com
 GibsonHousePress
 @GibsonPress
 @GHPress

FOR DOWNLOADS OF READING GROUP GUIDES
for Gibson House books, visit
GibsonHousePress.com/Reading-Group-Guides